an UNEXPECTED *turn*

STEPHANIE ROSE

AN UNEXPECTED TURN

STEPHANIE ROSE

That's What She Said Publishing, Inc.

Cover Design: Najla Qamber at Qamber Designs

Cover Photo: ©Regina Wamba

Editing: Edited by: Lisa Hollett—Silently Correcting Your Grammar

Proofreading: Jodi Duggan & Jessica Snyder Edits

ISBN: 979-8-88643-969-4 (ebook)

ISBN: 979-8-88643-968-7 (paperback)

080322

For Aunt Rosalie—

*I keep thinking I owe you a phone call and then remember I don't
have heaven's number.*
*Thank you for letting me be a kid and for being the star in all my
best childhood memories.*
*I pray you're happy now and you know how much we all miss and
love you.*

*And thanks for always leaving your romance novels around
Grandma's apartment for me to sneak read.*

This one is all for you.

ONE

JAKE

"Mikey, come on. Let's go," I told my son after I tapped on his door. I'd never thought I'd have to tiptoe around my own kid, but fourteen-year-olds changed moods every damn hour. At least, mine did.

"Mike. Mikey is a little kid's name." I caught his audibly defiant sigh as he heaved the strap of his backpack over his shoulder.

I stifled a laugh. The crack in his changing voice made the badass attitude he was trying to pull off fall short. If he spotted my amusement, it would only make his already shitty disposition that much worse.

"Okay, *Mike*. You need some breakfast in you before school. I can whip up some eggs for us if you want."

"I'll just pour some cereal," he muttered before pushing past me and shuffling down the stairs.

My sweet kid had turned into an ornery teenager, but I couldn't blame him. I'd be every bit as pissed off as he was if I had to start high school in a new town with a father he'd only known as a weekend dad for most of his life.

1

It wasn't that I'd never wanted more than that. I did, and God knew I'd tried. I'd spent most of my son's life fighting with his mother for more time with him after our divorce. Eileen wasn't a bad parent, but she often used our son to take her anger out on me. The one thing I never wanted was for Mikey to be in the middle of a savage custody battle, so I made the most of the time I did have with my son and kept current on all the child support payments to keep our relationship as amicable as possible.

When Eileen found a husband last year, things changed. I was able to take Mikey for long weekends and vacations without any resistance because his mother was too busy enjoying her new marriage to use our son against me anymore. Then, said new husband found a job across the country, and bringing Mikey with them wasn't "convenient at the moment." My son had told me about the disdain he had for his stepfather more than once, so moving in with me was his preferred option anyway.

Mikey had dealt with a lot of upheaval over the past few months—especially for someone his age. He had to leave the house he'd grown up in and the friends he'd known all his life, attending high school with strangers now. Five years ago, coming to live with me might have been an easier transition, but now it was just all-around miserable for him.

He'd moved in with me in early August. Since he was only five when his mother and I split up, he'd never entered this school system after prekindergarten. The one friend he'd had in our neighborhood moved away a few years ago, so he was starting his freshman year of high school as the brand-new kid in school and in town.

My kid oozed resentment and frustration, and all I could do was listen and guide him the best that I could. He wasn't the only one struggling through a new routine. I'd always wanted my son with me, but getting used to being a full-time parent to a now-troubled kid was no cakewalk.

I prayed the growing pains we both had would subside quickly—or at least eventually.

"I'll drive you this week," I said after we climbed into my truck. "The bus starts—"

"Monday, got it." He buckled his seat belt, another huff falling from his lips as he slumped in his seat.

"Look," I started and shifted to face him. "Mikey— Michael. Whatever your name is today."

I spied his lip twitch, and a tiny bit of relief slipped through me.

"I know this is tough. Visiting me here is different from living here. And it may be hard at first, but give it a chance."

"I know, Dad. It's just—" He shook his head, his gaze drifting out the window. "Nothing like being dumped by your own mother before you start high school."

"She didn't dump you." I hoped I sounded convincing, especially since my assessment of her move wasn't much different from my son's. She had the right to be happy and marry whomever she wanted, but it all happened so fast I couldn't blame my kid for having whiplash. "Things are changing for her right now, and she thought it would be easier for you if you stayed with me."

"Easier for *her*. Now, I'm stuck, and you're stuck *with* me."

"I'm not stuck." I reached across the console and squeezed the back of his neck until he swiveled his head in my direction. "I've always wanted more time with you, and I'm glad you're living with me. I'm with you every step of the way, and I don't feel even the least bit stuck with you. All right?"

He nodded, a tiny smile curving one side of his mouth. I

shared his nerves, but meant every single word. I'd do whatever I needed to make sure he was happy here. I didn't quite know what that was yet, but the slight attitude shift from this morning to now gave me a sliver of hope I was heading in the right direction.

"It's a lot bigger than my old school was."

"You'll get used to it. Try to remember the important stuff from the tour we took last month. Like the huge courtyard next to the cafeteria."

I smiled, but he didn't glance back at me.

"This is the same school you went to all those years ago?" he asked as we pulled into the parking lot.

"All those years ago?" I barked out a laugh.

"Well, you went here in the nineteen hundreds, right?"

"Jesus, Mikey." My jaw fell open as I gaped at my son. "I went here in the *nineteen nineties.*"

At forty-six, I was in damn good shape and never considered myself even close to being old—until my son made me feel ancient.

"Wow," Mikey noted, unaware of my shock and offense as his eyes swept over the main building. "Does it look the same?"

"I mean, they probably have electricity now, unlike in my day when I traveled to school in a horse and buggy. But from the outside, mostly the same."

He leaned over to give me a tight hug. I wrapped my arms around him and pulled him to me, as I used to when I dropped him off all those Sunday nights when he was little. This time, I didn't have to deal with the weekly crack in my chest after letting him go.

"It's all going to be fine. You'll see." I clapped him on the back before I pulled away.

I'd meant it for the both of us, and as I watched him walk through the large double doors, I prayed I was right.

The unease in my stomach didn't dissipate when I arrived at work. I was tempted to text Mikey to see how he was doing, but I didn't want to get him in trouble. Plus, checking up on him would only add to his nerves, so I'd deal with my jitters until dismissal.

I unlocked the door to the office, thankful my office manager and the guys wouldn't be here for the next couple of hours. Now that I had my son living with me, running my own contracting business and setting my own hours was a lucky perk. I rarely worked later than three or four in the afternoon, but my sister lived close enough if I had an occasional late night, though I hoped to keep those as infrequent as possible.

Sharing my daily life with anyone was a brand-new venture.

"Hey, Russo? Back from school yet?"

I cracked up at the gravelly voice drifting in through the door.

Keith, my best friend since high school, trudged inside and took the seat in front of my desk.

"Coffee would be nice."

"Then go to the deli across the street. Get me one too."

"I thought Russo's Contracting could do any job." He turned up his nose in mock disgust before his lips curved up. "How was Mikey's first day?"

"He got there." I shrugged, organizing some of the loose papers on my desk into job folders. "No clue beyond that. Hoping like hell for the best. What brings you out so early on your day off?"

"I can't sleep in anymore, too damn used to being up early. I thought I'd give Maya a break and drive the kids to school,

5

and I figured I'd come by on the way home and see if you were freaking out yet."

"Thanks for the sentiment—and the confidence," I said, quirking my brow. Keith had wanted to be a cop for as long as I could remember and joined the police department right after he completed the college credits he needed. He'd made it all the way up to chief of police, and I still had yet to see him take a real day off.

"I'm only here for moral support. No shade, I swear. I know how kids drive you crazy. Speaking of, my niece is staying with us for a while."

"Peyton? How old is she now?"

"Thirty-two." He shook his head and laughed. "But I guess she'll always be a kid to me."

"Wow, I haven't seen her in years. What made her move here?"

"She found a job at the high school. My sister is annoyed she's moving three hours away, but I'm glad to have her close by. These poor kids have to start school in August now, but they're running around the streets in May, so I guess it's all relative." He shook his head and laughed. "Will you relax already? He's going to be fine."

"I wish I were as sure as you are." I tossed the stack of folders I was trying to busy myself with onto my desk and rubbed my eyes.

"Stop worrying. I always thought Mikey would be better off with you, and he finally is. If it makes you feel any better, I'll tell Peyton to keep an eye on him. She's a guidance counselor."

"Oh, really? Good for her."

Keith shrugged and stood. "Good for her, I guess. I mean, I'm proud of her, of course, but whiny high school kids aren't my thing. Needy new cops are plenty."

"So, the twins will have to move out at twelve?"

"It takes someone special to want to deal with someone else's kids all day long. That person was never me. And right now, I need some coffee. Come on, Russo."

I didn't argue before I followed, locking the door behind me and heading across the street with Keith. I had a little more than an hour to stew over my own high school kid and how I couldn't be the next one to fail him.

TWO
PEYTON

"When is the new place ready?"

I cradled my phone in the crook of my neck as I got ready for school. Speakerphone would have been easier, but as big as my uncle's house was, the walls were thin, and I didn't have time to search for my earbuds. Not that my best friend and I were talking about anything secret, but I never knew what would come out of Claudia's mouth.

"In a few weeks, I hope." I fell back on the couch and swept my gaze around the basement. It would be nice to have my own kitchen again. Although, staying here wasn't the worst thing in the world. They used to rent this as a separate studio apartment, but my uncle had since turned it into his sanctuary. The pullout leather couch was a surprising dream to sleep on and I had my own full bathroom, but I was itching to move in to my condo. Camping out here when they already had young kids of their own to take care of didn't feel like the fresh start I'd wanted.

And it felt ridiculous to counsel high school kids when I was living like one.

"I'll be up there to help as soon as it is."

"That's not necessary, Claud," I protested, even though I missed her. Kelly Lakes was only three hours away from the boroughs, but far enough to get a little homesick from the culture shock.

"I miss you, and you need help. I've seen you try to put furniture together."

"I can't fight you on that one." We shared a chuckle. "The furniture is being delivered and assembled, but you can help me unpack if you'd like. My uncle already said he'd help me get settled in."

"I wish I had an Uncle Keith to give me a place to stay and help me move in to a new one."

"He is pretty great. It's helped."

"I still can't believe you moved all the way up there."

"It's mid-state. I'm a little more than three hours away from the city."

"But you lived in Brooklyn for your entire life." I cringed at her deep sigh, knowing what would come next. "You didn't have to leave your job just because—"

"Yes, I did. They didn't ask me to, but no one put up a big fight when I resigned."

I loved being a guidance counselor, and I'd loved my school. One stupid lapse of judgment didn't cost me my job, but I'd lost most of my credibility. My bad decision was shared by the two of us, but I'd borne the brunt of it. Each day, I'd come home wanting to collapse in frustrated tears, but I wouldn't let myself cry. I didn't deserve how I was treated, but I couldn't change it.

When I'd found a high school guidance counselor position open in Kelly Lakes, it seemed like the perfect solution. Whenever I'd visit my uncle and his family, it always seemed like such a quaint but friendly town. The quiet used to bother me in the past, but now I welcomed a break from the chaos I'd left back in Brooklyn.

When I was offered the job, I accepted right away and put it all in motion before I changed my mind.

"I hate what happened to you."

"Bad choices sometimes lead to bad consequences, but I'm fine now. Really." I hoped the chirp in my voice would ease her worries, even if she didn't totally believe me. "The different scenery is good for me. Small towns are very soothing."

I was almost done with my first week at school, and I already loved it. There were a lot of differences from my old school in Brooklyn. The building was much bigger and was surrounded by lush grass and rolling hills, compared to the concrete I was used to. Sports were a much bigger deal here than back in the city, with the flyers plastered along every wall already with different team tryouts over the next few weeks.

One huge and welcomed difference was getting used to the absence of eyes on my back or whispers whenever I approached. I was the new counselor with a clean slate, and the relief from all the old pressure already made my job easier.

"Well, you know what happens when a city girl moves up to a small town for a new job, right?"

"What? I'll meet the local veterinarian who's trying to save his family's farm and fall madly in love? I didn't move *that* far upstate, Claud."

"You never know. If you meet someone hot, faint. It seems to help move things along."

"You're ridiculous."

A laugh slipped out. No hot veterinarians for me. If I wanted good romance, I had the new Melanie Moreland book downloaded on my Kindle for later.

"I better get ready for school."

"It's adorable that you still say that. We'll talk later about what I can bring when I come up. I'm thinking white wine goes better with unpacking."

"Sounds amazing. Thanks, Claud."

I ended the call and dropped my head into my hands. This was a good choice. The right choice. I'd keep repeating it in my head until I believed it.

"Good morning," I greeted my aunt and uncle with a big smile. Faking it until I made it was my newly adopted mantra. "I'll miss the free breakfast when I leave."

"You could have all the free meals you want. I don't know why you're in such a rush to go." Uncle Keith gave me a half smile. "We told you that you could stay as long as you wanted."

I cut a look to Aunt Maya, her braids bouncing at her shoulders as we both shared a silent laugh. There was a ten-year age gap between my uncle and my mother, and when I came along, he was only a teenager. When my parents divorced and my father all but disappeared, Uncle Keith stepped up for us more than most men would have at his age.

He was the fun uncle when I was a kid, always up for an ice cream date or sitting on the floor to play with me for hours on end, but as I grew up, he became the protector I could always count on and the only real father figure I'd ever known. He was so thrilled I was here, but didn't know the whole reason why. Claudia was the only one who knew, and while I was sure Uncle Keith wouldn't judge me, I couldn't handle disappointing him.

"I know that, and I appreciate it. But I think eventually I'd get in your way. Even if you'd never tell me that." I lifted a brow at my uncle before reaching for a coffee mug.

"You would never get in the way. The boys love having you here," my aunt said, taking a seat next to me. "And we do too. But I totally get wanting a place of your own. Somewhere there isn't a framed jersey on every inch of wall space." She pursed her lips at her husband.

Aunt Maya's light-brown eyes almost glowed against her ebony skin. Their ten-year-old twin boys were a perfect combination of her and Uncle Keith. Brian was laid-back and reserved like his mother, but Aiden always had a million nosy questions like his dad.

"That's another reason." I reached across the table and patted my uncle's hand. "I took over your man cave. I'm sure you want it back, even if you don't mind my staying here."

He waved a hand at me. "I can always move that stuff somewhere else."

"Really? Where?"

I laughed at the lift in his wife's brow.

"I bet Kelly Lakes High hasn't changed at all." Uncle Keith snickered around a piece of toast. "That building is a hundred years old."

"It's had a solid reputation for a long time. I start meeting with my freshman kids today."

Aiden and Brian tore into the kitchen, both reaching into the cabinet at the same time for different cereal boxes. I enjoyed working with elementary and middle school children, but high school was my sweet spot. The freshmen and sophomores needed the most guidance and weren't as jaded or cocky as some of the juniors or seniors. I wasn't intimidated, but it was easier to help kids who didn't think they were too cool to accept it.

"Good morning to you, too, guys." Uncle Keith laughed, shaking his head. "Once they learn how to use the stove, they won't need us at all."

They both mumbled a hello at their father as they stuffed spoons into their mouths, milk dribbling down their chins.

"Slow down! You'll get a stomachache." Aunt Maya heaved out a sigh and dropped napkins next to their bowls.

"Oh, that reminds me. I'm not sure if I told you that Jake's son is a freshman. You remember Jake, right? I stopped by his office the first day of school, and he was probably just as nervous as Mikey."

I nodded and swallowed a mouthful of eggs, not wanting to admit how much I *did* remember his friend Jake. When I last saw my uncle's best friend, I was a high school freshman myself. Jake had been at a few functions my uncle had before then, but that was the first time I'd really *seen* him. I'd stayed with my uncle for a week one summer while my mother went on a work trip, and Jake popped over a few times.

It was more than fifteen years ago, but I could still picture the piercing blue eyes, chiseled jaw, and broad shoulders. He'd flash me a blinding smile, and I was too embarrassed by my braces to smile back. When he'd try to pull small talk out of me, I'd only stammer in reply.

I'd run into Jake eventually, especially since I recalled seeing a Michael Russo on my student list. I was certain that Jake was probably the kind of man who only grew hotter with age.

"His son is one of my students. Unless there's another Michael Russo in school, he's on my roster for the year."

"Poor kid. His mother moved away with her new husband and left him with Jake. After all the years of breaking his balls whenever it came to Mikey—"

Maya cleared her throat and motioned to the boys across the table. I bit back a smile when he responded with a sheepish grin.

"I mean, making it difficult whenever Jake wanted more than a weekend, now she has no problem dropping him off for good. Inside information you could use as his guidance counselor, I guess."

A wave of sympathy twisted my gut. I'd only been working as a counselor for five years, but it was long enough to hear some terrible stories. They ranged from the sad, like Jake's son, to the horrifying. Stepping in early was always key, and kids like Mikey struggled in ways that weren't always obvious.

I'd use the inside information and keep an eye out for him. Being in a new school and town, he probably could use an early friend.

"It is. He's at a tough age."

Fourteen- and fifteen-year-olds had it rough with the surging hormones and settling into that odd place between kid and young adult.

I sympathized even more now, feeling just as lost at thirty-two.

Maybe Mikey and I could bond over our common displacement in a new town. Mine was voluntary, but seemed just as forced.

My uncle pressed a kiss to the top of my head, breaking me out of my silent pity spiral. "If you want to stay, I can put my man cave stuff in storage."

I shook my head. "I appreciate the offer, but Derek Jeter can stay on the wall. I'll only be ten minutes away, so this isn't the last you'll see of me."

"Better not be." Uncle Keith stood and put his dish into the sink.

It was a comfort knowing my favorite uncle was so close by, but if I wanted the new life I'd dropped everything for, I had to do it on my own.

THREE
PEYTON

Chips on shoulders and hurt feelings had no place in school, especially in my line of work. While a teacher could be stern and unapproachable as long as their students learned from them, my purpose was to make a student comfortable enough to talk to me about anything, even if they didn't know me that well. I never let students walk all over me, although a few attempts over the years made me laugh. Some wanted to see me just to get out of class, and while I never refused any requests, I learned to decipher who was hiding their problems behind a little bravado and who was seeking a legal way to cut class.

"Ready for one more?" Arlene, the school principal and my new boss, asked from the doorway to my office. I'd only been working with her for a few weeks, but she seemed patient and kind, at least enough to not change the vibe of a room with her presence. All my last principal had to do was pass you in the hallway and both teachers and students stood straighter, as if we'd all been caught doing something wrong.

Back in Brooklyn, I knew our neighbors well enough to smile if we crossed paths, but I didn't carry on many conversations beyond small talk. Everyone was busy and always heading somewhere, but Kelly Lakes moved at a much slower pace. People not only had the time to get to know you, but they also made sure of it. My uncle entertained me with all the tales he'd heard from being chief of police, and I was sure people were just as interested in a single woman in her thirties moving to a new town.

I hadn't decided whether that was good or bad yet.

While my job was getting others to open up, after everything that had happened over the past year, I found it hard for me to do the same. It had always been easy for me to be social, but the fallout at my old school made me retreat into myself. I'd felt lighter since arriving at Uncle Keith's house and would have to coax who I used to be out in time.

Too bad the guidance counselor couldn't counsel herself.

Arlene motioned behind her. "This is Michael. He's new to Kelly Lakes too. Michael, this is Ms. Miller. We're very happy to have you both here this year."

My gaze landed on the tall, skinny boy now looking between Arlene and me. I had two Michaels left to see on my list, but I knew this was Jake's son. Those crystal-blue eyes were a dead giveaway.

"Nice to meet you, Michael." I shot him a smile as I stood and made my way around my desk. "Have a seat."

"I'll leave you to it." Arlene gave me a nod before she shut the door behind her.

"I'm glad I got to see you before the day ended."

His eyes met mine for a moment before darting all over the room.

"I know your father. He's my Uncle Keith's best friend."

"Oh," he said, his rigid shoulders relaxing a bit. "I think Dad mentioned that."

"How's your first week going? I'm in a new town and a new

school, just like you. Luckily, my uncle knows everything about Kelly Lakes, so I have a little bit of an inside track."

"Keith is pretty cool," Michael mumbled. "I haven't seen him since I moved here, but I remember he talks a lot."

"He does. As does my mother, so it runs in the family. When they're together, there's not much opportunity for anyone else to say anything."

A real laugh slipped out of him, and that familiar rush of euphoria and relief spread in my chest when a new student let his guard down a little.

"Enough about Uncle Keith. What can you tell me about school so far?"

"Nothing." He shrugged. "I don't know anyone."

"There are basketball tryouts on Friday. Great way to meet new people if you're interested."

His smile faded as he shook his head.

"I'm not into sports. I was in this robotics club at my old school, but I don't think there's one here."

"There is, just the sign-up isn't until the end of the month. I can talk to Mrs. Lopez about getting you in if that's something you'd like to do."

His head shot up. "Could you get me in? My old robotics club won a competition last year."

"Wow, that's awesome!" A blush crept up on Michael's olive skin. "I think so. It's open to all students, and with that kind of experience, they'll be thrilled to have you."

"Right. Everyone wants a new kid they don't know." He huffed, exhaling a long sigh.

"Michael, you're in a class full of new kids. Try to let that take some of the pressure off."

"If I'd stayed in my old town, I'd be in high school with all my friends. Freshmen are new to the school, but they all already know each other."

"Things change in a new place. It's not the huge disadvantage that you may think." I scooted closer to my desk, leaning in to get a better look at Michael. "Do you like to be called Michael or Mike?"

"Mike," he answered. "Although I doubt I'll ever stop my dad from calling me Mikey."

I bit back a smile at his groan. "Well, *Mike*. As I said, I'm new here too, in school and in town. Why don't we make a pact to get ourselves out there a little? There's a school barbecue on Saturday, but the park is open to the public. I'm sure your dad would bring you."

"My dad's done enough. He's already stuck with me."

I shook my head. "I know your dad, and I bet he's happy to have you living here permanently now. It's a lot of change, but change can be good if you give it a chance, right?"

He lifted a shoulder, fidgeting with the strap on his backpack. For a minute, I forgot who I was trying to convince.

"I guess it could." A long beat of silence lingered between us before he lifted his head. "I always liked visiting my dad. It's just different living with him. It's not that I don't like it, it's that . . ."

His chin fell to his chest.

"Whatever you say in here stays between us."

His head popped up, and his eyes met mine, searching my gaze as if he were assessing if he could trust me.

"My mom just kind of dumped me on my dad before she moved away with her new husband. I didn't want to move with her and my stepdad, but it would have . . . I don't know . . ." He shrugged.

"It would have been nice to be asked what you wanted to do instead of being told?"

He nodded. "I had to leave our house, all my friends, and she didn't even care."

"That's rough, Mike. I'm sorry. Leaving home is always hard, but it doesn't mean you can't make a new home somewhere else, right?"

He nodded, breathing out an exhale long enough to make his shoulders droop.

I smiled, resting my elbows on my desk. "So, I guess I'll see you at the barbecue?"

His shoulders shook with a tiny chuckle before he nodded.

I flicked my wrist to check the time on my watch. "I think Mrs. Lopez is free last period. You can ask her some questions about the robotics program now if you'd feel more comfortable."

His brows knit together. "Really?"

"Stay here. I'll see if she wouldn't mind a visitor. And you don't mind missing the rest of your last class, right?"

He laughed to himself, and I spied the strong resemblance to his father in his crooked grin.

I introduced Mike to Mrs. Lopez, and he was a completely different kid once they started chatting about the program. He asked all kinds of questions, his eyes lighting up when she told him about the different tournaments the club had participated in last year. His excitement was infectious, and before I knew it, it was five minutes after dismissal.

"It's a good thing the buses don't start until Monday," I told Mike as I led him outside the school's double doors. The building vacated quickly at the end of the day. My voice echoed down the hall. "I wouldn't want your father to worry."

"I would have gotten a text if he was." Mike scoffed as he scanned the parking lot.

"There you are. I started to worry that maybe I missed a side entrance." I didn't have to turn to the deep timbre to know where, or whom, it was coming from.

"Sorry, Dad. I was talking to the teacher who runs the robotics program. She said I could join next month."

Jake's mouth broke out into a wide grin. I could feel the poor guy's relief radiating off him.

"That's great, Mikey. I told you you'd like it here." When his eyes found mine, a familiar grip took hold of my tongue. Jake was twice as gorgeous as I remembered. The same broad shoulders and chiseled jaw were locked into my teenage memory, but now gray bristles mixed in with his dark hair and scruff dusted his cheeks. *Jesus, he was beautiful.*

I wasn't an awkward teenager anymore—or shouldn't have been. But the temptation to hide my face and the redness I knew was singeing my cheeks was still just as potent.

There was no time or place to entertain a silly crush, not then and especially not now, as his son was one of my students. My teenage fantasies were not only wrong, but now professionally inappropriate.

Been there, done that. Zero interest in revisiting what I considered to be my lowest point.

With Jake's eyes holding mine for what seemed like a yearslong moment, my breath caught. I cleared my throat in the hopes of bringing myself and my morals back to reality.

"I'm sorry, I have no manners. I'm just so thrilled that my son looks like he had a decent day at school." There was that deep chuckle again. "I'm Jake Russo."

My heart fluttered at his blinding smile as he extended his hand. The last time I'd seen Jake, I wasn't much older than his son. His gaze had an intensity that I hadn't remembered, at least from when he looked at me all those years ago. It would probably stop as soon as he realized who I was, but I couldn't help enjoying it, even for only a second.

"Peyton Miller." I took his hand, stifling a laugh when his jaw dropped.

"You're kidding me." He didn't drop my hand, instead draping his other one over my wrist. Heat ran up my arm from where our skin made contact. "Your uncle said you were working here, but I . . ." He dropped our hands to run a hand through his thick hair.

"You didn't recognize me. I was about Mike's age the last time you saw me, so that would make sense."

"See? She calls me Mike. Why can't you?" A deep groan rose from Mike's throat.

"Sorry, Mikey." He smiled at me as Mike let out another groan.

"Mike and I bonded over being in a new school and new town, but I think we'll both be fine, right?" I raised a brow, trying to ignore the urge to glance at Jake in my periphery.

"Right." The tiny smile curving Mike's lips relaxed me and brought me back into the present, where I was a high school guidance counselor and he, along with the rest of the students, was my focus.

Or was supposed to be.

"I'll make sure you get the sign-up form for robotics, and you can come to see me anytime."

"Thanks, Ms. Miller," he said before climbing into the passenger seat of his father's truck.

Jake stepped closer to me, his hands stuffed into his pockets. If I didn't know better, I'd say he was as jumpy as I was.

"I'm glad you're here. It makes me feel better that Mikey—Mike—has someone looking out for him."

"That's my job." I hated my knees for wanting to melt at that stupid smile of his. "I'm here if either of you needs anything."

"I appreciate that." The husky rasp of his voice kicked up my heartbeat. As much as I hated the thought, I needed to figure out a way to get back out into the dating world, so I wouldn't swoon over fifteen-year-old fantasies.

"I'll tell my uncle you said hello."

He nodded, blinking a couple of times as his grin shrank. Maybe that slipped out because I needed to remind myself of another reason why it was wrong to be attracted to Jake in the first place.

"I may see him before you will." He held my gaze, his lip curling into a smirk.

"Ah yes. Aunt Maya says you guys are attached at the hip."

Which was why I shouldn't have been so fixated on the way his full lips spread into a smile or how his T-shirt stretched across his broad shoulders.

"Have a good night, Peyton. I mean, Ms. Miller." My name rolling off his tongue still triggered that wave of goose bumps down my neck. My stomach fluttered when he turned his head one more time before climbing into his truck.

I needed to get a grip and stop my mind from playing tricks on me.

My focus needed to be on myself and the job I had to do, and mooning over the parent of one of my students, no matter if I'd mooned over him before, was inappropriate and unacceptable. The fact that he was my uncle's best friend made giving him more than a first look just plain wrong, no matter how enticing he was to the eyes.

If I was going to make a better life for myself here, I needed to heed all the lines I wasn't supposed to cross, and Jake Russo was the definition of off-limits.

FOUR

JAKE

"This is stupid. I see all the same kids at school,"
Mikey grumbled, hands stuffed into his pockets, as
we made our way into the park.

"Yeah, but maybe you'll get more of a chance to talk to
them today. We don't have to stay long. Just try."

Try was a constant plea with my son. Try to forgive the
mother who dumped him with his father. Try to like a brand-
new school and make new friends.

But try was all either of us could do.

"Mike! I'm so glad you made it."

We whipped our heads around, and I spotted Peyton
jogging over to us. She wore a simple tank top and jeans,
tempting my eyes to sweep along all the curves I wasn't
supposed to notice on my best friend's favorite niece. After
she'd told me who she was that afternoon, I drove home in an
uneasy silence, but my son was too busy rambling on about
the robotics program to notice.

The memory of the kid I'd met so long ago contrasted with
the woman she was now. The shock might have worn away,
but when she'd met my eyes for a moment before turning her

23

attention back to my son, an attraction had pulsed between us along with guilt turning my stomach.

"Turns out, the robotics club is here and having an unofficial meeting next to the ball field," Peyton told my son in a loud whisper. "I told Mrs. Lopez I'd keep an eye out for you and send you over when you arrived." She folded her arms, pushing up the swells of her breasts enough to create a slight strain against her neckline—right where I shouldn't have been looking.

"Yeah?" The light in my son's eyes caught me right in the chest when he looked back at me, a little more hope in his gaze than I was used to seeing. I'd almost forgotten the guilt over gawking at his guidance counselor, thanks to the rush of happy relief flooding my veins.

"Go," I said, giving his shoulder a playful shove. "This is what you came for. I'll get some food and a place to sit. You can find me whenever you're done."

It had been so long since I'd seen a real smile on my son's face, I'd almost forgotten what it looked like.

"Thanks, Ms. Miller," Mikey said before jogging over.

"Yes. Thank you, Ms. Miller," I said with a deep sigh. "I was praying he'd start meeting kids and not be so miserable, and the robotics program has been all he can talk about the past couple of days."

A smile crept across her lips. I couldn't look at her eyes, her body, and now I was mesmerized by the graze of her teeth across her bottom lip when she lifted her head. I needed to get a plate of food so I'd have something else to focus on.

"The new people in town have to look out for one another. Right, Mr. Russo?" She shrugged.

"Ugh, please." I cringed. "You know me, and Mr. Russo was my father. Please don't make me feel old like my son likes to do and call me Jake."

She laughed, a gorgeous smile spreading her mouth.

"Okay, *Jake*. As I said, new people need to look out for one another."

Her overpronunciation of my name shouldn't have sounded so damn sensual, and I shouldn't have been so viscerally attuned to it.

"Who's looking out for you?" I asked, lower and huskier than I meant to.

"Besides my uncle?" She smirked, looking me over with a raised brow.

The uncle who would kick my ass if he knew I was lusting after his niece.

"Well, he counts for a lot."

A laugh slipped out of her before she exhaled a long sigh.

"That he does. He's been really great about letting me stay with them, but it's crowded enough and I don't want to take away his sanctuary. When I move in to my own place, I think it will start to feel like home."

"Want to join me for a plate of food, or do you have to stay with the school?"

I nodded to the cluster of what looked like faculty behind her. The right thing would have been to excuse myself and eat alone, getting as far away from her ~~as~~ possible.

"I don't have to. We're all free to roam around and~~e~~ gets ~~lat-~~ ever we want. I could sit with you for a while un~~'~~bottom back." She sucked that full and probably pi~~ll~~~~'~~ lip into her mouth. have been

A plate of food at a school barbec~~ue~~ ~~ning~~ I'd done dangerous, yet it seemed like the m~~h~~ of us not sa~~~~ in I couldn't remember how lon~~~~ ~~nd~~ an empty ~~h~~

I followed her over to the~~~~ anything as we filled up ~~~~

"Where's your new place?" I asked, trying to break through the uncomfortable silence.

"In town, the condo complex on Maple, about ten minutes away from Uncle Keith. It's still not ready yet, but when I get the keys, I can start moving stuff in."

"Do you need any help moving? The back of my truck holds a lot."

Yes, Russo. Offer to spend even more time with her.

"I don't think so. I need to hire movers to take my stuff out of storage, and Uncle Keith will help me bring the rest of my stuff in his van, so we should be covered." She brought a water bottle to her lips, and I averted my gaze when a drop ran down the side of her mouth. "Thank you, though. That's sweet of you to offer. If any of that changes, I'll be sure to let you know."

Peyton was young, too young for me, and she worked in my son's school as his guidance counselor. If that wasn't enough, simply thinking of her like this would ruin a friendship I'd had for most of my life.

So why couldn't I stop doing it?

"I don't mean to pry." Peyton leaned her elbows on the table. "But how are *you* doing through all this adjustment?"

"Did Mikey say anything?"

I stilled, the ever-present knot in my stomach since my son
ome to live with me coiling a little tighter.

for winced. "Anything he tells me is between us unless it's
new e of his safety, but Uncle Keith told me about the
tough. the both of you were thrown into. Must be
the past her gaze on me as she speared her fork into
lashes gra her plate. When she looked down, her long
to keep my ek bone. I cleared my throat, attempting
topic on my son.

"I worry about him. I always wanted more time with Mikey, but forcing it is just making him miserable."

"I wouldn't say that. I can tell he thinks very highly of his dad. The misery you may see is probably from new surroundings and new people. Again, I can relate." She cocked her head to the side. "I knew Mike was your son right away. Same eyes and smile."

"Well, I had no idea who *you* were. Sorry again about that."

And sorry for ogling you before and after I remembered who you were.

"It's okay." Her giggle was almost musical. I needed to stop finding every little thing she did so goddamn adorable. "It's been a long time since you've seen me."

"Sure has." I smiled back at her, a little tension easing between us. "I'm surprised you recognized me."

"As if I could ever forget what you looked like." Her fork stilled before it got to her mouth, her eyes widening a moment before she cleared her throat.

"So I made a good impression on you all those years ago?" I couldn't help teasing her after a blush bled into her cheeks.

"What I meant was . . ." She dropped her face into her hands, pinching the bridge of her nose. I burst out laughing when she peeked at me through her fingers. "I meant you look the same. I'm thankfully not the same awkward teenager with a mouth full of metal. So I take it as a compliment you had no clue who I was." She laughed as her smile grew, more relaxed than when I'd met her yesterday.

"I wasn't expecting the beautiful woman standing with my son to be the same best friend's little niece from all those years ago."

Her eyes held mine for a long moment before she blinked

and took another swig of water. Maybe this was stress. My worry over my son was making me imagine things, like Peyton staring at my mouth when I swiped my napkin over it. She all but admitted that she had a crush on me, but I wasn't sure if it was past or present, and why the hell was I so damn curious to find out?

"If you don't mind my asking, how are *you* doing since you moved here?"

"Okay, I guess." She lifted a shoulder. "I always liked coming back here to visit, even though I haven't been here in a long time. It's a nice little town. When I saw the job opening at the high school, I applied on a whim. When I got it, I packed up and moved pretty quickly." She huffed out a laugh before tilting her head back to gulp the rest of her water. My eyes fell on the graceful slope of her neck, following her hand as she swept her dark hair off her shoulder.

I flexed my fingers back and forth into a fist under the table to shake off the urge to touch her.

"I'm sure it's an adjustment being here. Kind of a culture shock from Brooklyn, right?" I reached for my water bottle, and I took a long pull, shutting my eyes as I willed myself to cool off and stop drooling over the gorgeous but forbidden woman sitting across the bench.

Again, what the hell was happening to me?

When I brought my head back down, Peyton furrowed her brow as her eyes bored into mine. Her eyes were almost hooded as we sat there in silence, gazes locked as the rest of the park faded away.

"What's wrong?" I finally asked, my voice raspy, since my mouth was already parched again.

"Sorry, um . . . your shirt is wet." She handed me a napkin and draped a hand over her eyes. I looked down, and sure enough, I'd dribbled the water down my shirt. So much for cooling off. The heat in her eyes burned me right up, and I was this close to asking to see her again—despite how I should have been staying as far away from her as possible.

"Oh, Peyton, there you are!" An older woman with long blond hair and cat-eyed glasses rushed over to our table. "I wanted to introduce you to some parents when you have a moment."

"Oh, I can be there in a minute—"

"Go ahead. I can clean up the plates."

Her nose crinkled before she glanced behind her. "I probably won't be very long."

"No worries. I only came as a driver, anyway. You're here to meet new people too." I nodded toward the woman behind her. "Like I told Mikey, go make the most of it."

A slow grin spread her mouth. *Fuck, she was pretty.*

"I guess I should take my own advice. Thanks, Jake."

I allowed myself thirty seconds to watch her walk away before I threw our plates into the trash.

With my son living with me now, I was sure that dating had to go on the back burner for the foreseeable future. It didn't bother me. I was happy with the perpetual bachelor life, which my sister, Kristina, liked to tease me about.

If Peyton were anyone else, this odd pull I felt toward her wouldn't unnerve me so much. I could ask her to have dinner with me, watch the corners of her eyes crinkle when she laughed, track the swipe of her tongue over her bottom lip, and not be ashamed for wanting a taste.

But she wasn't, so I couldn't.

FIVE

PEYTON

"When was the last time we saw Jake's son?" Aunt Maya mused to Uncle Keith as we set the table for dinner.

"I think he was small," Uncle Keith said as he stacked the boxes of pizza on the side table. "Maybe six or seven. Jake mostly kept it to just the two of them when he had Mikey on weekends. You don't mind that I invited them tonight, right, P?"

"Of course I don't mind." I cleared my throat when my reply came out defensive. "It's your house. I'm just a temporary squatter." I chuckled as I set the glasses around the table, wincing at how accurate of a description squatter was for me at the moment. We were already almost two weeks into the school year, and I was still camped out on my uncle's couch.

"You are not a squatter. I just meant that Mikey is one of your students, and after a long week, you may not want to feel like you have to be *on* on a Friday night."

I laughed and shook my head. "I don't feel like I have to be on. Mike is a good kid, and Jake is your friend. I'm happy you invited them."

Even if my uncle's friend made parts of my body pulse when they weren't supposed to. I had to get used to being around him without the flutters, and tonight would be perfect practice. Simply eating with him at the barbecue was torture. I'd almost forgotten how to chew as I tried to will my eyes away from the sinful roll of his Adam's apple each time he swallowed.

Watching Jake eat shouldn't have been the almost-erotic experience it was, and while he was at my uncle's table, it absolutely couldn't be. Maybe staying out of his line of sight would help, although I doubted I'd be able to resist a glance or two.

He was an old crush, and I was feeling vulnerable in a new place and new job. As long as I kept that in mind, maybe I could get through tonight and the rest of the year as his son's guidance counselor.

"Would you mind getting that?" Aunt Maya asked when the doorbell chimed.

"Sure," I said, inhaling a deep breath and letting it go slowly as I made my way to the door. This was no problem. I'd have a slice, make some small talk, and retreat to the basement without seeming rude. I'd be polite, amiable, and keep the dirty thoughts and feelings to myself.

"Hi, Peyton. I guess we keep running into each other." Jake's wide smile stole my breath the minute I opened the door. He wore a black T-shirt over worn jeans that hung on his hips. Simple and casual, but so damn sexy that my eyes strained from the need to roam down his body. My gaze landed on his mouth for a second before the deep rumble of my uncle's laugh reminded me of where I was and who I was with—and why I had to try harder to stop looking where I shouldn't have been.

"Who is this dude? That young man can't be Mikey."

31

"It's Mike," I said to my uncle over my shoulder while flashing a grin at Mike. He smiled back at me, a tiny blush staining his cheeks.

"Thanks, Ms. Miller." His lips curved in a sheepish grin as he passed me to come inside.

"Ms. Miller?" My uncle laughed. "I'm not used to seeing my niece in counselor mode."

Jake's smile faded, cutting me a quick glance before giving Aunt Maya a hello kiss.

"Glad you guys came! I was just asking Keith when was the last time we saw you. I didn't recognize you either." She grinned at Mike. "Ah, the monsters smell pepperoni." She glanced toward the loud rumble on the ceiling before the twins stomped down the stairs.

"Easy, guys. You sound like two elephants." Uncle Keith grabbed their shoulders as they raced to the table and turned them both around. "Mike, this is Aiden and Brian. Guys, this is Jake's son, Mike. After we eat, you can take him upstairs and show him the three game consoles you made us buy."

"Hi," they both said in unison before jetting toward the boxes of pizza.

"Men of few words," Uncle Keith sighed, shaking his head.

"Eh, I'm used to it." Jake squeezed Mike's shoulder. The pure love in his eyes for his son, despite how Mike grumbled when he tried to pull him closer, made my heart squeeze.

As if I needed another reason to swoon over this guy.

He was so worried about not doing the right thing for his son, but he obviously loved him too much to fail. I'd been working with kids long enough to know how to spot the good parents, the ones who didn't care, and the ones who pretended they did for appearance's sake.

"Did you ever meet Mike before he was your student?" Aunt Maya asked me after we settled at the table.

"No, the last time I'd seen Jake was when I stayed here that summer when I was fifteen."

Aunt Maya squinted back at me. "Really? You've been back since you were fifteen."

"I have, but Jake was never here when I was. We've managed to dodge each other until now."

I made the mistake of glancing across the table, my heart fluttering against my rib cage, thanks to Jake's megawatt smile.

"It's true. Why, I had no clue who she was last week." Jake smirked at me.

"You didn't?" Uncle Keith chuckled. "It's been a while since you've seen her, but to me, she looks the same."

"She most certainly does not," Aunt Maya said, her eyes narrowed at her husband. "I'd just met you a couple of years before that, I think. We hadn't even been married a year. You were pretty then, but you're a knockout now."

I'd loved Aunt Maya on sight when I first met her. Even as a young teenager, I was ashamed of the cold reception my family had given her when my uncle first brought her to meet all of us. I had sat next to her at my grandparents' dinner table in uncomfortable silence when we started chatting like girlfriends. I didn't visit them as often as I would have liked over the years, but she was always that perfect balance of parent and friend whenever I needed a sympathetic ear.

My family came around, in part thanks to an ultimatum from my uncle, but no one was as close to her as I was.

I'd tried to tell her the reason I'd left Brooklyn so many times since I'd arrived here, but like my uncle, it hurt too much to disappoint her.

"You're very kind, but knockout is stretching it."

"No, it isn't." Uncle Keith leaned back in his seat with a heavy sigh. "The day you met me at the office, all the guys were falling all over themselves to talk to you until I set them straight."

"Set them straight? How?" Aunt Maya squinted at Uncle Keith, shooting me a quick side glance.

"I told them she was my niece and to back off."

"Keith, get over it. She's your *adult* niece. What is she supposed to . . ." She trailed off when her gaze landed on Jake and Mike. This wasn't the best conversation to have in front of one of my students, friend of the family or not.

Or Jake. Not that I ever really expected anything to happen between us, even if I had replayed him calling me beautiful a hundred times in my head.

When I peered down at the end of the table, I caught Jake's gaze. His mouth flattened into a hard line as his eyes held mine. So much for ignoring him tonight.

Was it just my residual crush, or was something really brewing between us?

But in the end, what did it matter? Nothing could happen, and my uncle had given us an unintentional reminder of why.

I managed to get through dinner, not saying much, but Jake and Uncle Keith were too deep in conversation to notice. The twins ran upstairs after they devoured three slices each, leaving Mike at the table in between his father and my uncle. I held in a laugh at how Mike seemed to be hanging on Uncle Keith's every word, and I headed to the kitchen to clean up.

"Could I help you?"

I almost dropped the dish I was holding when Jake startled me in the kitchen.

"No, thank you, I'm just rinsing and loading." I held up the plate in my hand. "I'm glad you guys came. Mike seems a lot more at ease."

"He is, thank God." Jake shifted closer, picking up a couple of dishes from the pile and handing them to me. "That's thanks to you."

"Me? I've only seen him once so far." I took the dishes from his hands, ignoring the jolt from where our fingertips brushed.

"You pointed him in the right direction of the robotics group, and he's already got all those kids in a daily group chat. He grumbles like a normal teenager, but he's not so miserable anymore."

I shook my head. "He would have found out about it anyway, but I'm glad he's making friends." I shut the dish-washer door, not looking back at Jake, but the hairs on the back of my neck let me know he was still behind me. "I don't think you have anything to worry about. He's going to be fine."

"Well," he started, cocking his head from side to side, "I think I'll always worry. At least for a while."

"Understandable." I fell back against the edge of the counter. "But no reason to worry right now."

"We'll see." His lips curled. "So I guess you're not allowed at the police station again."

I chuckled and shook my head. "Let's hope I'm never in trouble and Uncle Keith isn't around. They're all probably afraid to come near me."

He barked out a laugh. That smile, that twinkle in his blue eyes, it was unfair for one man to be that good-looking. Or at least, unfair to me.

"My aunt and uncle have a skewed version of what I look like. It comes from a place of love, but they're a little ridiculous."

"I disagree," he said, shaking his head as his eyes held mine again.

"What, that I can't handle a few horny cops? I handle

broody high school kids, which are more or less the same thing. I promise I can hold my own."

"I'm sure you can." His voice dipped to a husky rasp that made my pinkie toe jerk as if an electric current ran through me. "But you should look in a mirror sometime. You're every bit the knockout your aunt said you were."

Jake Russo had just said that I was a knockout, with enough heat in his eyes to halt my breath and my heartbeat. That couldn't have been right. I blinked a couple times, sure I'd heard wrong. I would have asked him to repeat that, but my gaping mouth refused to form any words.

"Finally, someone to listen to what Keith has to say without having to pretend!" Aunt Maya came into the kitchen with the last of the plates I hadn't noticed. "Mike can come over anytime." Her smile faded as she looked between us. "Everything okay?"

"Oh yeah," Jake said, clearing his throat before turning away from me. "Even though it's not a school night, Mike and I are going to head out." He kissed Aunt Maya's cheek. "Thanks for everything."

"Stop that, Jake. You're always welcome here."

"Good night, Peyton." His regular voice, the one without sex dripping from it, was back. He straightened as if a surge of tension shot across his shoulders.

"Good night, Jake. Good night, Mike," I called out to the living room.

Jake nodded before he padded out of the kitchen.

"Dessert was amazing. After these dishes, I'll go back downstairs if that's okay—"

"Everything all right?" She lifted a brow.

"Of course." I sputtered out a nervous laugh. "I'm good, really."

She eyed me as she opened the dishwasher door and shoved the rest inside.

As I'd always told my students, it was hard to tell anyone your problems when you couldn't admit them to yourself.

SIX

JAKE

"So what else can you tell me about school?" I asked my son from my side of the vinyl booth. I'd brought him to this diner hundreds of times on our weekends together, and he always ordered the same thing. The waitresses who knew him brought him a grilled cheese sandwich and french fries the second he sat down.

"I don't know," he mumbled around a fry. "It's fine, I guess."

"I know you love the fries here, but they may taste better if you stop to come up for air."

A smirk pulled at the corner of his mouth as he looked up.

"I'm just starving. Gym is forty-five minutes at the end of the day. That's torture."

"They make you do physical activity?" I clutched my chest in mock horror. "For a whole forty-five minutes? Not a chance to look at your phone even once? You're right, that's pure torture." I stole a fry from his plate. "Remind me to call the school tomorrow."

"Very funny, Dad." He rolled his eyes. "Would it be okay if

38

I went over to someone's house tomorrow night? It's a birthday party right down the block."

"Whose party is it? One of the guys from the group chat?"

"Aaron."

"Aaron Score? The house right before the dead end? I worked on that house for weeks before they moved in." I laughed. "You can go. I'll take you to buy a present for him tomorrow before you head over."

"Cool." He went back to his fries, and I felt a bit unsettled at how easy it had been for the last month. He got on the bus in the morning, we had dinner at night, he gave me one-word answers like all teenagers when I asked about his day, but it didn't feel as tense or as forced as it had been when he'd first moved in. Had we turned a corner so soon? Maybe finding some friends was helping ease his hurt feelings about his mother dumping him here. Either way, I'd take it, even if I feared it wouldn't last long.

"Mike, I thought that was you!"

Peyton came up to our table, almost out of nowhere. Mikey straightened in his seat when he noticed her.

"Hi, Ms. Miller."

"Hello to you too, Jake." She flashed me a big smile, and I cursed the flutters that took off in my stomach. Forty-six-year-old men shouldn't get butterflies or be so damn captivated by a woman they hardly knew and had a million reasons to stay away from.

"Nice to see you, Peyton." I grinned when her eyes flicked to mine for a beat before turning back to Mikey.

"I'm picking up an order for the family. Uncle Keith was going to come, but I felt like heading out for a drive. It's a nice night to be out of the basement."

My smile matched hers, and for the moment, it didn't feel so wrong to like this woman. Well, maybe it still did, but it felt natural and good. *Really* good—reaffirming how much I needed to keep my distance.

"I suppose it is."

We all turned to my phone as it buzzed across the table. I cringed when I spotted my ex-wife's number flash across the screen.

"Eileen? What's up?"

"Is our son with you?" she asked, clipped and impatient even though she hadn't even said hello.

I eyed Mikey, no longer eating with the same gusto as he slumped against his seat.

"He is. Why?"

"I'd like to talk to him since he hasn't responded to a text in days. What did you do, have him block my number?"

"Hold on for a minute."

I stood, holding the phone to my chest.

"I need to speak to your mother. Why don't you sit with Pey—Ms. Miller for a minute until I get back?"

I cut a quick look to Peyton as I slid out of the booth. She responded with a tiny nod before I jogged out into the parking lot.

"You should know I'd never do that. Petty games were your thing, not mine."

"Right. You've wanted to take him away from me for years."

"Are you kidding me? I wanted more time with him, yes, but I'd never take him away from you, and you know that. He just needs time to adjust."

Memories of years of this ran through my brain and exhausted me. As much as I'd tried to appease her for our son's sake, it was never good enough.

"Why? Because I decided to live my life for me for once? I put in fourteen years, and I won't feel bad for wanting something for myself."

I pressed my palm to my forehead, trying like hell to calm the fuck down, but after the decade *I'd* put in after we divorced, I'd finally had enough.

"You *put in* fourteen years? Like raising our son was some kind of prison sentence. I would have split custody with you rather than just have him for the weekends, and you know that. Hell, I would have taken him to live with me a long time ago, but I never wanted to make him feel like he was caught in the middle. You want to live your life for yourself now, that's fucking great. But Mike has every right to feel however he feels about it. He'll text back when he wants to. Have a good night."

I stabbed the phone screen, groaning as I let my head fall back. When I shifted to go back inside, I found my son standing behind me. Peyton leaned against the back entrance, wincing when our eyes met.

I exhaled a long breath as I approached my son, rubbing the back of my neck as if that would force the right words out. Once I spied the sad look in his eyes, I had no doubt he'd heard every word I said.

"Listen, Mike—"

"It's fine, Dad. You looked angry from the window, and I wanted to make sure you were okay. Whatever Mom said . . ." He kicked at a couple of rocks at his feet. "It's fine."

He didn't seem angry—that I could have handled. When he turned to trudge back inside, I wished for the days when an ice cream cone or a piece of candy was the solution to all his problems. I had no idea how to fix any of this for him, and it ate away at me.

"I overheard my mother having a conversation with my father once. I was much younger than Mike, though." Peyton stepped in front of me. "He had canceled again for a weekend, and I heard her say, 'Well, if she isn't your priority, she's mine.

Call back when you grow up.'" She snickered, her eyes darting from the pavement back to me. "That was the last contact we had with him, so we assumed he never did."

"I'm sorry, Peyton."

"Eh, it wasn't a loss in the long run. I was loved and spoiled by everyone else, and while it wasn't great hearing that I wasn't my father's priority, I always remembered my mother saying I was hers. Mike will remember you saying that you always wanted him. And whatever is going on with his mother, that's what he needs." She wrapped her hand around my bicep and squeezed. "You're a great father. He's lucky to have you. Stop beating yourself up, thinking he's not."

I reached up and covered her hand, not caring how I shouldn't be touching her or how this would look if anyone saw us.

"Thank you. I needed that professional opinion."

She grinned, and even in the dim lights of the parking lot, it was impossible to miss how gorgeous she was.

"Anytime. Plus, you called him Mike." She poked my chest. "I bet that's extra points too. I can ask to see him on Monday if that would make you feel better. I'd mentioned I'd be sched-uling some follow-ups with the freshman class anyway." The side of her mouth curved up, and even while pissed off and keyed up, I zeroed in on her lips.

One problem at a time.

"I still can't tell you what he says, but maybe I can offer some vague but helpful advice after." Her sweet smile soothed me.

"I would appreciate that."

Our gazes lingered that extra moment too long before she headed back to the takeout counter inside.

I did want my son. As clueless as I was about everything else, maybe that would turn out to be enough.

SEVEN

PEYTON

"**G**ood morning, honey! I hope the twins didn't wake you."

I smiled at my aunt as I shuffled into their kitchen.

"I was up, actually trying not to wake *you* up from jumping too hard."

One of the great things about the basement apartment was the open space. I cued up a boisterous cardio workout on my phone and had plenty of room to run back and forth. I'd checked out the gym in town, and while it looked modern and clean, it was full of too many people I already knew from school and around town. I missed the anonymity of my old gym in Brooklyn and the unspoken rule of no conversation during workouts.

"Nope, not at all. There are weights and bands down there too, if you'd like to use them. If you want to come to Pilates with me, let me know. I don't blame you for not wanting to go to the gym in town." I laughed at the cringe twisting her mouth.

"The gym is a little too small and friendly. I don't mind

working out at home. When my condo is finally ready, I'll have the space in my living room to do whatever I want."

I loved my family but hated feeling like a nomad. As the water beat down on my head in the shower, I'd been daydreaming about the shower rack I wanted to buy for my own bathroom. The house was great, the basement apartment was spacious and comfortable, but it wasn't mine. Although my aunt and uncle gave me all the privacy I wanted, I was still antsy to be on my own.

The twins rushed down the stairs when the doorbell rang.

"Goodness, if I could only bottle that energy." Aunt Maya sighed, tightening the band around her low ponytail before heading to the door.

"Mike, come in."

Mike and Jake crossed the threshold, Mike almost tiptoeing inside as Jake pulled my aunt into a hug.

"Thank you. Before Keith got called in, I planned a whole bunch of errands today, and I know my son doesn't like spending his Saturdays in the hardware store."

Mike rolled his eyes when his father glanced back at him.

"No problem. This isn't the arcade that Keith planned for them all today, but the boys have a ton of games to keep Mike busy enough to pass the time until you finish what you need to get done."

"Yes," Aiden said before rushing up to Mike. "We have a ton of games for you to be here all day! Come on!" He yanked Mike up the stairs by his hand until they disappeared on the second floor.

"Why don't you go with Jake?" my aunt suggested, drawing slightly widened eyes from both of us. "I'm sure you don't want to deal with three loud boys all afternoon, and didn't you say you wanted to pick up a few things for the condo?" She waved a hand at us. "Go. I'll stay back and make sure they have snack refills."

"I actually do need stuff, but I wouldn't want to impose."

He shook his head, his lips curving into a warm smile.

"Not at all. Plenty of room in my truck, and I don't mind the company if they aren't asking how long this will take and can we go home now."

I chuckled and nodded. "I'll do my best. Let me get my purse, and we can head out."

My aunt was sending me out to spend the afternoon alone with Jake. Seemed innocent enough, yet didn't feel that way. But I did need stuff for the condo, and while I loved my little cousins, getting out of the house on a Saturday while they both screamed at the TV screen seemed like a great idea.

Maybe an afternoon together doing boring things would take the power out of this pesky pull I'd felt toward Jake whenever I was within five feet of him.

When I spotted him leaning against the truck as if he'd stepped out of a suburban cologne ad, my high hopes crashed pretty quickly.

"I shouldn't be that long at the hardware store, and I can take you anywhere else you want to go," Jake said as he opened the passenger side door for me to climb in.

"Thanks, but I think I'm good. And besides, I'm sure after living with a teenager full time you'd like a little solitude on a weekend." I rubbed at my arms to quell the sudden shiver. "September gets cold fast up here."

A nervous chuckle fell from my lips, my shaking having nothing to do with crisp fall temps and everything to do with sharing such a small space with Jake.

He stepped into the driver's seat, flashing me a grin. The car smelled like spicy sandalwood, how I imagined Jake's scent would be if I climbed onto his lap and nuzzled into the crook of his neck. I cleared my throat and shook my head, trying to erase the intrusive thought from my brain.

"As I said, I don't mind your—the company." His wide smile shrank to a sheepish grin. "I wouldn't want to be in that house with all three kids either. My son gets very passionate about video games and never realizes how loud he's yelling."

"He'll fit right in with my cousins, then. Aunt Maya must own earplugs."

He chuckled, low and husky and unfairly sexy.

"Plus, I can show you the sights around town, make sure you've seen all five of them."

I laughed as I tried to buckle my seat belt. "Am I doing something wrong? It's not clicking in."

"The lock is tricky," he said, reaching across my body until it clicked. "There, got it!" When he lifted his head, both of us stilled. Now that I was close enough to breathe him in, he did smell of sandalwood and soap. His body was draped over mine, but neither of us was as quick as we should've been about backing away. His arm grazed my breast as he finally eased off me. My surge of desire was replaced by relief and a trace of disappointment.

I was breathless when he started the car and clueless as to how I'd convinced myself that being in proximity to Jake for the whole afternoon would be a good idea.

"Mike should have fun today." I cleared my throat when my voice screeched. "The twins have that new virtual reality game that's kind of cool. I tried it a few times, but they both got a little annoyed trying to teach me how it worked."

Jake smiled, keeping his eyes on the road.

"Mike has one of those too. I thought at least the boys might keep him busy enough not to brood."

"Has he been doing that at home? At school, he seems fine."

He lifted a shoulder. "I guess no more than usual. I've just been watching him a little more closely after that phone call with his mother last week."

I nodded, hating the tension knitting his brow.

"Off the record, I can tell you when I brought him in to chat he didn't mention it once. It was all robotics and his new friends and a camping trip they may be going on. Superficial stuff, and he didn't seem broody to me."

Jake nodded. "So either he's getting used to the fact that his mother dumped him with me, or he's learning how to hide it better." He shut off the engine after we pulled into a spot. "Either way, I hate it, and I don't know what to do about it."

Before I could help myself, I draped my hand over where he still held the steering wheel. "I hate it for him too, but from what I can see, you're doing everything right. This is his normal now—*you're* his normal. Since he seems to be acclimating to it, maybe you could try to relax. Just a little." I pinched the air between my index finger and thumb.

His lips curved, the slow smile making it up to his eyes when he glanced back at me. "I guess I could always try."

The blue in his irises was even more translucent in the sunlight. I was used to concerned parents unloading their worries on me, but I'd never wanted to leap over the console and wrap my arms around any of them. But Jake wasn't just any parent or just my uncle's best friend. I'd never gotten to know the man behind my teenage crush all those years ago, and now that I was learning about the beautiful heart inside the gorgeous package, he was that much harder to resist.

But I had no other choice.

EIGHT
JAKE

"This is adorable," Peyton said, scanning the space as we stepped into Mary's, a tiny coffee shop near my office.

"Adorable?" I laughed. "Four tables and a counter make it adorable?"

She shrugged as we settled into seats at a table toward the back. "It's cozy. Just like I'd expect from this town." She smiled, picking up one of the placemat menus. "So, what's good here?"

You.

I took a long moment to answer her question, too fixated on the lock of hair falling in front of her face and the inappropriate urge to reach forward and tuck it behind her ear.

Stopping my eyes from roaming up and down her body for the past few hours had given me a splitting headache. Now that she'd peeled her jacket off, the temptation to look was that much worse. In leggings and a long-sleeved T-shirt, she was every bit as gorgeous as when I'd last seen her.

And I still wasn't supposed to notice.

She chewed on her bottom lip as she studied the menu, calling even more attention to that pretty mouth and those full lips. I'd had the silly thought that maybe spending an afternoon with her would take the edge off the attraction, but all it had done was make it worse.

"Hey Jake, who's your friend?"

Mary, the owner and main waitress, smiled while glancing between Peyton and me. She always reminded me of my mother, although maybe a few years younger. She was petite with fiery red hair and a matching attitude. Her kids had moved out of town, but she'd never leave Kelly Lakes or this shop.

"Mary, this is Peyton. She's a new guidance counselor at the high school and Keith's niece."

"Chief Keith is your uncle?" Mary's hand flew to her chest. "Aren't you a pretty little thing? Did your uncle's friend offer to buy you lunch?" Mary cut me a look I didn't like—as if she'd just caught my hand in a cookie jar. Or maybe that was because it felt that way.

Peyton was forbidden sweets, and hell if all I'd wanted to do was take a bite.

"He doesn't have to do that. Everything looks so good."

"Your uncle gets the grilled chicken BLT for lunch when he stops by," Mary said, her eyes again flicking to me.

"I'll have the same, I guess," she told Mary as she peered back at me. "What's your usual?"

Pining for my best friend's niece, then spending hours talking myself out of it.

"Turkey club," I answered, turning my head to Mary. "And an iced tea."

"Two, please." Peyton smiled and leaned her elbows on the table.

Mary nodded, scribbling on her pad before ambling back to the kitchen, swiveling her head to us once more.

Jesus. It didn't take much of a spark for the rumor mill to be lit around here, and Mary's mouth was always moving. This place was small, but enough people came in and out on a given day.

There was nothing wrong with having lunch with Peyton —or there shouldn't have been. Maya had practically pushed us out the door together. It was a given that Peyton and I would keep crossing paths, either at the high school or at Keith's. In Kelly Lakes, I ran into everyone I knew all the time, but I didn't seek any of them out like I kept doing with the beautiful woman sitting across from me.

"You don't have to buy me lunch." She shook her head. "Especially after driving me around all afternoon."

"I would have offered if Mary didn't put me on the spot first. And I keep telling you I didn't mind."

"I guess you come here often if you have a usual." Her full lips spread into a grin.

"My office is across the street. We usually order from here a couple times per week. So, what are your plans for the rest of the day?"

"I have a few lessons to plan, so hopefully the twins will be tired out from showing Mike every single game they have. I love them all, but I will be *so* happy to be in my condo when it's ready."

"I didn't know guidance counselors taught classes," I said, my eyes catching how her top stretched across her full breasts and the pattern of lace I could make out under the material.

"It's not really a class. It's a wellness workshop. We had a lot of them at my old school, and I volunteered to plan the first one this year. This one is on anxiety management. How to recognize it, what you can do, topics like that."

"I don't remember any of that from when I was in high school."

I did a quick math equation in my head, subtracting

Peyton's age from how many years ago I was in high school, and my stomach turned over at the answer.

"Mental health isn't such a vague concept anymore in schools, thank God. This workshop has group exercises that I'm sure they'll all groan at me for, but most get into it after I push them a little. And the really anxious students who are too embarrassed to ask for help will hopefully get something out of it." She lifted a shoulder. "That makes doing work on a Saturday worth it. The school offered extra credit to the students who stay after school to attend, so hopefully that, along with the free cupcakes we keep pushing, will make some of them show up. If I can get enough butts in the seats, maybe I can convince the guidance department to make it a regular thing."

She cracked a wide grin, nodding a thank you to Mary when she set down our iced teas. If I were a student, I would have been the first in line to sign up.

"Those kids are lucky to have you."

She shrugged, stirring the iced tea with the straw before taking a sip. I never thought I'd be jealous of a plastic straw until she slid it past her perfect lips. I shifted in my seat when my cock twitched in envy too.

"I'm just doing my job."

"I'm sure there are a lot of guidance counselors who just go through the motions. You care about the kids, I saw it right away with Mike. Thanks to you, he's got a cluster of friends already and I barely get a hello and goodbye, but I'm okay with that."

"I've seen him around school with a little posse. I'm so glad he found his people."

"How about you?" I asked. "Have you found your people yet?"

Peyton's head jerked up as Mary came back to the table.

"Here you go," Mary sang as she dropped our plates in front of us. Peyton grabbed her sandwich, too hungry, I guessed, to note Mary's eyes still on us.

"Thanks, Mary," I said, my attempt at giving her a hint to stop looking us over and help the other group of customers that had just wandered in.

"My job description is to help guide them, so I've always taken it very seriously."

"Do a lot of kids come to see you with their problems?"

"Some. I always tell every student I have an open-door policy. If students are in crisis, I can call them in to check on them during classes. One girl likes to eat her lunch in my office sometimes. Some of the mean girls were giving her a hard time yesterday, and she needed a reprieve."

Even the way this woman chewed was sexy, moaning around a couple of bites and swiping her tongue across her lips. I inhaled a slow breath and forced myself to get a grip.

"I almost became an English teacher instead, but this gives me a satisfaction I wouldn't get from just teaching a class. It's a privilege being a student's safe place."

"Because you're like your uncle. Why every business here knows him personally. He's all about helping people too."

Keith was always there for me. When my father had a heart attack behind the wheel, he made sure to get to my house before anyone called to tell me he was dead. He was there through my divorce, hooking me up with a lawyer he knew would help me protect my rights to my son when Eileen was going off the rails. He'd even stopped by sometimes in between his shifts to check on us since Mike had moved in with me.

I owed him better than to drool over the woman he thought of as a daughter.

Her warm brown eyes lit up. "My uncle is the best person I know, so if you think I'm like him, that is a huge compliment."

"Other than his ball-breaking ways, I think you are."

She burst out laughing, and it was the best sound in the world.

"You didn't answer my question. Did you find your people yet?"

She dropped her chin to her chest for a moment before lifting her gaze.

"I've made friends with some teachers at school, and I've met them for drinks a few times. I'm kind of displaced at the moment until my condo is ready, but that all comes in time. I guess there's only one bar in town." She eyed the sandwich before taking another big bite.

"There may be a couple of small ones by the highway, but the one you probably went to is the one everyone goes to. Sometimes it's better to go a town or two over if you want a night out without eyes on you the whole time."

"I love how this place is like a Hallmark movie." She wiped the napkin across her mouth. "Kelly Lakes is only a few hours away from the city, and there's one supermarket everyone goes to, one coffee shop, and one diner. I can see wanting to have a couple of drinks without everyone knowing where you'd been the next morning."

"Depends on how wild and crazy you want to get when you go out."

My brows jumped when her eyes met mine.

"Wild and crazy hasn't described a night out of mine in a long time." She shook her head as she lifted her glass.

"I'm sure guys have been all over you since you moved here."

Her brows creased as she chewed.

"Not really." She pursed her lips. "Other than the new

officer at the police station, who was reprimanded for trying to talk to me. My uncle *is* awesome, but he's a jerk when he wants to be. Poor guy."

"Did he ask you out before your uncle scared him away?"

Where the hell was I going with this? Her love life was none of my concern or business, even if the thought of her dating anyone made me bristle.

"Uncle Keith didn't give him a chance." She chuckled. "But I'm not ready for that yet. I want to make a home for myself here before I add anyone else." She bunched her shoulders into a shrug. "I'm focusing on me for right now."

"Did you leave someone back in Brooklyn?"

She stilled, gently setting her sandwich back on her plate.

"I can honestly tell you that other than my mother and best friend, I left nothing and no one behind in Brooklyn."

I heaved out a sigh, disgusted with myself for poking where I shouldn't have been in the first place and upsetting her.

"I'm sorry, Peyton. I shouldn't be asking you who you're seeing or used to see."

"It's okay," she said, smiling as she gave my arm a quick squeeze. "The point is, I have nothing to tell. Which is kind of sad."

I flashed her a grin when she crinkled her nose, a ridiculous wave of relief relaxing me. Eventually, she'd date someone her own age and I'd have to get over myself.

Right or wrong, I was happy that day wasn't today.

"What about you? Is Mike living with you full time messing with your bachelor lifestyle?" A wry smile drifted across her lips.

"Despite the rumors, living with a teenager doesn't cramp my style."

She squinted at me, a skeptical frown pulling down her lips.

"Are you sure about that?"

I leaned back, a smile tugging at the corner of my mouth.

"Why, you're not?"

"Maybe I'm judging." Her cheeks flushed pink. "I know you're a nice guy, and a man who looks like you doesn't always take advantage of it just because he can."

"A man who looks like me?" I coughed out a laugh as I leaned forward, resting my elbows on the table. "And what would you mean by that?"

"I didn't . . . I mean . . ." She groaned and draped her hand over her eyes. "Stop looking at me until I can figure out a way to explain what I just said without making an idiot of myself."

I couldn't help but laugh as I peeled her hand away from her eyes.

"I don't think you're an idiot. I'm flattered. And that's why I thought the single guys around here would be beating a path to your uncle's door. Like I've said, you're beautiful, Peyton."

After playing it safe with women ever since my divorce, why was this one always tempting me into the danger zone?

"Thank you," she whispered, darting her eyes everywhere but mine. "This was nice. Thanks for bringing me with you today."

"No need to thank me. It was nice for me too. This must be why the kids like you. You have a calming presence."

She sputtered out a laugh before slurping the rest of her iced tea. As much as she captivated me to the point that I forgot how to act and speak, she did calm me. So much so that I dreaded having to drive her home.

What if I didn't? What if I asked her to spend the rest of the afternoon with me so that I could find out why she felt like she'd left nothing behind? Who hurt her and how could I make it right?

I couldn't ask that because it was already impossible to keep the distance that should have been between us. Each time I wanted more, and each time it was harder to cut myself off.

When Mary dropped off the check, I fished two twenties out of my wallet and tossed them onto the table. "That should cover us." I hoped it was enough of a generous tip for Mary to keep her mouth shut about what she thought she saw.

"Jake, stop. You can't treat me."

"I can and I did. Ready?" When she walked past me, my hand flew to the small of her back as we headed outside. The urge to touch her in some way was too intense, and I reached out before I could stop it. That had been happening between us all day—again why, after I dropped her off, I needed to work harder to stay away from her.

I needed to, but I knew I wouldn't. It was strange dreading my own next move.

"And listen," I began once we climbed into my truck. "You have people in this town other than your family. You're more home than you think."

Her face crumpled for a moment.

"Thanks, Jake." She reached out to squeeze my hand, the same nerve endings firing where our skin touched. I gave it a squeeze back and pulled out of the space.

I wished she'd show me something that would make me dislike her or want to back off, other than my best friend killing me over how I felt about her.

Wishing away how I felt about her was pointless because everything about her lured me in.

NINE
PEYTON

"This was a nice little turnout," Deirdre, one of the sophomore counselors, noted as we packed up the leftover cupcakes and snacks. I'd skipped lunch to see a student and had barely had enough time to help get everything ready for today's workshop. I wanted to shove one of the chocolate cupcakes into my mouth to silence my growling stomach, but I was so happy with the number of students who showed up, even if they had been bribed to come here.

"It was. I was glad to see some familiar faces today too."

"Me too! It's like maybe we're getting through to some of them." Deirdre had the same happy satisfaction in her features that was blooming in my chest. After months of my hands being tied to truly help kids in my old school, I'd forgotten how much I'd missed this.

"Ms. Miller?"

"Oh hey, Selena!" Selena was one of my freshman students. Tall and pretty, but always made her way down the halls with hunched shoulders. I remembered being the awkward tall girl until sophomore year when most either caught up to or passed me, but before then, I had the same shy stance as I headed to and from class.

That, unfortunately, was something that stayed all too constant. Teenagers, especially girls, were conditioned to hide the best parts of themselves, all for the sake of not wanting to be different.

"Thank you for . . . this." Her voice was timid as a smile crept across her lips. "It all made a lot of sense."

Her mother was a recovering addict but, from what I'd heard from Selena when she'd come to see me, had done a solid job of turning her life around. The stigma of the past was something they both suffered from, and high school kids could be vicious and unforgiving.

"I am so glad you felt that way. Everyone gets anxious, and the little things we went over today can help a lot."

"And thank you for today." Her smile faded. "I'm sorry I interrupted your lunch."

"Please don't apologize, Selena. That's what I'm here for. If you'd like, maybe we can schedule one lunch per week to check in, but my door is always open to you."

"That sounds good, actually. I shouldn't let them bother me, I know."

I shook my head, giving her a smile when she lifted her gaze.

"You feel how you feel, and high school can be rough for anyone. That's why we're all here." I nodded to Deirdre as she packed up the last of the food.

Selena smiled before ambling out of the classroom, her head a little higher than when I'd seen her earlier today. It was hard not to worry about students in crisis, but getting them to trust you enough to seek you out . . . To me, that was half the battle. In those moments, it always felt as if I were right where I was supposed to be.

Lately, those moments helped me find a little peace as well. The more I got to know my students, the more Kelly Lakes began to feel like home.

"I knew you'd be popular," Deirdre noted from behind me as she hoisted her purse onto her shoulder.

"Why would you say that?"

"The freshman counselor before you was a little . . . rigid. Even I tensed up talking to her." She chuckled. "You actually enjoy these events, don't you?"

"I do. They can be a pain to put together, but even if only one or two students show up, at least we helped someone, right?"

Deirdre nodded. "Absolutely. Here." She handed me the plastic container of cupcakes. "You said you skipped lunch, and you look a little queasy."

I shrugged. "I'm fine. And thanks. I won't eat all of them, but my cousins will be excited when I bring these home."

I found Mike heading down the hallway. I had been happy to spot him in the back of the room before we'd divided into groups, but I didn't want to embarrass him by making a big deal of it.

"Hi, Mike," I said when I caught up to him. "I was glad to see you here today."

"It was good, actually. There were some kids I hadn't met yet who seemed cool."

"See, that's a win-win, right?"

A real laugh fell from his lips, not something I had to work to cajole out of him like when we first met in my office.

"School still going okay?" I was curious about what brought him to the workshop. We were already over a month into school, and he seemed to be acclimating all right from what I could tell, but I worried that maybe there were more issues between his parents.

"Yeah, I think so. It's school, I guess."

I chuckled as we stepped outside into the parking lot.

"School is school, for sure. Thanks for staying late to come to the workshop."

"Dad said it would be good for me, and it would be good for you if people came."

"I see," I said, smiling when I spotted Jake's truck in the parking lot.

"How did it go?" Jake asked as Mike climbed into his passenger seat.

"Good," was all Mike replied. "It actually wasn't too bad. You didn't have to worry. Kids showed up."

I spotted a blush on Jake's cheeks as a grin split his mouth.

"I thought I'd help with butts in the seats."

It would've been helpful if this guy could've stopped being nice and so damn attractive, even a little.

"But seriously, I'm glad it went well. Mike seems okay, but I know he's still getting used to things," he whispered, glancing back at his son. Mike was already glued to his phone, not looking back at us.

"As I told you, usually they all get something out of it. And he even told me that he'd met new kids today, so I'm glad it was worth it for him."

"I had no doubt, if you planned it."

There was something in how his eyes held mine that made a shiver roll down my spine. I almost forgot where I was and who he was. Getting lost in his gorgeous eyes was dangerous territory, but tempted me all the same.

"Well, I better go. Thanks again . . ."

I turned too fast, the one granola bar I'd had before running out the door this morning no longer sustaining me as the parking lot spun around me.

"Shit. Peyton, are you okay?"

I blinked and found myself in Jake's arms, worry crinkling his brow as he peered down at me.

"Yeah, I didn't really eat today, and I guess my body is telling me that wasn't a good idea."

His full lips pulled into a frown as he shook his head.

"You can't take care of these kids without taking care of yourself first. I should tell your uncle on you so he forces you to eat in the morning." His blinding smile caused butterflies to swirl around my empty stomach, but that reminder of Uncle Keith should have been enough for me to push off his chest and step back. Maybe dizziness was to blame for me not moving quickly, but as I breathed him in, milking this glorious second for all it was worth, that was too big of a lie to even tell myself.

"I promise I won't do that again." I let out a nervous laugh as I eased away. "I'll have a cupcake in the car before I drive home. I'm fine. I swear I'm not usually the dopey girl who forgets to eat."

He smiled, triggering a weakness in my knees that had nothing to do with what I did or didn't eat today.

"Are you sure you're okay to drive?"

"I am. You don't have to worry—or tell on me." I shot him a grin as I backed away toward my car. "I need to do a better job of keeping up my strength before I move in to my condo next weekend. I swear I won't skip lunch again."

"That's right." Jake nodded. "Congratulations."

The air was always charged with something I couldn't pinpoint when Jake and I were together. Whenever we parted ways, a slew of confusing emotions swirled through me, the most puzzling ones regret and guilt.

His eyes held mine, still so blue and bottomless, luring me in until that familiar point when one of us would back away.

61

"Bye, Mike!" I called out, even though I knew he wouldn't hear me. "Take care, Mr. Russo."

His lips twitched into a smile.

"Take care, Ms. Miller."

I climbed into my car, my loud groan reverberating against the windows. Unwrapping a cupcake, I remembered Claudia's joke about fainting in front of a hot guy because it helped. It was a silly trope I'd never believed in, but falling into the arms of the man of your dreams did move things along—or made them even more uncomfortable and confusing than they already were.

I needed to put myself out there eventually, but I was still finding my way and hesitant after my last relationship imploded.

I hoped I'd start shaking it off soon and all of that would come in time.

But no matter when it did, it couldn't come with Jake.

TEN

PEYTON

"Could you please slow down?" I pleaded with my uncle as he jogged ahead. When he'd invited me to go for a run this morning, I didn't expect to have to sprint to keep up.

"You think this is fast?" Uncle Keith swiveled his head, chuckling and not even a little out of breath.

We passed lawn after manicured lawn until I spotted the entrance to the park at the end of the road. I hadn't realized how small this town really was when I'd come to visit. Everyone congregated in the same areas, and while that was a nice notion, it also didn't leave a person much privacy. My old neighborhood had its hot spots, but I felt much more on display here.

"Can we have a seat for a second?" I panted, pointing to a lush section of grass that seemed perfect to pass out on.

"We have to get you into shape, P." Uncle Keith looped an arm around my sweaty neck.

"I thought I was in decent shape until just now." I trudged into the park and plopped on the patch of grass. "I guess you have to be super fit to deal with the criminal element of Kelly Lakes," I teased before I dropped my head between my legs, still trying to catch my breath. When I lifted my head, I spotted a few bodies near the ball field and way off in the distance by the basketball and the handball courts.

"You'd be surprised." He rested his elbows on his knees, his lips quirking as he turned back to me. "It may not be as active as Brooklyn, but we get our fair share. So, tell me." He tapped my ankle. "How's it going so far? You're not running back to your old school in Brooklyn, so I guess that's a good sign."

I hoped he hadn't noticed me tensing at the question. Running back to my old school would always be a hard no, but I still couldn't tell him why.

"Pretty good, I think. The principal is nice, and the students have been great. Parent workshops start next week, and I volunteered to help run them. Hopefully, we get a decent turnout. The first student workshop went pretty well." I shrugged. "I'm told football is a big deal at Kelly Lakes High, so I have to show my face at the games when they start."

"Good, but don't spread yourself too thin either." He lifted a brow at me. "Get used to everything first."

"What obligations do I have? Other than moving in to my condo. I like keeping busy."

When the words were out of my mouth, they tasted rancid. It was one thing to know I didn't have anything going on here besides work and my family, but saying it out loud highlighted how pathetic it was.

"I know that." He shrugged. "I'd just like to see you get out there a little more."

"When I'm settled, I'll get out more. I promise." I patted his arm.

His mouth spread into a wide smile. "It's nice having you

here for more than just a visit. We're all going to miss you when you're out of the house next weekend."

"It's nice being here," I told him honestly. It still didn't feel quite like home yet. This felt more like a vacation, which was my intention for coming here. I could have just applied at another school in a different borough, but I didn't realize how much distance I'd needed until I found the job opening for this high school. Being here with Uncle Keith made me think of simpler times, like when spending the day with him made all my problems fade away—at least for the moment.

"And I'll be around. I'm only going ten minutes away."

Maybe I'd run *to* him as much as I ran *away* from Brooklyn and all the memories that were still fresh enough to sting.

"Everyone was always jealous of us. Still are. I hear it in your mother's voice when she calls and asks how you're doing with us *up here*. Like she didn't grow up here before she followed your father to the city."

My head fell back with a groan. "Sounds like her."

"She just misses you. It's not like when I took you to Coney Island that day."

"Oh my God." I sat up, that day so long ago, yet fresh in my mind now that Uncle Keith brought it up. "They were all so mad at you. That was the best day, though."

I was eight, and my father had just moved out. Uncle Keith and my grandparents came to stay with us for a weekend, and I remembered the relief of having family there to fill the awful silence. Mom had been so quiet since he'd left. It unnerved me to the point I couldn't sit still. Uncle Keith offered to take me out for the afternoon to get a hot dog, and we jumped on the train to Coney Island. He let my mother know when we got there and didn't take me back until after dark.

"I brought you back so pumped up on sugar, you were bouncing off the walls. I got serious shit from all of them for it, but I never regretted a single second. Seeing you smile all afternoon was worth it."

Maybe this was what I'd been seeking. That day had been a reprieve from how tough life had suddenly become, and I'd taken this job looking for the same thing. For solace, for distance, for Uncle Keith.

I leaned forward and kissed his cheek. "You were always the best."

"I can't argue with that. And if you want to date one of the cops at the station, I won't get in your way. At least I can scare them if I have to."

I laughed at his evil grin.

"Come on. Let's jog back. I'll take it slow so you can at least still see me in the distance." He tapped my ankle and popped off the ground.

"Well, thanks for the sympathy. And I'm not looking to date anyone at the moment, so no worries."

As I followed him out of the park, Jake's face flashed in my mind. I could never go there, but all the times I'd considered it twisted in my gut a little more today.

Uncle Keith wouldn't give his blessing to date his best friend. And after all he'd done for me my entire life, I couldn't hurt him like that.

Lack of control had already cost me dearly—and this time, the price would be even higher.

ELEVEN
PEYTON

This is fine. Really. All totally fine.

I lied to myself over and over again, but I couldn't make myself believe it. An overnight storm had caused a flood in my ground-level condo, destroying the floors and possibly some of the kitchen cabinets the day before I was set to move in. While I was no expert, I was fairly certain I saw the beginnings of mold along the living room wall.

When I called my insurance company after I headed here to check out the damage, I had anticipated the hassle of putting in a claim. In another shitty turn of events, they would only cover a small portion of the damage because "ground-up" floods needed to be covered by additional policies—policies I didn't have.

Before I even moved in, my brand-new condo needed an overhaul I couldn't afford.

I'd loved this condo from the first time I'd driven up here to check it out. The fact that it would be the first place I owned, not simply rented, thrilled me so much that it almost felt as if the past few months were meant to be. I was supposed to be here in this new town and school, regardless of how it happened.

As water seeped into my sneaker while I trudged around my new home, my move didn't seem so right. Karma had followed me when I'd made the silly attempt to escape it.

The only silver lining was that I hadn't unpacked anything yet. After my awful call with the insurance company, I was thankful to get a delay in the furniture delivery and made a quick extra payment to storage.

Instead of living it up in my new place, I was headed back to my uncle's basement, at least for the next few nights. Rather than helping me move in as we'd planned, he was on his way over here to help me clean up what was left of the flood so the place could air out. And I was left trying to figure out where and how to get the money for the repairs I needed.

I had no time to panic or dwell, but my nose burned with frustrated tears as I made out the rumble of Uncle Keith's truck and the gravel of the driveway crunching under his tires.

"So, the place is a little wet?"

I turned to my uncle with a sad laugh.

"Welcome to my disaster." I forced a smile despite the crack in my voice.

"Stop," Uncle Keith said, wrapping his arms around me. "It's not a disaster. We'll get this cleaned up and fixed."

I shook my head, sniffling into my uncle's chest.

"Insurance only covers a little of it. I looked up what it would cost for new flooring and cabinets, and I can't afford it. At least not now."

"That's why I'm going to help you."

My head shot up. "You can't do that."

"Why can't I?" The corner of his mouth curving up. "What kind of favorite uncle would I be if I didn't?"

"I wanted to do this move on my own. I thought I had it all handled, but—"

"You couldn't have seen this coming. It happens, P."

I shook my head. "You have your own family to worry about. I priced out the work I'd probably need online, and I can't take that money from you."

"First of all, I know a contractor who would give you a good price, so don't worry about whatever Google told you. And second, you're not my family?" He bent his head to meet my gaze. At over six feet, he towered over me.

"I still remember when your mother first brought you home." He crossed his arms and joined me as I leaned against the edge of the sink. "I had no clue what to do with a baby, but your grandmother made me hold you even when I refused."

I looked away from his sad smile. I had enough emotion scratching at the back of my throat today.

"I said I was afraid I'd break you. But as usual, no one ever listened to me, and they handed you—this little, pink-dressed football with hair—to me anyway. You gave me a big yawn and cuddled into my chest, and then I wouldn't give you back until they made me." He cocked his head to the side. "I consider you my own just as much as the boys." He grabbed my hand and squeezed. "That's why I was thrilled when you said you were moving back here. This—" he motioned to the drenched floor beneath us "—is a setback. That's all. I'll help you fix it."

Uncle Keith always knew the right things to say to make me feel like whatever was bothering me wasn't so bad after all. I'd trusted him before anyone else, but I couldn't shake the sour pang in my stomach.

"It would be a loan. I'd pay you back."

He waved me off as he left the kitchen.

"We'll clean up what we can tonight and finish tomorrow if we have to."

The paper towels I'd put down only a few minutes ago were already soaked through. I'd been trying to clean up since I arrived early this morning, but it was no use. The water had stopped coming in, but I couldn't get a handle on what was left.

"Cheer up, buttercup," Uncle Keith said, chuckling as he tapped my chin with his knuckle. "It's not as bad as you think and not a disaster. Got it?"

"Got it," I sighed, my chest deflating with a tiny bit of relief. Even if I'd wanted to do everything myself, refusing my uncle's help would just prolong my misery and lead to rotting floors.

I followed my uncle to the door until we heard a tap on the other side.

"Right on time," Uncle Keith said, flashing me a smile over his shoulder.

I squinted at him as he reached for the doorknob. Maybe Aunt Maya was coming by to help? When he opened the door, my heart fell into my stomach as I locked eyes with Jake.

Of course. *Jake* was the contractor he knew who would give him a great price.

I hated him seeing me at what felt like my lowest. Bone-deep disappointment loomed over me like another rain cloud. All I wanted to do was go back to my uncle's house and cry under his Giants blanket until I had to go to work on Monday morning.

"Here he is." Uncle Keith slapped Jake's shoulder and pulled him inside. "Please take a look around and tell my niece it's not as bad as it looks. Maybe she'll believe your professional opinion more than mine."

Jake shot me a crooked smile.

"I'm sure it's not. And at the risk of sounding arrogant, I can fix pretty much anything. I'll take a look around, but you can calm down. You're in good hands." He tapped my arm and made his way past me into the kitchen.

"I have some mops in the car. You said you were bringing the wet vac?"

"Yes," Jake told Uncle Keith. "It's in the back of my truck. We can start with that and mop up the rest."

"See that?" Uncle Keith squeezed my shoulder. "We already have a plan. Tell her."

I nodded, not lifting my head when a loud ringtone went off.

"This is your aunt." He held up his phone after he dug it out of his pocket. "She wanted me to call to let her know how everything was. Let me take this and get the vac."

I sucked in a long breath and rubbed my eyes, as if that would somehow stop the tears from burning my nose. I didn't want to cry in front of Jake or anyone. Maybe I'd jetted up here so fast so I wouldn't have the chance to think of all that had gone wrong over the past year, and now that I had no choice but to be still, the reminders and the shame washed over me. It was an overdramatic reaction, but one I couldn't fight, as it all snaked down my cheeks.

"Oh no, please don't do that."

Before I realized it, Jake wrapped his arms around me and brought me into his chest. His very hard chest and thick, strong arms. Instead of pushing him away like I should have, I let my head drop and softly cried into his shoulder. His spicy cologne and woodsy soap filled my senses as I relaxed, sliding my arms around his waist as I sank deeper into him.

"I can already tell this won't be an issue to clean up and fix." He grabbed my arms and pushed me back, tilting his head until I lifted my watery gaze to his. "Yes, I'll have to fix the floors and replace the carpet, but the water hasn't been sitting here long enough to cause much damage. This is not the big deal you think it is. Please don't cry, sweetheart," he crooned as his thumb swiped at a tear. "I'll fix it all for you."

I sucked in a gasp when he cupped my cheek, skimming his thumb back and forth along my jaw. This comfort was already too intimate, but I found more than sympathy in his eyes. I spied the same heat I'd been trying to reason away as a crush, now coming to a boil at the notion of it being recip-rocated.

The tears halted along with my heartbeat. My lips parted on instinct when Jake's gaze fell to my mouth. My shaky hands skated up his arms and met at the back of his neck. We drifted back toward the edge of the sink as we eased closer, the distance closing between us as his breath fanned against my chin.

"Fuck," he whispered, husky and low, as his hooded eyes locked with mine. The kitchen could have washed away around us, and I wouldn't have noticed or cared. I nodded, silently agreeing with how inevitable this was and having zero inclination to stop.

One more centimeter and his lips would be on mine, and despite how it shouldn't happen, I wanted his mouth more than I wanted air. Despite the bad memories this flood brought up in my troubled brain, the fight to resist Jake and how I felt about him whooshed out of me. I no longer saw or cared about what was wrong with pressing my lips to his because it felt too right.

"How the hell do you work this, Russo?"

We jumped apart at my uncle's voice.

"The one we have isn't this damn complicated. See, Peyton, I hired you a high-end contractor with state-of-the-art equipment."

I forced a smile as Jake followed my uncle, not looking

back at me as I tried to catch my breath, my panties now as wet as my eyes.

In a way, this was all a good distraction. I was no longer dwelling on the possible mistake I'd made rushing to Kelly Lakes or the original disaster that had brought me here. I was too busy focusing on all the dirty mistakes I wanted to make with Jake, but wasn't supposed to consider.

He ambled around the condo, going room to room and pointing to things and whispering to my uncle while I looked on. I didn't pay much attention to what they said, only nodded when they looked back at me.

"It doesn't look like any more is coming in, but it was enough to soak through the floor and ruin most of the carpet. The good news is the bedroom seems more or less okay. We'll start on the flooring, and we can figure out the cabinets after. But I want to take care of that wall before the mold gets out of control. I'll replace the hardwood floor, and you can come by the office to go through some carpet samples."

"He's not supposed to tell you the prices so you can pick what you want."

I exhaled with a loud groan.

"Uncle Keith, stop it—"

"Yeah, yeah." He came over to me and kissed my temple. "Let's clean this up so we can go home and eat." He stalked out the door, leaving Jake and me alone again in the kitchen.

"Thank you for coming by, and for doing this." I cleared my throat as I eyed my open front door. Had Uncle Keith not said anything when he'd come back in, he would have found his best friend and me lip-locked in my flooded kitchen. That was a brazen and thoughtless move on both our parts, but until that moment, my uncle's presence hadn't been stopping us. Neither of us caring or even remembering that he could come back at any moment spoke volumes about how dangerous the crazy attraction between us had become.

"My uncle is too much."

"That he is. But he's the best friend I've ever had." I spied a deep furrow in his brow as he blew out a long breath. "He'd literally give anyone the shirt off his back, and he loves his niece." He shuffled over to me, his shoes squeaking against the damp floor. "I'm happy to help him give you a nice place to live."

Our almost-kiss still lingered between us, an almost-kiss we had to forget almost happened.

Too bad that was impossible.

"Thank you." The words came out breathless and gravelly, like flirty sandpaper.

He cleared his throat and slid his hand to the back of his neck, taking two long strides away from me.

"My pleasure."

I wanted his pleasure. I wanted his mouth and his hands and everything else I wasn't supposed to crave from him. I had hoped getting in over my head was an isolated incident that I'd left behind me. Now, the repeat performance was all too familiar and all too easy to fall into.

His eyes darted away from mine and back toward the door.

At least we were aware now that we weren't alone.

I could handle a one-sided crush, but Jake actually wanting me back was something I'd never considered and didn't know how to resist.

TWELVE
JAKE

"Jesus, Russo," Keith panted as he ran past me. "What the hell did that ball ever do to you?"

When Keith asked me if I was up for a game of handball this morning, I'd almost said no. He'd asked me to come to his niece's condo to fix the damage yesterday, not cause more by making out with her in the kitchen. What the hell was I thinking, pulling her into my arms like that?

I wasn't.

When she started to cry, I couldn't stand it. I pulled her to me, first to calm her down, then she felt so good against me I couldn't let her go. When she peered up at me, those gorgeous, red-rimmed eyes regarding me like I hung the moon, I almost did what I swore I wouldn't. Even though our lips didn't touch, we'd turned the corner I'd been trying to avoid since I'd seen her in the high school parking lot.

I wasn't sure if I could look Keith in the eye today, but I couldn't ignore him forever—or for long. I agreed and did everything I could to smack the shit out of the ball rather than stop to think about what I'd done . . . and the little regard I had for doing it again—only following through next time.

Peyton was in my brain all night. I'd gotten too close, and that moment in her kitchen, right as I was about to lose control and taste her mouth, was all I could think about.

Every time I'd try to shut my eyes, I'd replay and finish that almost-kiss, picturing how soft her lips would be against mine or dragging soft kisses down my chest or wrapped around my cock.

I dove for the ball, almost flipping over as I smacked it again. As much as I tried to force them out, those five minutes in the kitchen lived rent-free in my head.

Who the hell was I? No woman had ever gotten under my skin like this, including the one I married. I would've agreed to rebuild Peyton's entire fucking condo if she wanted me to, anything to get that despair out of her eyes. Then I spied the heat and the longing, and I couldn't stop myself. I gave thanks to my best friend's big mouth as he'd come back into her kitchen.

"What's wrong, Chief McGrath?" I grunted out as I slammed the ball again. "Can't keep up?"

"I'm keeping up fine," he said through gritted teeth. "I just don't have a vendetta against the ball or the wall."

"Seriously?" I hoped the usual smack talk would distract me. "How do you run after bad guys if you're that slow?"

"I make the younger ones do it for me," Keith said before grabbing the ball as it bounced toward us. "I don't know what got into you, but I need a break."

I nodded. "Yeah, that actually sounds good to me." I'd pushed so hard, my legs were jelly under me as I followed Keith toward the other side of the court where we'd dropped our bags.

I opened my gym bag, rooting around for a water bottle, and took a seat next to Keith on the concrete. The early morning air had a bite to it, the temps already dropping low right after Halloween, but I'd worked up such a sweat trying to expel the lust and guilt from my system that my skin burned despite the chill.

"Thanks again for yesterday," he said, still panting a little before he chugged down the Gatorade he'd brought. "I figured it wasn't as bad as Peyton said on the phone, but trusted you'd know for sure." He huffed out a laugh. "Poor kid."

Kid. Peyton wasn't a kid, and technically, there weren't that many years between Peyton and Keith or as many as you'd normally think would be between an uncle and his niece. The age gap between Peyton and me was the same, but she most definitely didn't seem like a kid to me. She was one hundred percent woman—and off-limits for exactly that reason.

"It's not so bad," I told him, not acknowledging how he'd referred to Peyton as a kid, or else I'd have to do battle with the wall again. "I'll get it all fixed for her in no time."

"What I thought. I'd hate for her to have another obstacle."

"Another obstacle?" I wiped the sweat off my brow as I jerked my head toward Keith.

He winced as he craned his head toward me. "I don't know this for sure, but my sister and I have a feeling something happened to make her move up here."

"Like what?" My back went rigid against the fence I was leaning on.

"That's the thing, we don't know. She'd always told me how much she loved the school she worked at and all the different things they had her involved in. Then, all of a sudden, she needed a change and was heading up here. I'm happy to have her close, but I wish I knew why. My sister doesn't think she was seeing anyone, so she doesn't believe a bad breakup sent her up here, but I don't know. It worries me."

He exhaled a long breath, his gaze drifting over the rest of the park. Keith was never one to say or admit when he was worried. I trusted his instincts more than anyone else's, and after witnessing Peyton almost collapse in sobs over a flood, was there more to it than that? She'd told me that she left nothing and no one behind in Brooklyn, and now Keith's concern alarmed me even more.

I cupped my forehead, pressing into my temples as the overpowering urge to save her from something I didn't even know about barreled over me.

I was fucked in a fucked-up situation, but too invested and tempted for more of Peyton to walk away.

Maybe Keith shouldn't have worried about what happened *before* Peyton moved here. For someone always so annoyingly intuitive, he kept missing what was becoming all too obvious between his oldest friend and his niece.

"I'm surprised you're not using police intel to find out."

"They frown on snooping on family without a warrant. But all kidding aside, it's crossed my mind to do a check on her old school. Could be that I'm just too protective when it comes to Peyton, but I trust her to tell me eventually if something was up. Come on." He popped up with a groan. "You're buying breakfast today since you tried to kill me."

"All right." I stood and slung my bag over my arm. "Don't hate me because I didn't age like you."

"I'm as young as I ever was. I just need some hash browns and coffee if I'm going to play against a psycho contractor." He dropped a hand on my shoulder. "I don't hate you for trying to kill me. If you have to go, may as well be your best friend who does you in."

I faked a laugh as my stomach bottomed out.

He'd hate me for what I felt for his niece, and how it was becoming a question of when—not if—I'd do something I couldn't take back.

THIRTEEN

JAKE

"Why are you looking at me like that?" My sister, Kristina, squinted at me from across the table.

"What way am I looking at you?" I held up my hands in surrender. "I'm happy for you."

Or I was trying to be. My sister was *dating* her husband. They'd been separated on and off for what felt like forever, but after he'd moved out the last time, he'd suggested dating his wife of fifteen years and the mother of his two kids. I liked my brother-in-law well enough, and after what happened to my marriage, I gave them credit for not giving up.

I didn't have regrets about divorcing Eileen, but I'd never wanted my son to grow up in the cross fire.

"Don't worry about what I think or whatever anyone else thinks. You do you."

"Very philosophical, big brother."

Kristina was six years younger than me, almost my twin except her hair was a lighter brown and her eyes were green. She was a pain in my ass until I moved out at twenty-one, but we'd become close as we grew older. Sometimes, I just had to work on not reacting like a big brother trying to fix everything when she came to me with problems.

I was tempted to talk about mine for a change, but I wasn't ready to say them out loud yet.

"I have my moments." I motioned for the waitress to come over and refill our drinks. When Kristina had sent an ominous text asking if we could talk tonight, I had no idea what it was about. Before Mike had asked to go to Aaron's house again, I'd offered to bring her to the bar and grill in town in case my son couldn't hear whatever she had to tell me.

"What about you? When are you going to find someone?"

"Kris, I'm not in the mood to talk about this again. Mom brings it up every time she calls. I had someone, years ago. You saw how that worked out."

"Because your ex-wife was a bitch. I'd never say that in front of my nephew, but I think the poor kid knows by now." She scoffed as she turned to face me. "I'm so glad he's finally with you full time. But one bad marriage doesn't mean you have to swear off women forever."

"I see women, Kristina. I've been a little busy trying to make my kid feel better in his new home. Dating can always wait. It's not a priority."

She laughed to herself as she sipped her refilled glass of wine.

"What?" I narrowed my eyes at my sister until she set down her glass.

"Dating was never a priority for you because it was too damn easy. My friends still drool over you. It's annoying."

I laughed. "I'm not a manwhore, little sister. But I'm not a monk either. As far as finding someone beyond a few dates." I shrugged. "I'm set in my ways, that's all."

And the woman I wanted to date, I couldn't touch—even though she was all I could think about.

"Set in your ways? Finding someone good for you would be good for Mikey in the long run."

"Jake?"

I swiveled my head to a familiar, sweet voice. I found Peyton and a woman with long black hair standing next to our table.

"Peyton, hi. This is my sister, Kristina."

Peyton reached across the table to shake her hand.

"Peyton is Keith's niece," I said to Kristina.

"Nice to meet you." Kristina lifted an eyebrow at me when she took Peyton's hand.

"You too." Peyton smiled and dropped Kristina's hand. I swiped my tongue along my bottom lip on instinct when I caught her staring at my mouth. A blush bled into her cheeks, and I forgot about my sister, Peyton's friend, and the public in general. All I cared about was tasting the lips I craved, but was cheated out of so many times.

"Hi, I'm Claudia Ng." Her friend extended her hand to Kristina.

"I'm so sorry," Peyton said, pressing her palm against her forehead. "This is my friend Claudia. She came up to help me unpack what I could before your crew gets to work in the living room and kitchen."

"Nice to meet you, Claudia." I stood and shook her hand after she greeted my sister.

"Gets to work?" Kristina looked me over with a raised brow.

"My new condo was flooded the day before I was supposed to move in. Most of the floors are water-damaged. My uncle hired your brother to fix it until I could pay him back." Her red lips, the ones I almost tasted a week ago, curved in a grin. "Uncle Keith is annoying that way."

"I know your Uncle Keith well." Kristina nodded. "We

could never shake him when he was in school with my brother. Always around."

"Sounds like my uncle." Peyton laughed before her gaze flicked to mine, and her smile faded. We still had that same problem of looking everywhere but at each other, though glancing back enough to make it tense.

Tonight was even worse. I tried not to notice her painted-on jeans and blouse low enough to tease a little cleavage. It was another picture I didn't need in my head as I planned to camp out at her condo for the next week or more.

"I'll let you guys enjoy your dinner. It was nice to meet you, Kristina."

"Very nice to meet you both," Kristina said, her eyes flicking to me for a second before she smiled.

Claudia waved before they followed the hostess to a table.

"*Keith's niece*?" My sister gaped at me once they were out of earshot. "The one he's always talked about like she's his third kid? Holy *shit*." She blew out a long breath and fell back against her seat.

"Holy shit, what? That I'm working in her condo? She just told you Keith hired me."

"He didn't hire you to eye-fuck each other like I just saw."

"Shh." I craned my neck around the restaurant. "For Christ's sake, keep your voice down."

She rolled her eyes. "They can't hear from all the way over there. But do you really think it's not obvious? Even her friend looked between you two like you were about to pull Peyton onto your lap. Keith really has no clue?"

I groaned, rubbing my eyes before I shook my head. This was exactly what I'd been afraid of—someone picking up on whatever was brewing between us.

And of course, that someone had to be my sister.

"I hate that this is my first question," Kristina said, glaring at me with wary eyes. "But how old is she?"

I scrubbed a hand down my face.

"Thirty-two."

She leaned back with a slow nod. "Okay. Not that young."

"Young enough." I took a long pull from my beer.

"Keith may shoot you."

I let out a sad laugh. "I wouldn't blame him if he did."

"So this is . . ." She tapped her fingers on the table, chewing on her bottom lip. "A little icky maybe, but not so terrible. You're adults, right?"

"The last time I saw her before a couple of months ago, she was fifteen."

She shrugged. "You weren't interested in her then."

"Despite how it looked," I began, having no energy for a hollow denial, "nothing has happened between us." My chin fell to my chest when my sister shot me a glare. "Not really, anyway."

"Yet. And you'll be working on her condo, alone. Unless you send some of the crew, which I'm guessing you won't." She chuckled before squeezing my arm. "I want to see you happy, and God knows I can't judge anyone's love life, but make sure you understand all the repercussions before you start something with your best friend's niece."

"And my son's guidance counselor at school."

Kristina's jaw went slack. "Well, damn. Maybe dating isn't so easy for you after all."

"We're not dating, Kris."

"You've said. Not dating *yet*. I support whatever you do, big brother." She exhaled a long sigh. "Just make sure you know what you're in for."

My gaze followed Peyton and her friend as they slid into seats at a table by the bar. I could make out her profile and the graceful slope of her neck. Watching her from afar wasn't going to cut it much longer.

I *wasn't* sure what I was in for, despite what my sister warned me, but the real danger of it all was that I was starting not to care.

FOURTEEN
PEYTON

"Wow," Claudia said when we settled at our table.

I picked up my menu, ignoring her wide, dark eyes in my periphery.

"It's nothing."

"Nothing?" She pushed my menu down. "Since you've moved up here, all we talk about is your school, furniture, and other boring crap that wasn't worth our time when *that* was going on."

"Nothing is going on, Claud."

Her brows shot up to her hairline.

"I call such bullshit. He tracked you all the way to the table, and he's still looking back now. I felt like I was interrupting something between the two of you, and I was only standing there."

"It really looks that . . . obvious?" I dropped the menu and rubbed my eyes. Whenever Jake and I were in the same space, the attraction pulsed so hard between us it was stifling. Keeping it to myself was excruciating, but if Claudia noticed it in less than ten minutes, that meant others did too.

"Yes, it does. So, what's the problem that you wouldn't bring it up? Even to me?"

"What's the problem? Claudia, he's my uncle's best friend. It was one thing to crush on him when I was younger. But now? Too much is at stake." I shook my head and took a big gulp of water.

"Your uncle was always cool. A lot calmer than your mom."

I managed a real laugh for the first time in what felt like days.

"He is, but this may be his breaking point."

"Okay, for argument's sake, maybe your uncle will freak out." She leaned forward, resting her elbows on the table. "I feel like there's another layer to your hesitation."

"I'm his son's guidance counselor. How's that for a layer?"

"Hmm," was all she said.

"What? You don't think that's a big deal?"

She chewed on her bottom lip as she studied me.

"Yes and no. I think you're amazing at what you do, but you're not his son's teacher. Yes, you're there to help him, and I know you have seminars with students and individual meetings, but dating his father doesn't give him an unfair advantage. You can't fail him or anything. Maybe it has the potential to be awkward, but I'd bet no one would care."

"This is a small town. Everyone cares and knows everything. I can't go back there again."

"Back where, Pey? You can't be comparing this to you and Travis. That was completely different."

"I'm building my reputation here, and another scandal is not what I need. I can hear all the whispering already. The brand-new guidance counselor at the local high school starts a torrid affair with the father of one of her students, who also happens to be her uncle's best friend, that uncle being the chief of police."

"Torrid affair?" She burst out laughing. "Dipping into historical romance books again?"

I smiled despite myself.

"Okay, maybe people don't usually speak torrid terms in this century, but if I gave in to this, Claud, trust me. It would be torrid as hell." I snuck a look back at Jake, catching his gaze for a second before we both turned away.

"Shit, that's hot."

"Please stop and figure out what you want to eat. We have a long day tomorrow."

She waved a hand.

"We have plenty of time, and you aren't blowing me off that easy. When you said nothing 'really' happened, does that mean it did or almost did?" Her eyes danced. "Well?"

"There was an almost-kiss," I admitted. "After the condo flooded, I was emotional and frustrated. It felt as if I was still being punished."

"You aren't," she snapped, "because you didn't do anything to be punished for. But before we rehash that old argument, keep going."

"He came over with my uncle to assess the damage, and when Uncle Keith stepped outside, I burst into tears. Jake tried to comfort me, and before I knew it, we were backed up against my sink. My uncle came back in, and we broke apart. We didn't kiss but came very, very close."

"Wow."

"You keep saying that." I sighed, craning my neck toward the bar in search of a waiter. "I think I may have daddy issues when it comes to men."

"Why, because your father split when you were young? I

think that man is hot as sin, and my father was always, *always*, around."

I chuckled at her eye roll.

"Or because Travis was older too? So, you have a type." She shrugged. "Nothing wrong with that."

"Dating a man more than a decade older never works out for me."

"It didn't work out *once*." She held up a finger. "And he was an asshole who lied to you and let you take the fall. Is Jake a good guy?"

"*So* good." I exhaled with a groan-like whimper. "You should see him with his son. He's been a great friend to my uncle for so long." I twisted the stem of my water glass between my fingers. "How could I do this to them?"

"Jake is a grown man. You can't do anything to him." A wicked grin curved her lips. "Well, I mean, you can, but from what I just witnessed, you wouldn't have to twist his arm or anything."

"Very funny," I shot back, even though the thought of doing things to Jake had me breathless and flushed. This couldn't happen, yet it seemed as if it already had.

"My God, you should see yourself now." Claudia snickered and lifted her glass. "Need some ice?"

I should've taken a handful of ice and dropped it right down my pants to douse this growing ache that was about to get me into even more trouble.

"Get me a rosé when the waitress finally comes. I need to use the restroom."

I left Claudia and stalked down the tiny hall toward the bathrooms. She was a good friend who never pulled any punches, but after what I'd confessed to her, I needed air. I made a living helping kids face their problems, and all I wanted to do was run from mine.

But I couldn't run in a small town. I couldn't run from my uncle, and I didn't *want* to run from Jake. That was the biggest problem of them all.

I was so into my thoughts that I didn't watch where I was going and ran right into whoever was leaving the single-stall bathroom.

"Peyton! I'm so sorry. I didn't see you there." Jake's sister looked me over with a concerned pinch in her brow. "Are you okay?"

"It's okay. I'm sorry, didn't realize where I was going."

Seeing her up close, I spotted the resemblance to her brother. She had the same dimple poking her cheek when she smiled and the same big eyes, only hers were green, not blue.

"My brother seems to have the same problem." She glanced back to where I assumed Jake was still sitting.

My chest deflated as I darted my eyes away. A confusing concoction of relief and panic swirled in my belly.

"It's been a very long time since I've seen Jake look at anyone like that, if ever. Do you care about him?"

"Yes," I admitted without thinking.

"Good. You're both about to make a mess." She coughed out a laugh and tapped my elbow. "Make sure it's worth it."

FIFTEEN

PEYTON

"I think we should throw you a housewarming party."

"No, that's not necessary," I told Deirdre as I shook my head. "That's a very generous and sweet offer, but I have more stuff than I know what to do with from my old apartment."

"But it's not *new* stuff," Erin, one of the senior math teachers, said from across the lunch table in the teacher's lounge. I'd found a cluster of friends to eat lunch with on the days a student didn't ask to see me, and I looked forward to those forty-five minutes every day. They'd been friendly and welcoming when I'd first met them and not opposed to sharing a little tea about the students, staff, and some parents. While gossip wasn't the most productive activity, it was helpful to have some insider information when I had to deal with strife between students.

"Did she agree to the party yet?" Cam, the PE teacher and baseball coach, smirked as he took a seat next to me.

"Not yet, but almost." Erin chuckled.

"How about this," Deirdre suggested. "What if we promise

not to bring presents, but bring food and booze instead? It could be just like this, but louder and without the time limit."

"Okay, that's different. Once the work is done in my condo, you all have a deal."

I'd forgotten how nice it was to have camaraderie at work. After everything came to a head at my old school, I'd had two friends left once the dust settled. Thankfully, one of those friends was the head of the guidance department and gave me a glowing recommendation when I applied for this position. I meant what I'd said to Jake at lunch that day—other than my mother and Claudia, it didn't feel as if I was leaving much behind.

My new school and town were finally starting to feel a bit like home. Dwelling in the past wouldn't help me in the present, but I had enough going on to distract me from getting sucked in.

Like new friends—and new contractors alone with me in my tiny condo this weekend. The back of my neck heated at the thought of how small my space would get with Jake in it.

"Well, hopefully it's soon. You have me until baseball season starts. Then my weekends are dedicated to games, practice, and crying alone in my beer on a Saturday night."

"Judy doesn't cry with you, Cam? Isn't that part of marriage?" Erin teased.

"Don't get me wrong, I love coaching, but I'm not given a whole lot of support sometimes. It's not as if I'm royalty like the football team."

"Ugh, please," Deirdre groaned. "They walk around with such swollen heads now, I wonder how they make it into the classrooms."

"Encouraging your team is important, so I get building them up—to a point." Cam sighed, shaking his head. "But

Coach Lewis reminds me too much of the bad guy from the *Karate Kid* movies."

I snickered in agreement until I spotted Arlene frowning in the doorway.

"I'm so sorry to interrupt your break, but I need Peyton and Deirdre to come with me. A few of your students got into a fight at lunch, and it's still a little heated."

Our chairs screeched across the floor as we rushed into the hallway to follow Arlene.

"Who got into a fight? Is anyone hurt?" Deirdre asked as she jetted ahead of Arlene.

"A couple of punches were thrown from what I understand. They had an issue in the lunch line."

"Can you give me some names?" I asked, breathless as I rushed to keep up.

"Aaron Score and Michael Russo were the freshman students. Brad Sutton and Jared Marks tried to push them around in the lunch line and didn't expect Aaron and Michael to fight back, according to the cafeteria workers I spoke to after the fight broke up."

She pursed her lips before exhaling a loud groan.

"The football team is becoming an issue, especially with the younger students and the ones in academic clubs," Arlene said to Deirdre. "That's not the school I'm running, and their coach may need a reminder," she whispered before pushing open the door to her office.

Deirdre glanced at me, shaking her head before we followed Arlene inside.

I was worried about both of them, but hearing Mike's name sent my heart crashing into my stomach. I'd have to call Jake and tell him what happened, and I prayed I wouldn't have to tell him that Mike was seriously hurt. Arlene would have mentioned if he was, but I wasn't sure if her idea of seriously hurt matched mine.

The two sets of boys were spread out on opposite ends of the office. Hal, one of our security guards, stood in the middle of the room, a scowl on his face daring the kids to try anything. I would've laughed if I weren't worried sick.

The older boys held bloody tissues up to their noses, while Aaron and Mike didn't seem to have any serious injuries. A raw scrape trailed down Mike's cheek and Aaron's shirt was torn, but I exhaled in relief when I didn't notice any more blood.

"Let's hear it," Deirdre said to Brad and Jared. "This is the third time this month I've had to come and de-escalate a fight where you're both involved."

"We're the ones bleeding." Jared's muffled voice came through the tissue pressed against his face. "Talk to them."

I strode up to Aaron and Mike. Aaron focused on his shaking knee, while Mike's red and glossy eyes met mine.

"What happened? Talk to me."

"For the past couple of weeks, all they do is bother us," Mike started, glaring at the boys across the room.

"Bother you how?" I urged, still looking Mike and Aaron over for any more injuries.

"Since they were switched to this lunch period, all they do is say nerd this, loser that, and bump into us when they pass us. We told one of the monitors, and they said to shake it off." Mike looked away and shrugged.

I cut a look to Arlene and Deirdre as rage boiled in my stomach, my usual reaction when bullying was dismissed as boys being boys, but I stayed silent.

"Today, Brad pushed the tray out of Liam's hand, and he tripped and fell. When we told them to stop it, they put us each in a headlock and asked what we were going to do about it. We managed to push them away, but they pushed us back hard, and we hit them," Mike said, his voice small. "I meant to just push them away, but I guess I punched him in the nose."

"You guess?" Brad said, his nostrils flaring over the tracks of dried blood. "Are you stupid or something?"

"I know I don't have to remind you that fighting is forbidden in this school. Brad, Jared—" Arlene stepped toward them. "You're suspended for three days." She turned to Aaron and Mike. "I'm going to have to suspend you both as well, but I'll give you one day of suspension and two days of detention."

"You can't be serious. That's all they get?" Brad seethed and pushed off the wall he was slumping against.

"That means we can't play this weekend." Jared turned to Deirdre, his eyes wide and desperate.

"Yes, it does," Deirdre said, her voice calm and cold. "Your coach can call me or Principal Swift if he'd like an update on how his players are behaving and how he'll have no eligible players left if it keeps up. Come, I need to call your parents to pick you up."

"Come on, guys." I motioned for Aaron and Mike to follow me. "You can wait in my office as I call your parents." I'd never condone fighting and understood Arlene's obligation to punish both sides, but I was still proud of Aaron and Mike for standing up for themselves. It took guts to go back at older and bigger guys who were picking on you, and I hoped that as far as these boys were concerned, Brad and Jared would think twice about antagonizing them again.

I also had a conversation planned with the cafeteria monitors about turning a blind eye to trouble between students. And by conversation, I meant I was filing a complaint report and hopefully getting them both written up for not doing their jobs.

Aaron's mother was substituting for the day, and once I reached out to her classroom, she grabbed her son from my office and headed home. Mike stayed silent, rubbing his cheek with a hiss after Aaron left.

"Do you want some cream for that?" I asked, dipping my head in hopes he'd meet my gaze.

He looked away with a shrug. "No, it's fine."

"I'm not supposed to say this, but I think you were pretty brave today."

"But I'm suspended anyway." He dropped his head forward and rubbed the back of his neck.

"I have to call your dad. Sit here and relax, okay?"

I waited until he gave me a reluctant nod, and I ducked outside to the empty hallway, calling up Jake's contact information in my cell. We'd exchanged numbers to stay in touch when he began working on the condo, but having his name in my phone seemed too familiar and intimate, even if it was for a business reason.

When the call connected and started to ring, I sucked in a deep breath. This call was always harder when it was a family you knew well—and a father you cared about more than you should.

"Peyton?" I cringed at Jake's puzzled voice in my ear. "What's going on?"

"Hi, Jake. Mike was in a fight. He's fine and was defending himself, but school policy dictates that he has to be suspended anyway. He can come back to school on Monday and will have to serve two days of detention next week. But he has to go home now."

"Shit." His heavy sigh made my chest squeeze. "You're sure he's all right?"

"Upset and shaken up, but other than a scratch on his cheek, he's physically fine."

"Thank God. But I can't get him now. I have a truck full of equipment to drop off at the office first."

"He can stay in my office until you come. I'll see if I can get him to calm down a little before you get here."

"This shouldn't take long to drop off. I can be there in twenty minutes. Is that okay?"

"I'll make it okay. Just get here when you can."

"Thank you. This means a lot. Tell my son I'm not mad and we'll talk about it all when I get there.

"No problem. I'm sure he'll appreciate that."

"And Peyton, I'm glad he has you with him. And don't say you're just doing your job."

"Okay, I won't." A wide grin split my cheeks despite my worry for them both.

"Your dad is on his way," I said to Mike after I shut my office door behind me. "I hope you remember that you can talk to me. And the next time you complain and it falls on deaf ears, this office is always open to you. I'm happy to be the bad guy to keep my students safe."

He leaned forward, scrubbing a hand down his face before he swiveled his head toward me.

"Aaron punched him on purpose, I think. I just swatted him away and landed on his nose by accident."

"Fighting isn't allowed, as Principal Swift said, but you were defending yourselves and your friend. That took guts."

"Dad is going to kill me." He sighed before he dropped his head between his knees.

"Your dad specifically told me to let you know he wasn't mad. He's upset because you're hurt, but not upset at you."

He nodded slowly and rubbed his eyes.

"I didn't want to bother you. It's not like I'm not used to being picked on." A sad smile pulled at his lips.

"First of all"—I stood from my chair and took the seat

next to Mike in front of my desk—"it's my job, so you aren't bothering me. And second, you should never get used to being picked on. I am here to help you, and so are your teachers."

I spied a tiny nod from Mike. I tapped his sneaker with my foot to make him look up.

"So, next time this happens, what are you going to do?" I lifted an eyebrow and tapped my finger on the armrest.

A smirk twitched at the side of his mouth, and at that moment, he looked so much like his father that my heart squeezed.

"Tell you because it's your job and I'm not bothering you."

"There you go."

Our heads whipped around at a loud knock on my door. When I creaked it open, Jake burst into my office, taking Mike's face in his hands.

"Let me look at you."

"He's okay," I whispered, feeling like an interloper in my own office as I glanced between them both. "Just a little shaken up. As I told Mike earlier, this is off the record, but he was pretty brave today. Fighting should never be the answer, but I think he did what he had to do."

Jake grabbed the back of his son's head and pulled Mike into his chest. His body slumped against his father with palpable relief.

"I'm sorry, Dad."

"What did Pey—Ms. Miller just say?" Jake shifted him back and squeezed the back of his neck. "You did what you had to do. I wish fighting was never necessary, but unfortunately, it sounds like it was today."

"But I'm suspended . . ." Mike rubbed his eyes.

"I know, but we'll deal with that. In the meantime"—Jake smiled, his eyes still on his son—"let's go home, and we'll talk about it. But I'm not angry with you, I'm mad that it happened. Okay?"

"Okay," he said on a long sigh.

"Are you hungry? It sounds like you didn't get to eat lunch today."

"I'm fine, Dad." Mike picked up his backpack from the floor, slowly hooking it on his shoulder. The poor kid seemed exhausted in every way.

"Wait for me outside. I need to talk to Ms. Miller."

He nodded and looked back at me. "Thanks, Ms. Miller. For . . ." He trailed off, lifting a shoulder. "For everything. I promise I'll say something sooner next time."

"Of course." I tried to give him an easy smile and not give away how upset I was for him. "And you better."

"Thank you for staying with him," Jake said, rubbing the back of his neck after Mike stepped out of my office. "I've been sick to my stomach since you called, but so damn relieved he was with you until I could get to him. I know he's fourteen, but he's my . . ." My eyes followed the roll of his throat when he gulped. "I never regretted babying him all his life more than right now."

"Only children get babied. I have firsthand experience." I grinned and, although I shouldn't have, reached out to wrap my hand around Jake's wrist. "But for what it's worth, remember that Mike didn't back down today. He defended himself. Babied or not."

Something in his eyes made my breath catch in my throat. Regardless of where we were, I wanted to grab the back of his neck and pull him to me as he'd done with his son moments ago, then press my mouth to his and kiss it better like he almost did for me in my kitchen.

His eyes holding mine, he peeled my hand from where it was still wrapped around his wrist and brought it to his mouth, all the air rushing out of my lungs when he pressed a kiss to my knuckles.

"Thank you," he whispered, our gazes lingering for a long moment before he left my office and told Mike, "Let's go."

I pressed my hand to my chest, my breathing quick as my heart thudded against my palm. I traced the top of my wrist, still feeling the wet warmth of Jake's lips and the scrape of his stubble when he pulled away.

This thing between us grew bigger every time we tried to shut it down. We were overpowering, all-consuming, and just a matter of time.

SIXTEEN
JAKE

Mike seemed to take his day of suspension in stride, and although he was supposed to be punished, I let him lounge around doing whatever he wanted. I did feel better that he defended himself, but I worried about retaliation. I trusted that Peyton would watch him, but she couldn't be everywhere. His principal assured me the same, but I almost offered to donate free contracting work if I could hang out at the school for the next few weeks.

In all fourteen years that my son had been alive, I'd never been this crippled by helplessness.

I wished for the days he was little enough for me to wrap my arms around him and shield him from bullies, growing up, and parents who disappointed him.

I had no reason to be at Peyton's condo tonight. I'd sent my workers in while she was in school to replace the floors and cut out the beginnings of mold from the bottom of the wall in her living room. Although I had that primal need my sister had called me on to fix it all myself, I wanted it to be finished for her as soon as possible. The job was more than halfway done, and I didn't have to bother her by stopping by on a Friday night to install the new drywall against the wall.

Kristina said we were a *when*, not an *if*. Every time my eyes fell on that gorgeous face or roamed along Peyton's beautiful body, or when she gave me a glimpse as to how big her heart was, I wanted us to be a *now*.

I wanted that so fucking much I could no longer think straight or make good decisions.

And being alone with Peyton for an entire evening was the worst decision I could possibly make.

Aaron's mother offered to have Mike over for pizza because she didn't want them to feel punished either. With the unexpected extra time on my hands, I found myself texting Peyton to find out if she was home, telling her that if I installed the drywall now, it would help the guys finish quicker next week.

It wasn't a total lie, but the reason I'd reached out was because something in me needed to be near her—and that something was a hell of a lot louder than my conscience warning me away.

Despite how wrong it was to want her, I couldn't stop. My resolve had cracked right down the middle, and no matter how many times I reminded myself why it couldn't happen and the ripple effect of chaos after if it did, it was falling apart and I couldn't stop it.

"Hey," Peyton said as she answered the door, her loose T-shirt draping over one sexy shoulder. My eyes drank up every gorgeous inch of her body, over the black leggings that clung to every curve. Averting my gaze higher didn't help. Her chestnut hair was piled on top of her head, with little curls falling over her face and highlighting her cheekbones.

"Come in. Your crew has made good progress so far." She smiled and my skin tingled, the tiny hairs on the back of my neck sticking up as if I'd just tripped a live wire. This was the first time since our almost-kiss that we'd been completely alone.

"So I've heard." I scanned the space, happy to see the guys did a great job. You'd never know the entire place was flooded. "I'll only be here for a little bit. The wall should take me no time."

"No rush. Can I get you something to drink?"

"No thanks," I said, my eyes glued to where the sleeve of her shirt drooped lower as I stepped inside.

Her lips stretched into a tiny smile. "How did Mike handle suspension today?"

"Okay, I suppose." I leaned against the edge of her sink. "I let him do what he wanted for the day once his schoolwork was done. Was today a mess for you?"

She shrugged.

"The boys he got into it with are a problem. The football team, in general, is becoming an issue, in part because of their coach." She shook her head with a heavy sigh. "I had the cafeteria monitors written up for not reporting Mike's complaints, and I'm hoping our principal is going to deal with the team as a whole, but I'm personally going to keep an eye on all of this."

"Thank you. You've looked after Mike from day one, and I can't tell you how much I appreciate that." I dropped my gaze to the floor. "I wish he would have told me."

"Unfortunately, kids expect this to happen when they shouldn't. Saying boys will be boys is bullshit. I have a bullying workshop I'd planned for later in the semester, and I think I'm going to bump it up to now. It's a good time for a reminder."

I returned her tired smile.

"You're pretty amazing at what you do, in case no one over there has told you yet."

She lifted a shoulder. "I tend to care too much, which keeps me up at night sometimes."

"I'm sorry you're losing sleep over it, but clueless fathers like me are very grateful."

"You're anything but clueless. You're incredible." Her gaze found mine as the air crackled between us. She was closing that safe distance we always tried to keep between us, holding my gaze and breaking our unspoken rule of not getting too close or looking too long.

I jerked back on instinct, but as the sink was behind me, there was nowhere to go. I could leave the drywall here and send one of the guys to come back and install it.

Too bad my feet were rooted to her floor and I couldn't go anywhere.

"I don't know about that, but *you're* pretty fucking incredible," I rasped, barely blinking as our gazes stayed locked.

"Incredible. Right." She let out a sad laugh. "All I do is run and hide instead of taking what I want."

"What do you want?" I asked, both dreading and hoping for the answer that was about to change everything.

Her throat worked before she sucked in a long breath.

"You." Her breathless whisper knocked the wind out of me.

"Peyton, you . . ." I licked my lips, my mouth suddenly parched. "You can't say that."

Peyton inched toward me, every centimeter lost between us kicking up my heartbeat. This was exactly what I'd been working to avoid, yet I kept gravitating toward her at the same time.

A groan rose from my throat as I exhaled.

"I knew I shouldn't have come here today," I said, more to myself than to her.

"Why?" Her voice fell to a low whisper.

My heart hammered in my ears as she eased closer.

"Because I'm hanging on by a thread here, sweetheart."

"So, maybe we should both let go."

I caught her hand when it skimmed down my cheek.

"You're all I think about, no matter how much I've tried to stop." My own voice dipped to a husky rasp as I nuzzled her palm instead of peeling it away as I should have. "But do you really think it's that simple?"

"No. That keeps me up at night too." Her shaky breaths filled the silence between us. "It's too hard to fight this anymore."

"Peyton, please—"

"I think about you all the time too. I know I shouldn't, but every time I try to stop, it's that much harder." Her pleading gaze was about to be my undoing. "Maybe it's wrong, but I'm exhausted, Jake. Aren't you?"

"You're young," I managed to whisper as her other hand drifted down my chest.

"Thirty-two isn't that young. What's wrong? Are you afraid you'll corrupt me?" A tiny smile ghosted her lips, but her eyes burned with lust and want and everything I'd been pushing away since the second I laid eyes on her again.

"You're going to be sorry you said that." I grabbed the back of her neck and finally hauled her to me. I plundered her mouth, thrusting my tongue past those lips that tasted even better than I'd imagined. I slanted my mouth to go even deeper, both of us clawing at each other to get closer after having fought for so long to stay as far apart as possible.

"I tried. Fuck, I tried." I pulled the rubber band out of her hair and wove my fingers in, gazing down at her flushed cheeks and swollen lips. I wanted to strip her, claim her in every way with every part of my body.

I broke the kiss, grabbing her face as I pressed my forehead against hers.

"You know we can't go back after this."

I was offering an out I'd already known neither of us would take. Her hooded eyes lit up as they locked with mine, her hands meeting at my neck as she inched closer.

"Promise?"

I swiveled her around, pressing her back against my front for her to feel exactly how much I'd wanted her all this time. My hands roamed her body, coasting down her thighs. I swept the hair off the back of her neck and dropped slow, open-mouthed kisses across her nape. The sweetest whimper fell from her lips as she melted into me.

She wasn't the only one losing sleep.

"You're perfect, sweetheart. So fucking perfect."

"Touch me, Jake. Please . . ."

"How? Like this?" I cupped both her breasts, teasing the nipples until they pebbled against my thumbs.

Her head dropped back against me as she arched forward, pushing her full breasts farther into my greedy hands.

"So beautiful." I dove into her neck, running my mouth along the crook of her shoulder and smiling against her silky skin when she jerked in my arms. "You taste even better than I imagined, and I imagined you all the damn time."

"You did—yes, right there . . ." She reached behind to loop her arm around my neck, pulling me closer.

"I did," I whispered before grazing my teeth over her earlobe. "I never stood a chance."

She peeled one of my hands off her breast and shoved it inside her leggings. I cupped her pussy, already soaked through the lace against my palm. When I slid my hand inside her panties, I sucked in a gasp, leaning forward to stop my knees from giving out.

"So wet, you're killing me." I crushed my mouth to hers

again as I teased my finger up and down her slit, my finger already drenched as I swirled it around her clit. "This all for me, sweetheart?" I murmured against her lips. The little bump was as hard as I was, Peyton shuddering against me with every swipe around and over it.

"All for you, Jake. All you," she croaked out, spreading her wobbling legs as she pressed my hand deeper into her core. My brain short-circuited, robbing me of the little self-control I had left.

I took her mouth in another bruising kiss before dropping to my knees.

If I was going to hell, I'd enjoy every damn second of the ride.

I hooked my thumbs into the waistband of her leggings and pulled them down with her panties, with no patience even to get them to her ankles before I dipped my head and took her pussy like I'd taken her mouth. I devoured it, letting my tongue glide along every soaked inch before licking all the way inside her.

I was too high on this woman, too consumed by how she tasted and how she shivered in my arms as I went deeper, to remember all the reasons I wasn't supposed to have her. I grabbed her ass with both hands because I still wasn't close enough or deep enough. I was dizzy, common sense vanishing the moment she'd confessed she wanted me as much as I tried not to want her.

Reason, logic, and repercussions no longer mattered. At that moment, nothing mattered but the woman in my arms. It was as terrifying as it was exhilarating.

I continued the sweet torture until her thighs quivered against my face. I swatted the side of her hip, urging her to come in my mouth and give me what I'd craved for so damn long.

"Jake," she shrieked, her legs going rigid as she rocked against my mouth, moaning and pleading until she folded forward, her eyes shut and her cheeks wet.

She scrubbed a hand down her face as her chest heaved up and down, her other hand still holding the sink for purchase.

I dragged her pants back up her legs, painting kisses up her thighs until I stood.

I kissed her slow and deep as she rode out the aftershocks. She reached for my belt buckle with her quivering hand and managed to pop it open along with my zipper. I hissed when she found my cock. It pulsed against her hand as she took hold and pumped up and down.

"Sweetheart, I'm close," I murmured against her lips. "I'm about to come all over you if you don't move."

"Good, please," she begged, as her hooded eyes held mine. It was all I needed to spill all over her hand. I crashed my lips to hers, the kiss as sloppy and desperate as we were, before my release rocked through me.

"Please know that I usually have more control than that." I pressed my forehead against hers. "It's been a long buildup."

"Same," she whispered, smiling as the rise and fall of her chest slowed.

I straightened, cupping her cheek. Now that my blood was leaving my cock and heading back to my brain, the jolt of reality sobered me right up. Judging by Peyton's widened eyes, her pupils still dilated and her lips swollen and raw from my kisses, she was slamming back to earth too.

I planted a kiss on her forehead. She exhaled a sweet sigh, her eyes fluttering as I rained more kisses down her cheek and along her jaw.

"Let me . . . clean up." I nodded to the sticky mess of my jeans. "And we can talk. Okay?"

She nodded, her silence unnerving me. I'd never thought Peyton would be the one to give in first, but I was only minutes behind her. We had a lot to sort out, but she was right. I was fucking exhausted trying to fight the inevitable.

I headed back into the kitchen after I washed my face and cleaned up as much as I could. I found her on her couch, rubbing the back of her neck.

"Penny for your thoughts?" I tried for an easy smile when she lifted her head.

"I'm wondering if all that was a dream or not. My reality is never that good." A blush painted her cheeks as she sucked in a deep breath, and all I wanted was her lips back on mine.

"It happened, all right." I sat beside her, still searching her gaze for what she may've been thinking. "What's wrong? Do you regret it?"

She met my gaze, relief coursing through me when she shook her head.

"No." She exhaled a long gust of air. "Not for a second. I just don't know where to go from here, you know?" Peyton cupped her forehead, resting her elbow on her knees. "I didn't plan on telling you all that, but once I started, I couldn't stop." She turned her head and squinted at me. "I guess I'm a little embarrassed for being so forward."

"Did I fight you?" I tapped her chin with my knuckle and smiled when she lifted her head. "I wanted it every bit as much as you did."

She worried her raw bottom lip between her teeth before shifting toward me.

"Jake, I—"

The loud buzz of my phone in my pocket halted what she was about to say.

"You better get that." She was stalling, but in case it was my son, I peeked at the screen anyway.

Mike: *Aaron is sick, and I forgot my keys. Can you come home to let me in?*

"Mike is locked out, forgot his keys at home." I rubbed my temples and shook my head. After all this time it had taken to admit to what was going on, I had to run out before we could talk about it.

"I get it." Her disappointed smile gutted me. "Go ahead."

"He's still sorting through yesterday. I don't want him to be alone, or else I'd come back."

"It's fine, Jake. Really." She stood from the couch. "I know he's your priority, and that's how it always should be. And it's better you deal with one problem at a time."

"We're a problem?"

"We're a mess." She choked out a sad laugh. "Like your sister told me we would be. I bumped into her by the bathroom that night we saw you."

"Of course she did."

She chuckled, planting a quick kiss on my cheek before ambling toward the door.

"Go do what you have to do and be with your son." She opened the door, peering up at me with an expression I couldn't decipher. "You can come back tomorrow to fix the wall if you have time."

I allowed myself another minute to take in her flushed cheeks and swollen mouth. She'd be in my head as she had been for months, only now I didn't have to wonder what her lips tasted like or the sounds she made when she came. I kissed her cheek and then the corner of her mouth. If my lips touched hers again, I was afraid I'd never leave.

I always knew that once I had a taste of her, I wouldn't be able to stop or give her up—and that was the worst consequence of all.

SEVENTEEN

PEYTON

"**W**hat's wrong?" Aunt Maya asked as I held my screen door open for her to walk inside.

"I'm fine," I chirped with a little too much enthusiasm. When the doorbell rang, I hadn't been expecting to find my aunt on the other side. I'd been keyed up all morning in anticipation of seeing Jake, and when I didn't see those blue eyes searing through me when I opened the door, both disappointment and relief washed over me.

"It's been a long week, but I'm happy to see you." I pulled her into a hug. "Where are all the guys?"

I cracked up when she rolled her eyes. "Keith took them to the park early this morning. They all need to burn off some energy. I thought maybe we could have breakfast if you're up for it. Plus, I'm a little nosy about Jake's progress."

Her lips curved as she glanced around the condo.

"It's getting there." My eyes kept drifting toward the door. I was already on edge, and Jake hadn't even arrived yet. We hadn't spoken about what happened between us—what I'd started. I was as shocked as he was when I blurted my confession, but once I began, it all poured out. I was half hoping he'd let me down easy and all I'd have to deal with was the humiliation of rejection.

The best orgasm of my life against my kitchen sink and figuring out what the hell to do about it after wasn't even close to where I'd expected it would go. Then he kissed me so sweetly after, assuring me that our quick finish was because he'd wanted me that much.

I was the one who put a pause on trying to figure out how to deal with all that was going on between us, ushering him out the door all too easily, a big contrast to how little I'd cared about the aftermath when Jake crashed his beautiful mouth into mine.

Claudia said I had a type, and I guessed it was men I shouldn't want but threw myself toward anyway.

Aunt Maya wore a light-pink hoodie and matching jogging pants, but she always looked like a model coming off the runway. She joked about my uncle's energy, but anytime they were together, it was easy to see how ridiculously in love they still were. The last time I fell for someone, I had to keep it to myself. How was I going to hide it from her when Jake and I were in the room with them? Or hide it from my uncle?

Rage bubbled in my gut as to why I had to hide it at all. Maybe that was why I was so intent on telling him how I felt. I had a silly hope in the back of my mind that maybe it could be different this time.

In reality, it would be worse. I could quit a job, but I couldn't quit my family. It made no sense, but I felt as if I'd let my uncle down. Out of respect for him, I should have found a way to resist. We both should have.

Despite the shame swimming through my veins, I didn't regret it, and I wanted more. I'd been in this exact position once before, and it seemed like one time too many.

My stomach folded at the chime of my door.

"That's probably Jake," I said, pushing a smile across my lips that, judging by her narrowed eyes, I didn't pull off as genuine. If I was bold enough to go after the man I wanted, I had to be brave enough to deal with what happened after. I sucked in a quick but deep breath that I hoped my aunt didn't see and opened the door.

"Hi, Ms. Miller." A stocky man with paint-stained sweatpants and a matching hoodie smiled back at me. "I'm Ralph. I work for Jake. He asked me to come here to install the drywall today."

"Oh, sure. Come on in."

"Thanks. Oh hey, Mrs. McGrath! How's the chief?"

"Exhausting." She chuckled. "Nice to see you."

"You too. How's the deck holding up?" he asked as he laid out all his tools in the hallway.

I was happy they were too busy making conversation to pay much attention to me. While I was relieved not to have to worry about my aunt picking up on anything between Jake and me, the sting of him not telling me beforehand that he was sending someone else and wouldn't be here was what threw me. He never said he could come back today, but was he blowing me off? He didn't seem to be last night, but a lot could change when a person had a chance to come to their senses.

Honestly, if he did, that was better for both of us. We'd learn to be around each other when we needed to be. I only had to worry about running into him at parent functions or if anything else happened with his son during school hours. If he was at my uncle's house, I could manage for the short time we'd be in each other's presence.

He didn't owe me any explanations. It happened, and now we had gotten it out of our systems. Talking it out wasn't necessary, especially since talking was what got me into trouble in the first place.

"You can leave Ralph here while we have breakfast. He's spent many days alone at our house doing renovations."

"Sure. You ladies go."

"Great, thanks." I grabbed my purse and plucked my jacket from the rack by the doorway. I hadn't spread anything out yet. I'd gotten used to avoiding all the lingering construction, but even that wasn't as extensive as I'd originally thought. It would all be over soon, and I'd have a brand-new and improved condo of my very own.

The thought should have thrilled me, not triggered an annoying pang gnawing at my side.

"Ready?"

Aunt Maya's voice ripped me out of my thoughts.

"Oh, sure." I forced another smile and followed her out my front door to her car.

"Where do you want to go? The coffee shop?" I asked as I fastened my seat belt, my gaze landing on Jake's company logo on the side of the truck parked in my driveway.

I had no idea what would have happened had Jake come by instead of one of his workers, but I'd been fantasizing about pulling him into my bedroom the minute I saw him. We'd have a whole bed, a locked door, and no family popping over to interrupt us. But he didn't show up, and I didn't know if he really had somewhere else to be or if what we had last night was as far as it would go.

Being open and honest was overrated. Living in uncomfortable denial was the better option, especially compared to the shit I felt like for putting myself out there, only to be hurt and humiliated *again*. The nerve endings between my legs were taking over my brain cells, and that needed to stop—now.

"Ugh, no. I'm not in the mood for Mary's attempts to gossip while I try to eat my eggs. The diner has a kick-ass Bloody

Mary." She frowned, lifting an eyebrow at me. "And you, my dear niece, look like you could use one."

The laugh falling from my lips surprised me.

"I could," I agreed, leaning back against the headrest and shutting my eyes for a moment. Somehow, I needed to forget about what was or wasn't happening between Jake and me for at least the day. My life as of late seemed to be work, thinking about Jake, and then lamenting how bad it was to think about Jake in the first place.

It was time to break this awful and pathetic cycle. I'd make sure to start accepting more invitations to have drinks after work and meet other people. Maybe dating one of the officers at the station wouldn't be so bad. I'd only be distracting myself, but going through the motions was better than remaining stagnant.

"Hey, did you drift off there for a minute?" Aunt Maya whispered as she nudged my arm. We were already in the diner's parking lot. I'd shut my eyes and obsessed for longer than I thought.

"I guess I did." I yawned for effect and stepped out of the car. She waved hello to the crowd leaving the diner as we came in, the host greeting her as if we were royalty before leading us to a table.

"I crack up at the reception I sometimes get as the chief's wife," she whispered as we slid into a booth. "Your uncle and I laugh and make up stories as to what illegal stuff they may be hiding by being so nice to me."

"I don't know about that." I picked up a menu. "Most people here seem over-the-top nice."

"And that's exactly it, over the top." She pointed a French-manicured finger at me. "Keith makes sure to stay in touch with the community so he can spot the trouble more easily. So yes, most are nice, but I guess more eyes are on us than others because he's so involved."

My stomach folded in on itself for a second. More eyes on them most likely meant, indirectly, more eyes on me. And more tongues wagging if I decided to date my uncle's best friend.

Opinions didn't matter to me, not really. It was when the opinions affected my job or how I tried to help the students entrusted to my care. I was over Travis, but not the fallout after.

"*Peyton.*"

Again, I jumped at my aunt's voice, too into my spirals to pay attention to anything or anyone.

"I asked you out to breakfast because I missed the girl time we had while you stayed with us, but I'll be honest, I'm worried about you."

"Worried? I'm fine." I waved a hand. "It's just been a lot, getting used to my job and dealing with the unexpected damage in my condo."

"From what I saw today, the condo is almost done and good as new." She pursed her red lips as she studied me. "It's been a long time since you were sixteen and would call me for advice about the boys you liked."

"Well, you were the only one I could go to. Mom was not the boy-advice type, and Uncle Keith would have driven down to Brooklyn to take me to school in his police cruiser."

"I was happy you chose me. I loved every minute of it."

Warmth flooded my chest as I relaxed. Aunt Maya was the only one who let me just be me in her presence. I didn't have to reassure her I was okay or ease her own worry about anything when it came to me. Since she'd married my uncle, I was always able to give it to her straight—until now.

"I'm too old to cry about boy trouble."

"There are no age limits on that." She dipped her head. "Do you think your uncle wasn't trouble when I met him?"

"No, I'm pretty sure he was lots of trouble."

Her shoulders shook. "We shocked the hell out of everyone too."

"I hate how our family treated you at the beginning."

She shrugged. "Your uncle didn't get the best reception from my family either. For a long time."

"Really?" I squinted at her. "Uncle Keith and Jason are always attached at the hip when you have anything at the house, at least from what I see."

"Now, yes, he's close with my brother. But when I brought home a white cop from upstate, dinner was just as silent and uncomfortable as it was at your grandparents' house. Sometimes people don't understand why two people fall in love, so they judge when they have no right to since they aren't involved. How we felt about each other was all that mattered, and I couldn't imagine a life without him."

I smiled at her wistful gaze. "You two are still adorable together. Gives the rest of us hope."

"Oh, it's not always easy, but my favorite moment of the day is hearing the key turn in the lock when your uncle comes home. Of course, that's a little relief too, considering his job, but it's still mostly excitement."

We gave the waitress our order of stuffed French toast and two Bloody Marys. I was all set to drown my troubles in carbs.

"I'm glad you found each other. Maybe someday I'll have a romance-novel type of love too."

"If you let yourself, yes, you will."

Her hay-colored eyes bored into mine, telling me without telling me that she already knew or had a good feeling.

"I'll be honest, coming here in the first place wasn't something I planned on."

I was free and easy with the confessions the past couple of days, and I felt another one coming on just as fast and unexpected.

"I realize that," she said, her brow furrowed. "Call it intuition, but I don't think you spotted the job opening and just decided to come here."

At that perfect moment, the waitress set two huge mason-jar drinks in front of us. I took a big sip, shifting the celery stick back and forth between my fingers before lifting my head.

"I loved my old school. Granted, it was the first school I worked at after my master's, but they let me basically run the guidance department. I had this reputation among students of being the one to come to with any problem, and I loved that. About a year ago, a new principal took over."

I shut my eyes for a moment, revving up the courage to tell at least the short version of the story.

"Travis was a decade older than me, but still a fairly young principal. He wanted to make it a blue-ribbon school but would always come to the events the counselors would organize. He told me he loved my enthusiasm and how I was making a real difference."

"Is this story going where I think it is?" She leaned forward, a deep crease in her forehead.

"Well, if you were thinking he told me he was separated from his wife and made me believe we could only meet at my apartment because the divorce that he had no real intention of getting wasn't final, then yes."

"Shit, Peyton. I'm sorry, honey."

My eyes darted away from the sympathy I knew I'd find in her gaze.

"But, of course, sneaking around never works for long. A teacher found out and told the school board, which was a little extreme, but she and Travis always butted heads. He resigned and left the district to protect his family and his wife, whom, again, he was still very much married to, and I stayed behind to take the fall. I kept my job, but it didn't matter because I couldn't do it anymore. They put a stop to any events, and any concerns I had for students were waved off. I knew I had to move or look for another profession." I let out a sad laugh. "And when I had the chance to move here, I thought it was a sign."

I scrubbed a hand down my face, both sick and relieved to tell someone other than Claudia about what led me here.

"It was. I hear wonderful things about you at the high school. And we love having you here. Sometimes unexpected turns lead you to where you're supposed to be." She stretched across the table and covered my hands with both of hers.

"I can't be another scandal, Aunt Maya." My voice cracked when I met her eyes. "How many times can I move?"

"Who said you would be? I don't know this Travis, but he sounds like the very worst kind of man, to lie and then leave you in the lurch like that. Not all men are like that, and the man I think we're talking about is one of the *really* good ones."

I agreed that Jake was one of the really good ones, whatever his reason was for not showing up today. Sure, he was gorgeous, but his big heart drew me in the most.

"You're not . . . disappointed in me?"

Age didn't matter when it came to the people you loved and wanted to be proud of you. I was in my thirties, but I may as well have been a kid again as I searched her face for a reaction.

"No, of course not. I'm angry you were hurt and had to leave a job you loved. As much as Keith would like to think of you as his sweet little niece, you're a grown-ass woman. You trusted the wrong person and didn't realize it until it was too late."

"Thank you." I swiped a tear off my cheek and rolled my eyes at myself. I'd come here to start over, not dwell in the past. But for the first time, it felt as if maybe I was taking a step toward moving on.

"I love you. No thank-yous." She nudged my ankle under the table. "So tonight, you're going to come over and see your cousins and enjoy my husband's freezing-cold barbecue because he thinks early November is still grilling time."

"We don't have to eat outside, do we?"

"Oh, hell no. And you are going to talk to me from now on and remember nothing is too bad that you can't tell me or that will make me not love you after. Got it?"

I swallowed thickly and nodded, letting out a long breath that seemed to shed a twenty-pound brick from my chest.

Maybe that job posting was a sign after all.

EIGHTEEN

JAKE

"Mike, that's enough donuts," I told my son as he settled into a chair in front of my desk with three piled up on a paper plate.

"I could always get more." Michelle, my office manager, waved a hand at me. "He's a growing young man, and the more he has, the less tempted I am to swipe one."

The side of Mike's mouth lifted in a small smile as he chewed.

"I suppose his thumbs will need the energy for his video games later."

Michelle had worked for me for almost the entire time we'd been open, close to twenty years. She was a close friend of my sister's and started only part time at first because she had a young daughter to take care of. But as her daughter grew and then went away to college, she asked for more hours. Now, she put in longer days than I did.

I'd brought Mike in with me for a couple of hours to sort out the week's jobs. And because I was a chickenshit, I'd sent someone else to fix Peyton's wall. It could have waited until Monday, but I had to keep up the ruse that it had to be done this weekend, not that I had to see her and sink my face between her legs before I even unloaded my tools.

Every time my life seemed sorted out, it just gave way to more chaos. Adding to the worry about Mike in school, I had no idea where Peyton and I went from here. I knew where I wanted to go—her taste and the sweet sounds she made had reverberated in my brain from the moment I'd opened my eyes this morning—but she'd seemed all too willing to see me out last night. Maybe she had regrets after confessing how she felt, or maybe I'd pushed too hard once I had her in my arms.

No matter from which angle I looked at the last couple of days—or if I was honest, the last couple of months—I was fucked without a way out.

"Are you all right, Jake?" Michelle asked, a sour expression pulling at her mouth. "Unless you're that into the final estimates, you seem a million miles away."

I laughed. I wished I *were* a million miles away, but unfortunately, I was right here and without a clue.

"I'm good, Michelle. Trying to sort this out so you don't get pissed at me and complain to my sister later." I shot her a smirk.

"I would never complain to your sister before I complained to you. It's sunny outside. You should go do something." She nudged my arm. "You're ruining my quiet Saturday afternoon."

I smiled until I spotted Keith and the twins through the front window. I'd hoped to have a little prep time before I had to look him in the eye again. I'd been guilty enough of becoming infatuated with his niece for so long that I'd almost gotten used to it. Now I'd looked *and* touched, and if Keith had any idea, he'd pound me into next week and never speak to me again.

And I wouldn't blame him one bit.

"I thought we'd come in to say hi since I saw your truck outside. I didn't know you worked on Saturdays."

"I do after a busy week," I said, still avoiding his gaze.

"Hey, Keith! There are donuts by the coffee machine in the corner, if you'd like."

I turned my head, laughing to myself at the twins' matching widened eyes.

"One," Keith said, holding up a finger. "Or I'll have to take you back to the park to burn off the sugar." He pulled a chair from in front of Michelle's desk and dragged it over next to Mike before he plopped down. "I'm sorry about what happened at school, Mike. But I heard you did the right thing." He squeezed his shoulder. "How are you holding up over there, Russo?"

"Fine." I shrugged, straightening the stack of papers in my hand. "I guess there is nothing we can do about it now. The school knows, and I have to take them at their word that they're handling it."

"I'm sure my niece is taking care of it. She's like her uncle and hates bullies, especially when friends of hers get hurt. You're in good hands, kid."

Keith cut a look at me, an oblivious smile stretching his mouth. I was in Peyton's hands last night, and I couldn't stop thinking how great they were. The hot-as-fuck memory flashing through my brain brought zero regrets, even in Keith's presence.

"Why don't you both stop by tonight? I'm having a barbecue, and it would be good for you not to stew at home over this."

"But it's November," Mike said, crinkling his brow.

"I have a double grill. I smoke everything all year long. Come by at seven . . . Guys, I said *one*." He cupped his hands over his mouth and stood. "Let's go."

A smile snuck across my lips when the boys scurried over to Keith with a donut in each hand.

"Relax, Russo." He dropped a hand to my shoulder. "Pick up some beer for us, and I'll see you guys later."

It would be good for us to get out, and I had to learn to live with what I'd done and would probably continue doing if Peyton let me.

Keith strode out with the twins behind him.

"Is that all right with you?" I asked Mike. "We don't have to go if you don't want to."

"It's okay," he mumbled. "Everyone keeps telling me I did the right thing. It was an accident."

"You defended yourself," I said, leaning forward. "Whether or not you meant to make contact. And I'd bet Keith is going to throw his weight around a little at the school so you don't have any more trouble. He's good like that." Guilt coiled tight in my stomach. "I'll finish up here, and we can get one of those ridiculous stacked milkshakes from the coffee shop and go wherever you want."

He smiled, a little wider and brighter than before. "It's good that you have so many friends here."

"*We* have friends here." I grabbed the last donut off his plate and took a chomp. "Office is all yours, Michelle." I stood from my desk, giving her a wave as we headed out.

Would I still have a best friend here once he found out? That I couldn't say with the same certainty.

"Do you go to Ms. Miller's condo a lot?" Mikey asked as we drove to Keith's later on.

"Not really. Most of the work in her condo was done while she was in school."

I'd been trying not to think about her all day, but it worked as well as all the other times I'd tried not to think of her the past few months.

Meaning not at all.

I finally understood the expression moths to a flame, because it was so hot between us I didn't see or care about the damage.

"Any reason why you're asking?"

He shrugged and turned his head to stare out the window.

"A few of the guys at school talk about her. I heard some of the sophomores saying stuff at lunch the other day. Something about the skirts she wears." He shrugged. "She's nice and pretty, I guess."

I smiled as I kept my eyes on the road. My son was on the young side of fourteen, still much more interested in video games than girls, but Peyton was hard not to notice.

I'd been trying for months.

"I'm glad I could help her out since she's been helping you too," I said as I pulled into a spot in front of Keith's house.

Mikey only nodded before he climbed out of my truck.

"I don't know how much she'll be able to help me on Monday," he muttered as we stepped across Keith's lawn.

"She said she was, and I believe her. There are eyes on this now, and you aren't alone. So stop thinking like you are."

He smiled when I nudged his shoulder. I was still worried about Monday too, but I had to keep it to myself for my son's sake.

"Why is Keith cooking outside? Isn't it too cold?"

"Like he told you, he cooks outside all year long. Come on," I said, looping an arm around his shoulder as we climbed the outside steps.

"There they are!" Keith marched up to us after we stepped through the front door. "Glad you came. I want you both to try to relax for a night." He dropped a hand on Mike's shoulder, smiling wide enough to coax a small grin out of him. Keith had a way of making you feel like whatever problem you had wasn't so terrible if you just looked at it from a different angle, and his niece took right after him.

Unfortunately, his niece was the one problem my best friend couldn't fix, because bringing her up would change everything.

I broke a lot of rules for Peyton, the worst one being unable to stay away from her. I was close enough to hurt all of us. There wasn't a better—or decent—way to spin that.

Now that Peyton had her own place, I didn't expect to run into her here. Maybe she'd gone for drinks with her teacher friends from school. She was gorgeous, single, and lit up any room she walked into. I'd watched her enough to catch all the eyes that followed her. She could have any man she wanted, so why should she stay home? My hand balled into a fist at my side at the thought.

"I don't think you know Ron, he's one of the new officers in the department. Just moved here from Connecticut. He stopped at the butcher for me today, so I thought why not let him stay for dinner."

"Nice to meet you." Ron extended a hand from where he stood next to Keith. I guessed he was in his mid to late twenties at most, tall and lanky like I'd been at that age. "I've never been to a barbecue in November."

"Most haven't."

Keith laughed when I shook my head.

"Your dad talks a lot of shit, but he's here every year for the wings I make for the Super Bowl," he said to Mike. "We'll eat when my niece gets here."

My stomach dropped, then clenched when Ron's eyes brightened.

"Peyton is coming? I didn't know that."

Keith frowned, shooting him a glare that would have been laughable on any other day. "I told her that if she wanted to date one of you clowns, I wouldn't stop her. But if you want to eat, don't drool over her in front of me."

My blood boiled at the shit-eating grin spreading Ron's mouth.

"Hey, everyone." Peyton's voice drifted in from the doorway. I turned, catching her gaze after she shut the door behind her.

I was used to the skittish way we avoided looking at each other, but I hated how she tensed up as soon as she saw me.

"How are you barbecuing?" She scrunched her adorable nose at Keith. "It's below freezing out there."

"You just say that because you're not used to being up here for the fall." He kissed her temple and drew her into his side. "You remember Ron from the station."

"Yes, nice to see you again." Her tight smile shrank a bit when she turned toward me. "Hi, Jake, Mike."

"Hi, Ms. Miller," my son said as I nodded hello. So much for a stress-free night. Tension and rage twisted in my gut, my muscles so tight it was as if my whole body flexed. I had to sit at the table and try to eat while watching this guy make a play for Peyton and not be able to do a damn thing about it. It wasn't as if she was mine, that I could pull her to my side and make it clear to everyone giving her a second glance to back the fuck off.

"Ms. Miller," Ron said, chuckling with a little too much enthusiasm. "I didn't know this dinner was so formal."

"Mike is one of my students."

She turned with a small smile, her eyes finding mine for a moment. She was so beautiful, and even though I wanted to punch Ron's lights out, I didn't blame him one bit for how he looked at her.

I followed Keith to the table, my teeth grinding when Ron took a quick seat next to Peyton.

Her eyes flickered to mine, but quickly darted away. She nodded at something Ron said, a polite smile playing on her lips. I knew her real smiles. I knew how soft her skin was and how sweet she tasted. I was a fool for pushing her away for reasons that should have still mattered, but didn't now. I had the overwhelming inclination to stand and hoist Peyton over my shoulder just to prove she was mine.

But she wasn't. And that was my fault.

This was not the time to act like some jealous boyfriend, although the way Maya leveled her eyes at me, I was too obvious. I almost wished Keith would notice so he could kick my ass and get it over with and I could take Peyton all for myself.

"Hi, Maya. Thanks for having us here tonight."

"You're welcome." She smiled at Mike, but regarded me with a concerned pinch in her brow.

I was done with sitting by and just watching Peyton—or pushing her away because it seemed like the right thing to do, but not at all what I wanted to do.

I only hoped I wasn't watching her slip right through my fingers.

NINETEEN
PEYTON

"You're a teacher, right?"

"Guidance counselor," I replied before I took a quick but generous swig of wine. Poor Ron was hanging on my every word, and all I could focus on was the searing heat from Jake's side of the table. I fought the urge to look. I'd felt his eyes boring into me since I walked through the door. I guessed Jake and Mike were surprise guests because my aunt wouldn't have blindsided me like that, but I had to suck it up and be an adult—even if I'd had the inclination to bolt as soon as I'd spotted him.

"Oh, like the school shrink?"

"No, school shrink is above my pay grade." I wanted to correct him about the outdated use of the word *shrink*, but I had enough trouble keeping up with the tension at this table tonight. "I'm like a combination of a teacher and a psychologist, I suppose."

"Peyton, we got the new Mario game. Want to play after dinner?" I met my cousin Aiden's sweet and hopeful eyes, barbecue sauce smeared all over his mouth. I didn't have the heart to tell him my plan was to run out the door before coffee.

"Not tonight, bud. But next time, I promise."

"Peyton takes care of kids for a living. She's here to visit and relax, so give her a break." My uncle tousled the tight curls on Aiden's head.

"My cousin isn't and could never be work." Aiden grinned at me as I spoke, his mouth full of meat. "I just can't stay long."

"Oh, do you have plans tonight?" I swore I heard Jake growl when Ron leaned in closer. "I was headed to O'Malley's tonight for some pool. Next to the chief here, they have the best wings."

"I've been there a few times with some friends, but I've never eaten there."

Aunt Maya winced as she surveyed the train wreck at her dining room table.

"Why are you two so quiet?" Uncle Keith squinted at Jake and Mike. "I may or may not have something to do with the extra guards at Kelly Lakes High this week. Punks have no place in this town, especially in the schools. You have an in with the chief, so relax, kid."

Mike laughed, nodding as he reached for a wing. He'd been picking at his food since he got here, everything from this week obviously weighing on him. I smiled when he glanced in my direction, worrying about him all over again and forgetting for a second how excruciating dinner had been up until that point.

My cousin Brian said nothing, staring at Ron and me as if we were some kind of zoo display. Or maybe that was just how I felt.

"So, you can cheer up too, Russo."

Jake only shrugged in response, tension radiating off him from head to toe. I'd heard it in the short responses he gave my uncle and the clench of his jaw I'd spotted in a weak moment of glancing back at him. Maybe he thought this was a setup, or that I agreed to come here and meet Ron. Jake and I weren't technically together, and the sting of him not showing up this morning, even if he owed me nothing, was still fresh.

Yet I couldn't shake the feeling I was doing something wrong by sitting next to another man with Jake only feet away.

"I wish I had a guidance counselor who looked like you in high school. Maybe I would have shown up to class more often."

We all turned to Uncle Keith, clearing his throat as he wiped barbecue sauce off his hands.

"I know, I know." Ron held up his hands, sneaking a smile at me as if we were sharing a private joke. "I'll stop."

I managed to swallow two pieces of London broil, my stomach churning too much to tolerate anything else. I chewed on a piece of bread to pad my stomach for the wine I needed to get through the rest of the night.

"I'm thirty-two, Uncle Keith. You don't have to throw the uncle weight around anymore. I can take care of myself."

He was simply sitting there, trying to enjoy a meal with his friends and family, but who he was and what he meant to both Jake and me deepened the shame of what had happened between us. At least, it did for me.

It wasn't Uncle Keith's fault. It was Jake's and mine for not respecting him, as we should have been all this time.

The second I met Aunt Maya's narrowed eyes, I regretted what I said. It had come out harsher than I'd meant it to as frustration at this entire screwed-up situation seeped out of me.

"Excuse me for a minute." I pushed my chair away from the table and headed upstairs. I opened the bathroom door and fell against it after it shut behind me. I shouldn't have lashed out at my uncle, and catching the hurt in his eyes made me even more disgusted with myself.

I leaned against the sink, my tired eyes staring back at me in the mirror. I shook my head at my reflection—the smart woman who prided herself on helping others with their problems, but couldn't solve her own. In fact, she was pretty damn good at creating more.

I ran and leaped at this new chance to begin again, and now I was tripping all over myself.

My head fell forward on a groan at a light tapping at the door. I had to apologize to Uncle Keith, but I wasn't ready to look him in the eye yet.

"Hey, I'm sorry. I'll be right out—"

I froze when I met Jake's gaze. His jaw was tight as he kept his eyes on me, gingerly shutting the door behind him and turning the lock.

"What are you doing?" The question came out on a long sigh. "This is a little brazen, even for us."

Jake said nothing as he came closer, grabbing me by the waist and swirling my body around until it was flush against his.

I pressed into his hard chest, but he wouldn't budge.

"So, you and Ron?" He nodded behind him as he skated his hand down my back, triggering a shiver along my spine.

"Me and Ron what? I had no idea he'd be here, and in case you hadn't noticed, it's been uncomfortable as hell dealing with his puppy-dog eyes, my oblivious uncle, and not having a clue how to react to being in the same room with you anymore. Not that I ever did. You need to leave."

"What if I don't want to?" He cupped my cheek, tracing my quivering jaw with his thumb. My visceral response to Jake pissed me off, yet there was nothing I could do to stop it. "What if I've had it with pretending?" My breath caught in my throat when the pad of his thumb skimmed my bottom lip. "You're not going anywhere with him tonight."

"Since when is that up to you? Look, we had a moment," I began, darting my tongue out to swipe across my dry lips, my entire mouth parched from the simmering heat in Jake's eyes. I wasn't sure if it was lust or jealous rage, but it shot straight to my core all the same. "Now, the moment is over, and maybe it's better to let it go—"

Jake cut me off with a kiss. A blinding, scorching kiss that set my whole body on fire. I should've pushed him away and escaped this bathroom with a little dignity and self-preservation, but when he slanted his mouth over mine to deepen the kiss, I couldn't care less about either.

"Jake, please," I gasped when we broke apart, too dizzy and aroused to remember the rest of my argument.

"Is that what you think? Just a moment?"

"What else should I think? I know you said we'd talk today, but when you didn't show up, I figured you were done. And maybe that's for the best."

"The best? You really believe that?" He ran his finger down my neck, the jolt from his touch shooting down my arm.

"I don't know what to believe."

"I'm not done. I'm not sure I ever could be done with you." He wove his fingers into my hair. "We had more than a moment, and you know that. It wasn't enough." His sinful mouth tilted. "I want more. I want *you*. You're right, baby. I'm exhausted. So fucking exhausted."

Our mouths fused together again, my fingers sifting through the hair at his neck as he hoisted me up onto the sink, hooking my leg over his hip. He was hard and heavy as he rubbed against all the right spots, drawing a needy whimper out of me. Nothing would be enough with this man, and it was terrifying.

"We can't do this here," I murmured against his lips.

"I'm coming to you tomorrow morning. Like I should have a long time ago. We'll go somewhere, we'll talk, and we'll figure this out. Until then," he rasped, cupping the nape of my neck and pulling me in for another kiss, slower and wetter, his tongue gliding against mine as it made long, deliberate strokes inside my mouth.

I was about to come just from Jake kissing me.

He dragged my bottom lip through his teeth before he backed away.

"Remember that. You can come back downstairs and sit next to your new friend before you tell him goodbye for the night."

I rolled my eyes. "Since when are you a caveman?"

His gaze softened as he feathered his hand down my cheek.

"Since you, I'm a lot of things, Peyton." He came back to my lips, his kisses quick but sweet before flashing me a panty-melting smile.

I watched Jake leave and went back to my reflection. My cheeks were flushed, my lips and chin were red and raw, but a smile stretched across my mouth.

Jake made me a lot of things too, and whether they were good or bad, I wasn't done either.

It was hard to run from disaster when you didn't want to be anywhere else.

TWENTY

PEYTON

"Claudia. Enough."

I scowled at my phone screen. It was barely eight in the morning on a Sunday, but I'd been up for a couple of hours—if I even slept at all. Her eyes twinkled even on the spotty video, as she rested her chin on her hand and smiled widely while I went through the painful dinner at my uncle's house that ended with Jake cornering me in the bathroom.

"This is the best."

I shut my eyes at the shrill of her squeal.

"This is just the hot thing I wanted to happen to you up in the country."

I shook my head, fidgeting on my couch as I tried in vain to get comfortable.

"I'm still in New York State, not the country."

"Honey, I was there." She tilted her head and clicked her tongue against her teeth. "It's the country."

"And by hot thing, you mean hot mess. I'm waiting for my uncle's best friend to take me somewhere to talk about how we can't keep our hands off each other."

"And then keep doing it." She waggled her eyebrows. "Okay, okay. My excitement isn't helping you. Answer this for me, if you take your uncle out of the equation, what is so awful about the guy you're into wanting you back? You're both adults. And the sexual tension between the two of you was delicious, so live a little and enjoy it."

"What if I can't help Mike in school because I'm dating his father and they think I'm trying to give him special treatment?"

I bristled, thinking of having to fight for credibility to do my job once again, especially after the fight Mike had just gotten into. I'd watch him, but I couldn't have eyes everywhere to stop it from happening again.

Worrying about my students was nothing new, but my concern for Mike went deeper than usual. I was privy to more of his backstory, but maybe Jake wasn't the only Russo I focused on too much.

"Couldn't they already make that argument since he's a family friend of yours? I understand that you want to be cautious, but if you stepped back a little, maybe you'd realize that it's not such a big deal."

"A lot easier said than done." I rubbed my temple, wishing it were that easy to revel in new passion without dreading casualties or repercussions.

"Did he say where he was taking you?"

"No, just to be ready at eight thirty." I flicked my wrist to check the time. The minutes had inched by so damn slowly since I'd gotten out of bed. I'd already been fully dressed for an hour.

"You never said how you got through the rest of dinner last night."

"I didn't," I sighed, draping my hand over my eyes. "I came back downstairs, apologized to my uncle, who, as usual, let me off too easy, and told everyone I wasn't feeling well. I managed to make it out the door before Ron asked for my number."

After those kisses from Jake, I couldn't stay at that table and not squirm in my seat for the rest of the night. I'd get a call from my aunt or uncle or both, asking how I was feeling at some point today. I was a terrible liar, but Uncle Keith always gave me the benefit of the doubt on everything.

There was no way to step back and not see the complications.

But there was no way I could step back from Jake. Not anymore.

"This is totally like one of those Hallmark movies, except you never see the couple get to third base in front of a kitchen sink. So, it's even better."

"Goodbye, Claudia."

"Love you . . ." she sang as I poked the screen to end the call.

I'd been reading into every touch and lingering glance between Jake and me for months, starting with our reintroduction in the parking lot. I'd blown it all off as my mind playing tricks on me, that he was just the nice, helpful, molten sex-on-legs Jake that I remembered, and I blamed my vulnerability for my growing attachment to him.

It seemed impossible to me that Jake wanted me back and was probably why my uncle hadn't noticed anything between us yet. Or maybe, like me, he *did* see something but brushed it off because his best friend and his niece together were too ridiculous of a notion to seriously consider.

Seriously considering anything with Jake had kept me up all night, terrifying me no matter which angle I tried to look at it from.

I jumped out of my skin at the sound of my doorbell. I took a quick glance at myself, the simple sweater on top of jeans and boots, and shrugged. I shouldn't have wanted to be sexy for Jake or encourage the heat I spied in his eyes, but I craved it as much as I'd craved him.

"Hey" was all I could say. He leaned against the doorjamb, his black jacket stretching across his broad chest and shoulders as if it was specially made for him. I let my eyes drink all of him in—the thick, dark hair that gathered at his neck just below his ears, the sparkles of gray at his temples making him even hotter, the dusting of stubble over his cheeks short enough to tease a dimple when he smiled. His lips curved as he swept his gaze up and down my body with a dirty intention he either stopped hiding or I finally allowed myself to acknowledge as real.

Talking rationally about what was between us, no matter how many layers of clothes I piled on myself, wasn't going to happen. The stolen glances and innocent yet forbidden touches had become a powder keg of foreplay.

Despite Claudia trying to talk me out of it, I still believed this was wrong, but I was in too deep to stop it.

"Hey, yourself." He leaned forward and pressed his lips to mine. Jake smiled into the kiss when I went in for another on instinct.

"Feeling better?" he rasped, sliding his hand to the back of my neck. Tingles went down my back from the graze of his calloused fingers against my skin.

"I am." I smiled when he yanked me closer.

"Good." He pressed a kiss to my forehead. "Let's go."

"Where's Mike today?"

"My sister is taking him and his cousins to the pancake house on the thruway. She offered to take him since she still feels as bad as I do about the fight he got into, and my nieces will probably love being along for the ride."

"Oh," I said. "You didn't want to go?"

His lips curved as he gave me a slow shake of his head.

"I think my son would like a break from me hovering over him, and I had important plans."

"Which are?" I lifted a brow, my dopey heart speeding up at being part of his important plans.

"Well, first, we're getting breakfast since I didn't have much to eat last night. I was too distracted by what was happening on the other side of the table."

I exhaled with a groan at his lifted brow.

"Nothing was happening on the other end of the table. But I didn't really eat either, so breakfast sounds good." I fought a smile as I pulled on my jacket.

"Then, we'll go somewhere and talk."

"Where?" I asked, eyeing Jake as I locked my door.

"Somewhere we can just be us, not what we are to someone else."

My stomach dipped at his reference to my uncle, but I said nothing as I followed him to his truck.

"So, another planet, then?" I smirked as he held the passenger side door open for me to climb into the seat.

Just as I was about to fasten my seat belt, Jake cupped my neck and pulled me in for a kiss. It was deep, wet, and just as possessive as when he stalked me into my uncle's bathroom last night. Yet, there was something different about it. He was proving something, trying to convince me with every stroke of his tongue. He kept a tight grip on the back of my head as if he were holding me in place so I didn't slip away. He should've known how hard it was to be anywhere else.

We traded whimpers and groans as the kiss kept going. I should have been aware of where we were and who could possibly see us, but I didn't care. As his lips moved against mine, all I saw and all I felt was Jake. The control and distance

I'd grasped on to all this time vanished, and I doubted I'd ever get it back even if I wanted to.

And I didn't want to.

In all the uncertainty and trepidation when it came to Jake and me, that was the one thing too sure to deny.

I fisted the collar of his jacket, ready to get out and drag him back to my condo where we wouldn't have an audience and wouldn't have to stop. He pulled away when I shifted toward the door, leaning his forehead against mine as he chased his breath.

"Fuck, you can kiss," he groaned and shook his head, still leaning against me.

"Back at you," I said in a breathless whisper.

He skimmed his thumb over my raw bottom lip and shook his head.

"*This* is why we aren't talking here." He nodded back toward my front door. "I want you for so much more than this, but you're so damn beautiful I can't help myself."

I bit my bottom lip as I held in a whimper. His mouth, his eyes, his words, this couldn't be my reality. I'd made Jake a teenage dream but never got to know the real man behind the gorgeous exterior. Now that I did, I wanted him even more, and it was still the best kind of surreal that he wanted me back.

Even if it came with the nagging voice in the back of my mind reiterating all that could go wrong.

TWENTY-ONE

JAKE

"Where are you taking us?" Peyton asked, her pinched brow in my periphery as I drove.

"Somewhere private."

She squinted at me when I turned my head.

"More private than my condo?"

I turned down the back road and pulled onto the patch of gravel where we all used to park. In the summer months, the lake was packed from early in the morning until almost midnight. It was the closest thing we had to a beach, but I used it to clear my head in the colder months when only the hard-core fishers would come this early.

"Private and where I won't be tempted to strip you before we can talk."

My head fell back with a laugh when her eyes darted to my back seat.

I cupped her chin and pulled her into a kiss, brushing her lips lightly in an attempt not to start anything I didn't want to be tempted to finish.

"That's why we didn't stay at your condo and why we're getting out of my truck. I'll grab a blanket from the back."

Peyton eyed me with playful suspicion before climbing out of the passenger seat.

"I'm still a city girl and haven't embraced the ice-cold outdoors yet like the locals." She shivered and grasped the paper coffee cup in her hands.

"You never played in the snow as a kid? Brooklyn has snow sometimes, right?"

She chuckled around the lid as she took a sip.

"Sometimes. My mother wasn't exactly the play-in-the-snow type, and in Brooklyn, the snow is gray and gross after about five minutes. Uncle Keith would take me sledding up here when we'd visit, but I didn't build many snowmen in my time." She shrugged, darting her eyes away as she probably felt the same twinge of guilt I did at the mention of her uncle.

"Well," I started after I pulled the blanket out of the back of the truck and shut the door, "after the first snowfall this year, we need to fix that."

She burst out laughing, her chocolate eyes twinkling as she peered back at me.

"You want to play in the snow with me?"

She shot me a sexy grin, but I didn't smile back. I cupped the nape of her neck and pressed my forehead against hers.

"I want to do everything with you. Feels good to finally admit it."

"That it does." She exhaled a long sigh and leaned into me.

"Come on." I kissed the top of her head and pulled her by the hand. "I usually come here alone this early in the morning. It's quiet enough to drown out the noise in my head."

I led us to a grassy area next to the rocks. The lake was still. It was cold but not frigid enough to spot any ice on the surface. I spread out the blanket and pulled her to sit next to me.

"It's pretty. I can kind of see why you'd want to come here, even in the cold."

Silence washed over us for a moment, and the only sounds for a few long minutes were the tapping of Peyton's nails against the side of the cup.

"I should have come back to your apartment Saturday morning."

"You don't need to explain," she said, crossing her legs under her. "Mike needed you, and to be honest, I needed a minute."

I shook my head. "I also didn't need to fix the wall on Friday night. I just needed to see you and didn't have the balls to come out and say it."

A smile tugged on the side of her mouth. "I had a feeling about that. I wanted to see you too. I was so worried about both of you all day Friday. Seeing my students fight always bothers me, but knowing the kind of kid Mike is and how it would upset you made me sick to my stomach."

"I got into my share of fights in high school. I worry because he's a young fourteen, and that's my fault."

"How is that your fault?"

"Because he's my only son, and I babied him because of what happened with his mother and me. I tried to make my marriage work, but . . ." I scrubbed a hand down my face, hating how this would come out. "My heart wasn't in it—not for a long time. When I asked for a divorce, Eileen lost it and has hated me ever since. My son has seen and heard a lot of things I wish he hadn't."

"Sometimes people are happier apart than together. When my father left, I was barely eight, and I still feel the relief."

"I never got in too deep with anyone after. I dated, but I was afraid of hurting anyone like that again, so I focused on Mike and tried to make the most out of the little time we had together on weekends. It was easier to move on if I made sure I didn't become invested in anyone."

She nodded, studying me. "I get it."

"No. No, you don't."

I scooted closer and pulled her to me.

"From the time I saw you in the parking lot with Mike, I haven't been able to stay away. I should have, for so many reasons." I chuckled. "But I couldn't. The fact that you're almost a decade and a half younger than me, my kid's guidance counselor, and the niece my best friend thinks of as a daughter hasn't stopped me. When I almost kissed you in the kitchen with Keith right outside, I knew—"

"That it was a matter of time. I figured that out a long time ago too." She set the cup next to the blanket, draping her arm over my torso and cuddling into my chest. "I think we moved on from mess to clusterfuck."

I cracked up, resting my chin on the top of her head.

"Sounds about right. What I'm trying to say is that I've never felt this way about anyone before."

Peyton lifted her head. "What way?"

I cradled her cheek as a long, defeated sigh fell from my lips. She was so damn gorgeous it almost hurt to look at her.

"That I would tell everyone and everything to fuck off just to have you for myself."

Her mouth parted when I skimmed my thumb over her lips.

"I almost stopped at your uncle's house first to ask his permission."

"Why didn't you?"

Without realizing it, we'd rolled back on the blanket. I hovered over her, settling between her legs. She feathered her hand down my cheek and over my jaw, triggering goose bumps along my shoulder that had nothing to do with the cold.

"Because," I murmured so close to her mouth that our lips brushed, "if he told me no, it wouldn't have mattered. I'd be right here anyway." Our mouths fused together. Peyton grabbed at the back of my jacket as I sank deeper into her. This kiss was slow instead of how ravenous I usually was whenever her lips touched mine. I wanted to savor her instead of devouring what I could before I lost it.

She pulled back from the kiss and shook her head.

"If we came here to talk, I need to tell you something first."

"Okay," I whispered, my stomach falling a bit. "What is it?"

"Could we . . ." She nodded behind me as she sat up on her elbows. I took the hint and climbed off her, bracing myself for whatever she had to say.

"Aunt Maya knows this, but Uncle Keith doesn't. Aside from her and Claudia, and my old school and most likely the entire school district I was in, no one else does." Her chest rose as she sucked in a deep breath. "I had a fling with the principal at my last job. I ignored a lot of red flags and took a professional chance that cost me, especially when I found out that my *fling* was an affair since he was married. He'd told me that he was separated and we had to lie low until his divorce was final, and I believed him." She turned away from me and rubbed her eyes.

"That's why you said you didn't leave anything behind in Brooklyn, and why you ended up here."

"It is. And, of course, people found out anyway. He quit and moved away, and while I was allowed to keep my job, no one would let me do it. My opinion wasn't taken seriously or even into consideration. I think the school board felt if I stayed behind, maybe it wouldn't seem like the scandal that it was, but trust me, I felt it every single day until I quit."

She ran a hand through her hair, coughing out a sad laugh.

"Anyway, I saw the job posting for the high school in Kelly Lakes, and I thought it would be a great way to start over. I'd be close to my aunt and uncle, far enough away from Brooklyn where I didn't have to worry about who did or didn't know, and I could stop feeling like the worst person in the world for what I'd let happen."

"Stop that." I slid my hand to the back of her neck, "You could never be the worst person in the world. I'm sure it killed you that you couldn't help your students like you wanted to."

She shrugged, shutting her eyes and leaning into my touch as I massaged her shoulder.

"Every time I go through this story, I always feel like whoever I'm telling doesn't see me the same way. I couldn't look my aunt in the eye for a few minutes after, and it's a little hard to look at you now."

"Hey." I inched closer and shook my head. "Other than wishing I could find this guy and kick his ass, nothing you just said changes anything. Thank you for trusting me enough to tell me."

A sheepish grin pulled at her lips.

"I swore I wouldn't do this again, that my new school would only see the best of me and I wouldn't make the same bad decisions that made me leave my last one."

Her eyes darted away again, and she dropped her chin to her chest.

"And you think dating the father of one of your students puts you back there again?" My hand stilled as my stomach dipped. I'd been all too aware of what we had against us and that her being my son's guidance counselor wasn't ideal, but I hadn't expected this. I didn't care, but it was obvious that she did, and I had no clue what that meant.

"No . . . Not exactly. It's not encouraged, but there's no rule that I'm aware of, at least not a serious one. I'm not his teacher, so I don't have the power to pass or fail him. But after Thursday, all I keep thinking is, what if these kids go after him again and I can't do anything about it because the school thinks I'm biased? It's probably a dumb thing to worry about, but that feeling of my hands tied behind my back when my students were in trouble . . ." She pressed her palm against her forehead. "I promised myself I'd keep my eyes open and not make the same mistake."

"So, what are you saying? That you don't want—"

"I'm saying," she said, the crease still between her brows, "that even with what I just told you, and how Uncle Keith is going to lose it when we tell him . . ." She sifted her fingers through my hair with the beginnings of a smile ghosting her lips. "I can't stay away from you either."

"Thank God." I grabbed the back of her head and took her mouth in a relieved as hell kiss. "You scared me," I murmured against her lips.

She smiled and cuddled into the crook of my neck.

"We need to be careful, but I'm at a loss as to how. It was one thing to crush on you before, when I was a kid—"

"You had a crush on me? I had no idea," I teased, smiling when she shot me a glare.

"Right." She rolled her eyes. "That week I stayed up here, I couldn't even speak when you were around. You came with us for ice cream one night, and I had trouble saying what flavor I wanted because you were *right* next to me, so I just pointed and ended up with vanilla instead of chocolate." The groan rising from her throat was fucking adorable. "But I couldn't say it was wrong because, again, my tongue wouldn't work while I was in your proximity. All these years later, I still remember that."

"Well, if it makes you feel any better," I started, rolling back on top of her, "I had a similar reaction when I saw you in the parking lot the first week of school." I nuzzled her cheek. "And your tongue works just fine around me now."

"What I'm saying is," she said, pressing her hands into my chest, "it all means so much more now. I never really got to know you when I was a teenager. You were just this ridiculously good-looking guy who always hung around my uncle. But I moved here and got to know the kind of man you are, and I meant what I said." A slow grin split her mouth. "You're pretty damn incredible." She heaved out an audible sigh.

"I don't want to sneak around, but if you feel more comfortable, maybe we . . . keep it quiet until Mike finishes the school year."

"It's November." Her brows shot up. "Do you really think we can keep this to ourselves all that time? Here? People already pick up on it. Your sister, Claudia, my aunt."

"I figured your aunt knew after I almost lost it at her dinner table."

She winced. "You mean when the whole table heard you grinding your teeth every time Ron tried to speak to me? I made it a point to not look at you through dinner, and even I couldn't ignore it. She knew before, although she realized it after she pushed us out the door together that afternoon. But she won't tell Uncle Keith until we do."

"If you want to keep it quiet until this fight Mike had blows over, that's fine. But we tell your uncle together. And soon. I'm still shocked he doesn't notice, but I don't want to wait until he does."

Telling him before anyone else did wouldn't stop him from hating me, but I owed Keith that much.

"So you're saying that you want to be secret lovers for a little while, Mr. Russo."

The last time she'd called me Mr. Russo, I'd felt every bit of our age difference. The throaty way it fell from her lips now made me, and the growing bulge in my jeans, appreciate it much more.

"I'm saying I'll take you any way that I can have you, Ms. Miller." I pressed into her, coaxing out a sweet little moan. "But secret or not, I'm not sharing you."

"Good, because I'm not sharing you either." She arched her back and pressed her lips back to mine. "Still such a caveman."

I laughed against her lips. I was a lot of things when it came to Peyton—distracted, possessive, and foolish.

Which one would pull us under first?

TWENTY-TWO
PEYTON

"The lake is nice. I can see why you love it."

I rubbed my hands together after I climbed back into the passenger seat of his truck. Jake's lips were glorious enough to distract me from the cold, but now that we weren't rolling around on top of each other, I couldn't shake the chill running through me.

"I loved it today because of the company," he said, taking my hands in his big ones and lifting them to his mouth. "But I didn't want you to freeze." He blew on our hands, the wet warmth from his mouth causing another kind of shiver.

"Thank you for bringing me here. And you're right, better to talk where it's too cold to get naked, right?"

He flicked his gaze to mine, a wicked grin splitting his mouth.

"Come here, I'll warm you up," he rasped, hauling me to him and covering my mouth with an achingly slow kiss. His tongue made long and languid strokes, seeking and exploring as I whimpered. When he slanted his mouth over mine to go deeper and harder, heat pooled between my legs as I melted against the seat.

I climbed over the console and onto his lap, straddling his hips and rocking against him as our mouths kept moving. Even with two layers of denim between us, I could feel his cock swell under me. He slipped his hands under my sweater and cupped my breasts. I went from freezing to on fire as I searched for the zipper on my jacket. Jake caught my hand and broke the kiss, panting as he dropped his head to my chest.

"No. Not like this."

"Well, no. We'll eventually run out of room and have to head to the back seat." I chuckled and dove back in for his lips, but he shook his head.

"When I make love to you, we do things the right way. In a bed, where I can have you all night, not fumble around in my back seat. As tempting as it is." He grabbed my face and pressed his forehead into mine. "What the hell are you doing to me?"

"I could ask you the same thing." A breathless laugh fell from my lips. "Want to go back on the grass and cool off?"

He tilted his head and laughed.

"I don't think it's possible for me to cool off around you." He pressed his lips to mine with a featherlight kiss and backed away. "Let me take you home."

I nodded and crawled back to the passenger seat.

"Why can't I get this? It buckled before . . ." I groaned, stabbing the fastener with no use.

Jake reached over me, taking the buckle out of my hand and pressing his lips to mine as he pressed himself against me, just like that first day in his truck, except we both leaned into it instead of freezing up. He smiled into the kiss as the lock clicked.

"That's what I wanted to do that afternoon you were in my

truck. I had you all to myself for a day, and I couldn't do a damn thing about it."

"You can now." I grazed my thumb along his bottom lip, still wet from our kiss. "The back seat isn't *that* small. You drive a truck." I looped my arms around his neck. "We could maneuver a little bit," I teased, holding in a laugh at the heat in his eyes, now thinned to slits. "If I got on top, we could save room."

"So another man could see you and watch you come? Absolutely fucking not." He growled and started the engine.

"You're no fun." I jutted my lip in a mock pout.

He leaned over and took my lip in between his teeth, giving it a nibble as he pulled away.

"My eyes only, sweetheart." He pecked my lips before putting the truck in drive and heading away from the lake.

A bed with Jake all night sounded like the best kind of dream. But at this point, it was still just that—a dream. He had a son at home who couldn't know about us, at least for now. We would keep running into each other, but when was the next time we could be just us? When would I be able to kiss him whenever I wanted to and touch him just because I could?

"Do you want to come inside? See my new wall?" I joked when Jake pulled up in front of my condo.

Jake shot me a crooked grin. My heart stuttered and then sank at the intrusive memory of the last time I could only see the man I was with at my home in secret. This wasn't that, and Jake was a good man and not a liar who was using me, but keeping what we had a secret, even if I agreed it was the best thing to do right now, still left a familiar and unwanted taste in my mouth.

"Mike isn't coming home until later this afternoon."

"So you have time, and we talked already, right?"

"We did," he said, tucking a lock of hair behind my ear and smoothing his finger down my cheek as he pulled away.

I inched closer and cupped his stubbled cheek.

"There is nothing I want more than to be in your bed all night, but all night isn't something we'll have any time soon. But we have a few hours, and I just want to be with you, wherever it takes us." As the words fell from my mouth, I wondered if they were desperate or direct? Probably both, but either way, they were true. If I was jumping into this, even with the risks we were taking looming over us, I wasn't holding back or wasting a minute.

"I want that too. So much, you have no idea."

"Then I think we should get the most out of every second we have."

Until they run out.

I pushed the nagging voice out of my head and stepped out of the truck.

"Peyton, hi!" Cheryl, my next-door neighbor, waved from her driveway. I was still getting used to friendly neighbors who knew my name.

I waved back as I unlocked my door, the heat of Jake's presence behind me curling up my neck under my sweater.

I threw my keys in the bowl on the kitchen table as Jake peeled off his jacket. His black Henley stretched across his chest as he hung up his jacket, his back muscles working under his shirt as he lifted his arms. My eyes drifted down to his worn jeans and boots. I wasn't used to allowing myself more than a friendly glance, but I let my eyes feast on him now. He was so breathtaking that I couldn't tear my gaze away.

That beautiful man was mine—and I was afraid to introduce him to my neighbor because no one was supposed to know.

"Looks good," Jake said as he stepped up to the new

drywall. "Once we get the carpet down, you'll never know this place was flooded." He smiled as he craned his neck toward me. "I told you I'd fix it for you."

"You did." I wrapped my arms around his waist. I was already bracing myself for the next time we had to see each other. Not looking at him in public was already taxing— seeing him and keeping my hands to myself would be torturous.

"And now, I have ground-up flooding insurance, so if this happens again, I don't have to cry into my contractor's arms."

He chuckled, deep and low enough to curl my toes in my fleece boots.

"Your contractor would have agreed to rebuild the whole place for you that night if it made you feel better." His laugh rumbled against my cheek as he kissed the top of my head.

I smiled and closed my eyes, breathing him in enough so I could remember it later.

"Thank God Uncle Keith's big mouth saved him from what he could have walked in on that day."

I spied the same wince of guilt that churned inside me.

"Think he'll hate us?" I lifted a brow and tightened my arms around Jake.

"Not you. Me?" He moved his head from side to side. "He might. I'm the one he'll be angry with, and I'm fully prepared to take that all on when the time comes."

"Why? Because you still think you corrupted me?" I rolled my eyes. "You didn't lure me into a van with candy. I'm very aware of what I'm doing and what I want." I smoothed my hands over the soft cotton of his shirt, lingering over his chest when his heart hammered against my palm.

"Yeah? What's that?" Jake's husky whisper sent a chill rolling down my spine.

I grabbed the back of his neck and brought his lips back to

mine. The kiss caught fire as Jake ran his hands over my body, down my thighs and up my back, landing on my ass as he pressed me closer. He dove into my neck, sucking and biting in all the right spots until I slumped against him.

For this heaven, I'd go to hell and back—although I wished that didn't seem like such a certainty.

Our lips kept moving as he walked me backward down my hallway and into my bedroom. I was impatient and nervous. Making love to Jake would ruin me, but there was already no going back.

I fumbled with the hem of his shirt, peppering kisses along his stubbled jaw and down his neck. "Let me see you," I whispered as I dragged his shirt up his torso until he pulled it over his head.

All the air rushed out of my lungs as I drank him in. He hissed out a curse when I painted kisses across his chest and skimmed my hand over the ridges of muscle along his stomach, hot and smooth under my fingertips.

"My God, you're beautiful, Jake," I croaked out.

A smile tugged at his lips before he hooked his thumbs into the waistband of my jeans and yanked me closer.

"Hands up," he whispered as he lifted my sweater over my head. His blue eyes went dark as his heated gaze caressed my body. "So gorgeous, I'm so fucking lucky."

The air was always charged between us, but this time, it was hard to breathe. Anticipation and desperation took over as Jake snapped, lifting me by the waist and dropping me onto the mattress, his mouth taking mine in a bruising kiss as he snaked his arm under me to bring me closer. I kicked off my boots as he unbuckled my jeans and ripped them down my legs. His mouth was everywhere, my body shifting beneath him as I swayed toward the trail of his lips.

"You're soaked, Jesus," he rasped in my ear as he slipped

his hand inside my panties. My legs flailed back and forth as his fingers worked me over, swirling around my clit before pressing inside me.

"Jake," I moaned his name as I sank my head into my pillow, unable to keep up with all the sensation. He pulled down my bra strap until I spilled out of the cup, taking my nipple between his teeth as he pumped his fingers in and out. Pressure pulsed between my legs and burst over my body, already so close to the edge it hurt.

"I feel you, sweetheart. You're close, aren't you?"

A strained noise I'd never heard fell from my lips as I nodded.

"Come on my fingers, beautiful." He curved his fingers inside me as he sucked my other nipple into his mouth. "Ride my hand and come."

I arched off the bed as I crashed, bucking into his hand. This orgasm was even more soul-shattering than the one against my kitchen sink. I rode the aftershocks and mewled into his mouth as he kissed me slow and deep enough to drive me out of my mind even as I was coming down from the high.

"*No one* sees that but me, sweetheart," he croaked out as we both reached for the buckle of his jeans. "God, I wish I could watch you come every single day."

I cut him off with a kiss. I wished for that too, but wanted to delay any nuggets of reality from barging into our perfect day.

He dragged my panties from where they tangled around my ankles. They landed on my carpet with a soft whoosh as he hovered over me, holding my eyes as his chest heaved up and down.

"What?" I panted out. I couldn't decipher the expression on his face. He peered down at me, seeming like he was going to devour me or say he had to stop. I was a breathless ball of need, and my brain would short-circuit if we didn't keep going.

"I'm not going to survive you, sweetheart." He hooked my leg over his hip, his gaze searing through me.

It made no sense to feel this much for someone over just a few months, but the fact that we were here at all meant it was too big to ignore.

Maybe that terrified him too.

He stood, fishing his wallet out of his pocket and dropping it onto my nightstand before he kicked off his jeans, followed by his boxers.

He jerked his head up as a gasp slipped out of me.

His cock was long and thick, bobbing against his stomach as he slid the condom down his length.

He came back on top of me, taking my mouth in a slow kiss as he settled between my legs. I was still drenched and impatient, but tears scratched at the back of my throat at his change in pace. It seemed like he was preparing both of us for not only being inside me, but for all it meant.

I was on board with wherever this took us as long as I went there with Jake.

He slid inside with one thrust, grunting curses in my ear as he started to move. He grabbed my leg and pushed it against my chest, the new angle drawing a long moan out of me and making my eyes roll to the back of my head.

"Okay?" he asked, squinting at me as sweat dripped down his brow.

"Fucking fantastic," I whispered, my voice gone as I dug my nails into his backside to push him even deeper.

"Peyton," he growled before he picked up the pace, driving into me hard enough for my mattress to squeak and my head-board to bang into my wall. "You're too perfect. Too tight, too

. . ." He trailed off, his forehead pressing into mine. "You were made for me, baby. Just me."

Our mouths came together again, our kisses sloppy and desperate, as I met him thrust for thrust, lifting my hips off the bed, greedy and begging for more. I'd never get enough of Jake. I'd have to get by on little scraps after today, but I'd worry about that later. Right now, my world was reduced to him, this bed, and how long I could hold out until the spasms rushing up my spine exploded.

"Come again for me, sweetheart." His voice was rough. "I need to feel you again. I need . . . Fuck."

I held on, raking my nails down his back as this orgasm ruined me more than the first. I'd heard of orgasms described as little deaths before, but had always found it to be a ridiculous notion until that moment. When you had them with someone important, the intensity shattered you each time—and you never got all of you back.

I reveled in the moment, Jake still inside me and the two of us nestled together as close as we could possibly get. Despite my past, I trusted him with every piece of me.

All of me was all of his.

TWENTY-THREE
PEYTON

"Are you hungry?" I asked Jake, propping my elbow on his bare chest.

"I could eat . . . again."

I giggled when he squeezed the inside of my upper thigh.

"Today is my food shopping day, so I don't have much." I rolled up to sit. "But I think I can find something."

"Stay here." He pulled me back by my wrist, brushing my lips with a quick kiss before he flung his muscular legs over the side of the bed. My eyes followed the flex of his perfect ass as he reached down to pull up his boxers.

"I feel your eyes on my ass, Ms. Miller." He shot me a smirk as he turned around.

"You'd be right, Mr. Russo." I pulled the covers up to my neck, feeling the chill against my still-naked body without Jake's heat to warm me up. "I'm still enjoying the novelty of staring at you whenever I want."

He climbed back onto the bed, his arms and legs boxing me in like a cocoon.

"I love looking at you too, so stop hiding from me." Jake traced my jaw with the tip of his finger before he hooked it in the space where the comforter met my neck and pulled it down.

"I'm not hiding. It's cold under here without a sexy contractor to keep me warm." I yanked at the covers in a pointless tug-of-war until the dusting of hair on Jake's chest tickled my breasts as the comforter bunched at my waist.

Another loud moan fell from my lips as he ran his mouth up to my neck.

"So beautiful," he whispered as his thumb drifted back and forth over my cheek. "We'll figure things out, I promise." He pressed his lips to my forehead, smiling at me as I exhaled a long, contented sigh, despite the twinge of worry over exactly *how* we'd figure things out.

"Part of me wants to run to my uncle's house right now, but the other part, the much larger part . . ." I grimaced as I peered up at him. "That part doesn't want to ruin today with an ugly fight."

His grin shrank as he nodded.

"I know, sweetheart. It may not be so ugly, he could surprise us, but I agree. Let's keep today like it is." He kissed the tip of my nose. "I'll be right back."

I breathed out a long gust of air when Jake left my bedroom, dragging a hand down my face as I wished I could be as optimistic. When the worst that could happen actually happened, I'd become well versed in expecting it all the time. As much as I tried, an outcome where my uncle would just shrug and tell us "That's great" didn't seem likely or even plausible.

I flung the covers off me and stood, no longer cold and losing the battle with myself to keep reality at arm's length until Jake left.

I was reaching for a T-shirt when I spotted his Henley on the floor crumpled up next to his jeans. I scooped it up and slipped it over my head, holding the collar up to my nose before I smoothed it down. I was on the curvy side, but his shirt still draped over me, the hem stopping at mid-thigh.

"Jesus," Jake hissed from behind me.

"Sorry." I shrugged before turning around. "I figured if I was going to be clingy until you leave, may as well go all in."

"You in my shirt is the hottest fucking thing I've ever seen. Be as clingy as you want, sweetheart."

I burst out laughing when I realized what Jake was holding.

"I forgot I bought those when Claudia was here. She has an ice cream cone fixation."

He strode up to me with a chocolate ice cream cone in each hand, holding out his hand for me to grab one. "I haven't kept cones in the house since Mike was little. I used to have a system of stacking the scoops, but I may be a little rusty."

"Thank you."

A groan rose from his throat when I took a long lick.

"I take back what I said. You in my shirt while licking an ice cream cone—*that* is the hottest fucking thing I've ever seen."

I laughed and sat on the edge of my bed.

"You're an animal, Mr. Russo."

"So, am I forgiven?" he asked as he settled next to me. "For cheating you out of chocolate that day?"

He snickered as he bit the side of the cone, already almost done with his.

"That whole day was traumatic." I sighed before taking another lick. "Ice cream sounded like a good idea until Uncle Keith mentioned you were going to meet us there. I was fifteen and he was taking me for ice cream like I was a kid, and then *you* had to be there."

"Well, I guess I'm sorry about that too."

I shoved his shoulder as he cracked up.

"I think he wasn't sure what else to do with me because I was older, and I didn't mind because being with him was still fun. But something about you being there for it made it embarrassing. I didn't want to be such an awkward kid in front of you."

"You weren't awkward, you were quiet. I have my own teenager now who hardly speaks."

"Then we went to mini golf, and I just put the ball where you both told me and nodded every time you tried to speak to me, praying you'd keep asking questions with yes or no answers. The whole thing, even now, is taxing to think about." I cut him a look, scowling as his lips continued to twitch. "Eating an ice cream cone around a guy you like is stressful. You have to worry if it's all over your face or dripping down your chin. You know what?" I moved over to the other side of the bed, turning toward my bedroom wall and away from Jake. "Don't look at me until I finish."

"Is that why you're eating so slow? I'm still distracting you?"

The bed dipped behind me, but I wouldn't give him the satisfaction of turning my head.

He came up behind me and leaned in, dragging his tongue up the side of the cone where the chocolate was melting onto my fingers, swallowing the rest of the scoop in one bite, holding my eyes as he licked his lips. My clit throbbed with every swipe of his tongue as if he were licking me instead of ice cream.

He took the empty cone out of my hand and put it on the nightstand. I whimpered when he sucked my fingers, one by one, into his mouth. Licking them clean and inching them out.

"Still tongue-tied, sweetheart?"

STEPHANIE ROSE

Our mouths crashed together as we fell back on my bed. I climbed on top of him and straddled his legs, a growl escaping him when his hand slipped under his shirt and he found me bare. I rocked back and forth, his cock hard and twitching against my core. I was about to lift his shirt over my head when his phone buzzed from where it still lay on the floor.

Jake glanced at the screen and winced. "It's Mike. I'm sorry."

I plucked the phone off the floor and handed it to Jake, quickly climbing off him before he could answer.

"Hey, is everything okay? I'll be home in a bit. I had to check on a job today. Tell your aunt and the girls to relax. I'll be right there, and we can order dinner. I would've thought a mountain of pancakes would fill you guys up until tonight." Jake laughed, an easy smile stretching his lips like it always did when he was with his son.

I loved how easily he showed his affection toward Mike and the strong friendship he had with my uncle. Uncle Keith had said more than once that he and Jake were more like brothers than friends.

And here I was, putting a wrench in all of it. Jake couldn't even tell his son where he really was all afternoon. I wasn't mad at him for lying, but hated that any time we spent together from now on would mean dishonesty to the people we cared about the most. I wished Jake had stopped at my uncle's house so this could have blown up already and we could deal with whatever came afterward.

I peeled off his shirt and grabbed my robe from the back of my bedroom door. Forcing a smile, I handed Jake his shirt and grabbed the empty ice cream cone from my nightstand, leaving my bedroom before Jake dressed.

Trudging up to my sink and tossing the cone into the trash, I tore off a paper towel and ran it under the water to bring it

162

into the bedroom and wipe away the sticky trail of ice cream from my nightstand. When Travis would leave my apartment, I'd feel empty, the disappointment heavy but dulling over time as it became familiar. This was different, as the decision to lie low—for now—was made by both of us.

I still hated being this crazy about someone and unable to scream about it to everyone I knew.

"Hey," Jake crooned from behind me as he wrapped his arms around my waist. "The last thing I want to do right now is leave—"

"You have Mike and your family waiting for you. I understand and would never expect you not to put your son first."

"And I love that about you, but that doesn't mean I wanted today to end. Soon, sweetheart. We'll get through this issue at school, tell Keith, and I can let everyone know you're mine. And we'll have so many more days just like this."

I nodded, pushing a smile across my mouth as my nose burned. Why was I so emotional? I'd never felt this way when I parted ways with Travis at the end of a night. Maybe something in me knew that it was all temporary, that his drawn-out fake divorce created distance between us that I not only accepted but maybe even wanted.

I didn't want to be temporary with Jake. I wanted today and any scraps of time I could get with him.

"You believe me, right, sweetheart?" He turned me around to face him and took my face in his hands. "This isn't what happened to you before. I'm not him, and I hate feeling like that's where your mind is going right now."

"I know, and I know you're not," I said, unable to mask the crack in my voice.

I believed him, but things wouldn't be as easy now that we had our clothes back on and were headed into the real world.

"I just . . . feel a lot for you, and if I'm being honest, it's scary as hell. And yes, this situation is a little more familiar than I would like, but not because of you. In a perfect world, I wouldn't have to keep the man I'm falling for a secret, and I wouldn't be responsible for my uncle losing his best friend."

He nodded, his chest deflating with a long sigh.

"In a perfect world, you'd come back home with me. You'd tell Mike all the right things to make him feel better about school like only you know how to do, meet my nieces, who will fall in love with you on sight, and I'd sit close enough to you at your uncle's dinner table the next time we're there so that there is no question that we are together—and he'd be happy that we're happy." He kissed me, closemouthed and featherlight, but lingering long enough to make my pulse race. "I have faith all of that will happen, but I'll take any world I can get right now as long as I have you in it."

"You have me." I snuggled against his chest as he held me tighter.

A slow smile spread across his face when I lifted my head.

"Then everything else will fall into place. You'll see."

I knew he meant every word, but I wasn't as sure. But I'd take any world with him in it too, even if it crumbled around us.

TWENTY-FOUR
JAKE

"Text me when you're on your way home," I told Mike as he slipped on his jacket by the door.

"I'm only at Liam's house for the night. What's the big deal?"

"I know you're all just going to congregate and play video games like you do on the headset, but eleven is the latest I want you home, and I want to make sure I'm here when you are."

"Where are you going?" Mike turned to me with a furrowed brow.

"I'm seeing some friends too. Why? Only one of us can have a social life?"

Mike's lips twitched as he shrugged.

"No, you can."

"Well, thank you." I pressed a dramatic hand to my chest. "I appreciate it. But like I said, home by eleven and text me."

He nodded and made his way out the door.

How would Mike react to Peyton and me? I hated lying to him about it, but it didn't seem like the right time to tell him.

I'd have to make sure to do it soon, as the last thing I needed was for him to be blindsided at school.

I hopped into my truck, ignoring the inclination to floor the gas pedal on my way to Peyton. I jumped on any time I could get with her, not wanting to waste a second. I wished I could take her out instead of holing up in her apartment, but I wouldn't do that until we spoke to Keith first. I had mentioned stopping by a few times, but he'd been knocked out from extra shifts and asked if we could make it next week.

I was antsy to get it—get us—out in the open and didn't want Peyton to tell him alone. It was me he'd be furious at, even though we were both adults. I never felt an imbalance due to the age difference between us. In fact, Peyton was ahead of me in so many ways—but he wouldn't see it like that. Oldest friend or not, his first instinct, once he found out, would be to kick my ass for taking advantage of his niece.

"Hey." Peyton gave me a tired smile when she opened her door, pressing her lips to mine with a long, lingering kiss before moving aside to let me in. "I planned to cook for you, but the school day lasted longer than I would have liked."

"I don't need a fancy dinner. I just need you for a few hours."

I gathered her in my arms and kissed her. Another smile that didn't make it to her eyes played on her lips.

"Everything okay?"

She nodded. "Just a long day. A lot more students stopped by than usual during my office hours. They had to put chairs outside my office for a couple of them to wait."

"So I'm not the only one itching to see you every day?"

I drew her closer and coaxed a real smile out of her.

"Sometimes it's hard not to absorb all their problems. School days can be difficult to shake off."

I kissed the top of her head as she leaned her cheek against my chest.

"I'll make you forget the best that I can tonight."

"You *are* good at making me forget a lot of things." She lifted her head and dragged kisses along my jaw. "Pizza work for you?"

A moan escaped me as she ran her lips down my neck.

"Anything works as long as I can have more of those lips."

I cupped the nape of her neck and hauled her to me. When I grazed my tongue along the seam of her lips, they opened on a soft moan. The kiss caught fire, and before I could blink, her shirt was off and both of us were fumbling with my belt buckle.

"I missed you so much," I murmured against her lips and delved a hand into her hair. "You taste so damn good."

She backed us up against the sink and popped the button of my pants open.

"We always end up here," she said, her voice low and breathless.

"We do, although the bed has more room—shit, just like that."

My cock pulsed in her hand with every slow stroke.

"The sink is special for us." Her eyes stayed on mine, hazy and hooded, as she picked up the pace. "Sure, we could do this in a bed, but this seems a little more fun."

I gasped when she dropped to her knees and took me in her mouth. I slammed my hand against the counter as she swirled her tongue around the tip, dragging kisses up and down my length before she swallowed me whole.

"Fuck, sweetheart. That mouth is so good." I grabbed the back of her head as her nails dug into my ass. She whimpered around my cock when I wove my hand into her hair and pulled.

"Did I hurt you?" My hand stilled in her hair as I fought the urge to buck my hips against her face and fuck her beautiful mouth.

"No. More." She buried her face between my legs until I poked the back of her throat.

I tapped her shoulder and tried to lean back when I was past the point of no return, but she only sucked harder until I spilled down her throat.

"I was supposed to make you forget your day." I laughed, still chasing my breath. "Not have you obliterate my brain cells."

Her eyes danced as she stood and pressed her lips to mine.

"You did. I love that I can make you that crazy."

"You don't know the half of it, sweetheart." I cupped her cheek. "How about we have pizza and then stay in bed until my son texts me?"

"Perfect." She dropped her head to my shoulder and wrapped her arms around my waist.

Every second of my time with Peyton was perfect, except for how soon it always had to end.

"Where did you tell Mike you were going tonight?" Peyton asked later as she lounged on the bed, my shirt so big on her it draped over one shoulder.

"Just out. He was more shocked I had somewhere to be other than home, waiting for him. I can't blame him, since that's all I've done since he moved in with me."

"How do you think he'll react? We have a good rapport in school and he's sort of used to thinking of me as a family friend too, but I hope we don't put him in a weird position."

"I don't think we will. But I was thinking about maybe meeting you somewhere. Pretending like we just ran into each other and have you spend a few hours with us. Get him used to you being around all the time."

"Are you saying that I should get used to being around you all the time too?" She quirked a brow.

I rested my elbow on the bed and slid my other hand to the back of her neck.

"Definitely," I whispered, and kissed the corner of her mouth. "All the time." I grazed my lips against hers. "I'm excited for that, but I admit, I kind of like this."

"Being in a little bubble all by ourselves?"

I nodded, drawing her closer when she lay next to me. "I wish I could take you out, not care who notices how close we are, but that will come soon enough. Until then . . ." I threaded my fingers into her hair as she hooked her leg around my hip. "It's nice having you all to myself."

My gaze drifted over her shoulder. "What's in the box?" I motioned to the large box leaning against the window and taking up all the space next to her bed.

"Another bookcase. It's supposed to be easy to put together, but when I look at the instructions, I get aggravated and stuff them back in the box."

"You're in bed with a licensed and bonded contractor. I can put that together in less than an hour."

She rolled her eyes but fought a smile. "I admire your confidence, but I wanted to put it together myself. I'll figure it out soon."

"It's already got a layer of dust on it." I sat up and kissed her forehead. "I'll get my tools from the truck."

"No."

She pressed her hands to my chest and pushed me back on the bed.

"I only get a little time with you. We aren't going to waste it on a bookcase."

"Sweetheart, I'll be right there." I cradled her cheek and nodded behind her. "I'm not going anywhere yet."

She tilted her head, narrowing those deep brown eyes at me as she kept her hands on my chest.

"Okay," I relented, raising my hands in surrender. "If that's what you want, maybe you can stack books on top of the box until you let me put it together."

I snickered when she shoved my shoulder and settled next to me.

"How about," I said, smoothing her hair off her forehead, "you take that back, and I'll build you one instead."

She lifted her head, resting her chin on my chest.

"You don't have to do that. You've done enough around this place. I'd like to enjoy you as my guest, not my contractor."

"I could be both. And no, I don't have to, but I'd like to." I trailed my finger along her spine. "But if you want to keep me in bed to have your way with me, I guess I can comply."

"How long do we have?" She yawned into my neck.

I peeked at the alarm clock on her nightstand.

"A couple of hours."

"Dammit." She rubbed her eyes.

"Go to sleep." I kissed the top of her head and pulled the covers over us. "You had a long day. And I wore you out a little while ago."

A tired smile drifted across her mouth, probably enjoying the same dirty memories of tonight that would be on replay in my own head after I had to leave.

"I don't want to waste tonight." Her mouth dipped in a frown as she peered up at me.

"Tonight was far from a waste." I picked up her hand and laced our fingers together. "Sleep, sweetheart. Good practice for when we have a whole night instead of just a couple of hours. And stop acting like we're racing against the clock. We have all the time in the world."

"Easier said than done." She skimmed her hand up my

chest as her eyes fluttered shut. "I'd love a whole night with you." She burrowed into my neck, a soft sigh falling from her lips right before her breathing slowed. "Wake me in a few minutes."

I wanted more than just one night with Peyton. In fact, I never wanted to leave this bed, or her.

That realization should have been enough to shock me awake, but I let myself drift off. Maybe it was too soon to be this sure, but I stopped worrying about what was supposed to be wrong between us when it all felt too damn right.

TWENTY-FIVE

PEYTON

"On nights like tonight, I remember the days when I'd be out until dawn," Erin mused with a wistful sigh before she took a long sip of wine. "I actually was a little jealous of my seniors before I dismissed them today."

Deirdre and I shared a smile as Erin's words slurred out of her mouth. The housewarming party my school friends had thrown was winding down. The remnants of charcuterie boards and dip littered my kitchen. Cam had to head home to help his wife prep for Thanksgiving dinner tomorrow and left Erin and Deirdre to linger over the last bottles of red they'd brought me tonight.

My own head spun from too much wine and not enough food. I dove into the alcohol a little too hard before I'd created enough padding in my stomach. Uncle Keith was picking my mother up from the train station in the morning and dropping her off here before he came back with Aunt Maya and the boys. Just enough time to pick at all the ways I was preparing the side dishes wrong.

I wanted to host Thanksgiving here and give my dining

room table a purpose other than a makeshift office for when I came home from school. Plus, I wanted to thank my aunt and uncle for all those weeks of free room and board. Aunt Maya was bringing the turkey—thank God—so I only had to synchronize everything else.

School let out early today, and I'd managed to finish all the baking I needed to do, already anticipating being too tipsy to go near a stove after my friends left tonight.

"Thanksgiving may be my least favorite holiday, other than the food." Deirdre chuckled. "It takes a long time to deflect the why am I still single and didn't bring anyone questions."

"I hated that," Erin agreed. "Before I married Will, I dreaded Thanksgiving. I think it's because dinner is the whole focus of the day, and Christmas has more distractions."

"I may have a reprieve from that this year, seeing as how the focus will be on how I moved upstate at what my mother describes as a moment's notice."

"So hopefully you can dodge the 'Can I set you up?' questions I get from family every Thanksgiving because I'm not seeing anyone."

"I am seeing someone," I said, shocking myself at how it just slipped out.

They whipped their heads toward me, my news seeming to sober them a bit as well.

Jake and Mike were heading up to his mother's house until Saturday morning, and then he was scheduled for an all-weekend job. I wished the someone I was seeing would be sitting next to me tomorrow as my mother counted the lumps in my mashed potatoes, but there were a multitude of reasons why that wasn't happening this year.

"*You sneak.* You never said anything."

"It's new." I shrugged. "We're keeping it to ourselves for the moment."

"Ah, I see." Erin nodded, shooting me a grin. "That little smile playing on your lips must mean you're still at the good part."

"Good part?" Deirdre asked as she swirled the rest of the wine in her glass.

"You know, that passionate, I can't think of anything but you and the glorious sex we're having part."

I sputtered around the rim of my glass. After a few drinks, Erin lost any kind of filter, but she was pretty spot-on. Jake would come over when Mike went out with friends, and we'd have that glorious sex until he had to go home. Each time he'd go, goodbye became more excruciating.

It would have been nice to be out around my family tomorrow, but Jake kept insisting that we tell my uncle together because he didn't want me to bear the brunt of it. Aunt Maya knew something was brewing between us and probably had a feeling that we were somewhat together by now, but I knew she wouldn't bring it up unless I did.

Mike's fight seemed to blow over, the football team now keeping themselves in check for the time being, but I still kept an eye on all of them. When I'd see Mike in school, he didn't appear bothered or fearful, so I hoped he'd moved past it. Other than an amazing man in my life whom I couldn't tell anyone about, life had reverted to a normal routine.

"So, who is he?" Deirdre shot me a wry grin. "And Erin must be right, because you haven't stopped smiling since you brought it up."

"As I said, it's new. When I'm ready, you'll hear all about it."

When I was ready was something I was anxious to find out myself. I was curious about what had happened when parents dated faculty in the past, but I couldn't ask them now. First, because that would tip them off a little, and second, because I didn't totally trust them yet. They'd basically catered this party for me tonight, but after almost every friend I had in my old school scurried away when I'd hit my lowest point, for the moment, I kept it superficial with work friends.

"I can see why you'd want to keep things to yourself. In this town, if you have coffee with someone and appear too close to each other, everyone starts to speculate."

My mind went to that afternoon in Mary's coffee shop that seemed like years ago, when Mary hovered over us. Maybe people were already talking, and when it finally came out about Jake and me, it would be an anticlimactic moot point. But I'd bet the age difference and connection to my uncle would give it some legs for a while, even if he wasn't a parent of one of my students.

I had a constant headache as the carousel of possibilities went around in my head.

"Not to talk work at a party," Deirdre said, turning toward me. "But I'd like to plan a parent workshop for when we get back from break. We could do it on one night for both freshmen and sophomores or separately, but judging by the past turnout rates, I think a combo night is fine. If you're interested."

"Sure! You know I'm always in for that," I said, already thinking of how I'd act at school around Jake. My mind went to old faculty meetings when I'd make it a point not to look at Travis for too long, even when he was speaking.

This wasn't that—not by a long shot. But the feeling of being in trouble at my job for who I was dating while at work kept taking me back to it. I reached for the Malbec and drained what was left in my glass.

"Let's help Peyton clean up the kitchen so she can plop into bed when we leave." Erin pushed off the chair and waved a hand at Deirdre.

"You guys don't have to do that." I stood, shaking my head as I grabbed a couple of garbage bags.

"Think your garbageman will be able to tell you had a bunch of teachers over?" Deirdre snickered as she held up the recycling bag full of bottles.

"Maybe." I chuckled, stuffing all the half-eaten snacks into the garbage bag.

"So then, what's one more?" Erin grabbed another bottle from the basket they'd brought me and popped it open. "I'm a guest at someone else's house this year and have no turkey to wake up for."

"Aw, but you'll miss the parade on TV," I joked, agreeing with a reluctant nod for her to refill my glass. I had dinner to prepare for, but the anticipation of aggravation tomorrow would get me up more or less on time.

"It's not that cop who knew you, is it?" Erin grabbed my arm.

"No," I sighed as I stuffed the last half-eaten container of dip into the trash. Uncle Keith had sent Ron to school one afternoon to check on the extra security guards he'd *strongly suggested* to Arlene to have at school for a couple of weeks to ward off any more trouble. Ron spotted me and lingered until I'd told him I had to prep for a class.

"Not him."

The inner workings of a small town amazed me. We had to beg for more security for a school I'd worked at during my master's, but here, the chief just had to make a suggestion to the principal to get anything done.

It was more proof of how Kelly Lakes and Brooklyn were different planets, how respected Uncle Keith was, and how he went the extra mile for the people he cared about.

I came back to the table and took a long gulp from my glass, a futile effort to numb the familiar but sharp pang of guilt when I'd remember what a great man my uncle was and how much he'd always meant to me.

"Well, I think you're all set," Deirdre said as she stabbed at her phone screen. "We'll get a car home and be out of your hair."

"Stop. This was really great. Thank you for doing this."

It *was* great. The past couple of hours were so fun and easy, it was as if I'd always lived here and had known my friends forever. In fact, I was getting so used to it that it made me nervous.

One of the worst things about how I'd left my old job was that I couldn't enjoy anything—not fully. Happiness for me always seemed to come with a caveat now or an inner warning that it wouldn't last. Jake and everything surrounding us had a lot to do with that, but would I ever truly shake that off?

"Of course. We're happy to see you finally settled in," Erin said as she pulled on her jacket. "I'm jealous of your amazing new floors. Your contractor must be awesome."

"He sure is," I sighed and gave them each a hug before they rushed out the door.

"Go have some more cake! It's almost your birthday!" Deirdre called out before she slipped into the back seat, and they drove away.

Every few years, my birthday landed on Thanksgiving. My family always made a big deal out of it when it did, but I couldn't look forward to it like I usually would. Having them here, with me, in the first home I could call my own, would be great, but the one person I really wanted to spend my birthday with wouldn't be here.

I smiled, thinking of how Jake's face had fallen when I'd told him my birthday fell on Thanksgiving. He probably felt the same way I did—that it was one more reason that we should have been together tomorrow and made it even more awful that we couldn't be.

I eyed the open wine bottle and shrugged as I poured another glass. Jake and I had made some big strides in the past weeks, but truly being together out in the open was a hurdle we hadn't cleared yet.

I opened the fridge and pulled out the C-shaped remnants of the birthday cake my friends bought me. I poked my fork in the corner where all the chocolate icing had pooled and speared a large chunk before bringing it to my mouth. My gaze dragged to my sink, all the sweet and dirty memories of Jake and me since that night we'd finally lost control washing over me.

It was hard to claim something, or someone, when you couldn't tell anyone they were yours.

TWENTY-SIX
JAKE

"You can't stay up all night," Kristina told Mike and Chloe, my niece, as they ignored her, focusing on *Super Smash Bros.* on the TV screen. "One more game and then shut it down."

"Mom, we're not little kids." Chloe's mouth twisted as her fingers raced over the controllers. "We're not going anywhere tomorrow—ugh!"

"I win *again*," Mike said, turning to his cousin with an arrogant smirk.

"That's because Mom distracted me. Rematch." She nodded at the TV as she shot my son a scowl.

Chloe was a year younger than Mike and always fell into some kind of competition with him when they were together. I enjoyed watching them squabble since he didn't have any siblings of his own. This was the first time Mike had been with me for Thanksgiving since he was small. Eileen offered to fly him out to have dinner with her husband and his family, but he passed.

Of course, I was told via text that his refusal was my fault, but I was done paying her tantrums any mind. I didn't doubt she missed her son, and if Mike had said yes, I wouldn't have stopped him, but he'd had enough decisions forced upon him this year.

"I play too!" My four-year-old niece, Emma, peered up at me as she pulled on the drawstring of my sweatpants. "I stay up too!"

"I don't think so, pretty girl." I scooped her into my arms and kissed her cheek. "Chloe and Mike are bigger, and you need sleep."

She looped her little arm around my neck, her wide blue eyes pleading with me as she frowned.

"Please, Unca Jake. I got lotsa sleep last night." She cuddled into my chest. My sister and I shared a laugh when a yawn escaped her.

Emma was the product of the last reconciliation vacation Kristina had with her husband. She was a lovable little beauty who already knew how to play us all to get what she wanted. She was also the only one of all our kids still innocent and too young to remember her parents arguing or splitting up. We spoiled her more than we probably should have to keep her that way.

"I don't think so. You can see Uncle Jake and play tomorrow." Kristina tucked a lock of chestnut hair behind Emma's ear. "Say 'good night' so you can get up early to see Santa on the parade tomorrow. Plus, we promised Daddy we'd call him before we went to sleep."

My brother-in-law was on his yearly hunting trip. They weren't living together again yet and claimed to still be dating. It had gone on longer than we all thought, and I was worried about Kristina. She said they were committed to working toward a better life together for the girls' sake, but I hoped they weren't holding on to one that didn't make either of them happy.

"Okay," Emma relented with a dramatic sigh. "Good night, Unca Jake."

"Hey," I said when she went to squirm out of my arms. "I need a kiss." I pointed at my cheek.

She smiled and pressed her lips to my cheek, giggling when I tickled her side.

"You feel scruffy." She scrunched her nose at me when I set her down, rubbing her own cheek.

"Uncle Jake needs to shave," I told her, smoothing my hand over my jaw. "Sweet dreams, pretty girl."

She swiveled her head toward me as my sister led her down my mother's hallway.

"And guys, try not to stay up until dawn."

After two grunts in reply, I shut the door behind me and headed down to the basement.

My parents had moved a couple of towns over after my father retired, into an over-fifty community, not wanting to keep a big and mostly empty house. Their townhouse had a guest room and a small basement for all of us to stay. I'd asked my mother if she'd considered selling after my father passed away, and she said no because, "Where would everyone sleep?"

She was excited to have us all home this weekend, so I'd deal with an air mattress for a couple of days for her sake.

"Where are you off to?" Mom stopped me at the top of the staircase. "Escaping the kids?"

Mom's eyes were green like Kristina's, but our resemblance was stronger. Her hair was dark brown thanks to weekly trips to the salon, and she was still stunning in her late seventies.

"I have to make a phone call. I'll be right up."

She caught my arm and leaned in.

"Mikey is okay?"

I nodded, fighting a smile. She was the only one my son didn't correct when she said "Mikey."

"He's fine. Having fun sparring with Chloe over video games, so I would expect the both of them to sleep in tomorrow."

She waved a hand at me. "You're all here, you can all do whatever you want." She patted my cheek. "Come to the kitchen when you're done."

I smiled and headed downstairs, searching for Peyton's number on my phone.

She had her own plans with her family, but I'd wanted to ask her to come with me for the weekend and hated the idea of not being with her for her birthday. I hoped next year would be a different story. We'd be out in the open and could maybe split the holidays between our families, or whatever couples did.

I didn't question whether we'd be together next year because I couldn't bring myself to think of us ending.

"Hey, baby," Peyton slurred as her face filled my screen. "How's it going? Miss me?"

"Sweetheart, are you drunk? Where are you?"

"I'm home. Alone. Silly. My friends gave me a party for my house, remember?"

"I do." I stifled a smile as she lifted her phone high above her head.

Her tiny T-shirt rode up her stomach as her limbs sprawled across her mattress.

"Must have been some party."

"They brought me a lot of wine, and I had too much of that and too little food. I want to spend Thanksgiving and my birthday with you. And every time I thought about it or wanted to talk to my friends about you, I had more wine." The screen fumbled before she placed the phone on her nightstand. I had a full view of Peyton's side, her beautiful body on display as her shirt bunched up right above the sweet curve of her ass.

"I miss you too, sweetheart. So fucking much. I hate missing your birthday. Believe me, I wish I were sleeping right next to you tonight."

A sleepy smile stretched across her lips as she crawled toward the phone.

"You wouldn't be sleeping if you were here."

I laughed at the tipsy waggle of her eyebrows.

"No, I wouldn't be. It's hard to keep my hands and mouth away from you."

Her eyes shut for a moment before her lips twitched into a sly smile.

"I *love* when you eat my pussy. Remember when you did it against my sink that first time? I came so hard I almost fell," she said, giggling into her elbow. "Your mouth is my favorite thing in the whole fucking world."

Shit.

I shot up from the edge of the bed to make sure the door was locked.

I'd never heard Peyton say pussy before, and while I wished that it wasn't while I was in my mother's basement, she'd started something, and I couldn't go upstairs until we'd finished it together.

"Your pussy is *my* favorite thing in the whole fucking world. What I would do to you if I were there," I rasped as I lay back on the bed, smoothing a hand over where my cock tented my pants.

"Like what?" Her throaty chuckle reverberated through my body and landed right on my dick as it pulsed against my palm.

"Well, first, I'd get that shirt off you and run my mouth all over you—everywhere. I'd start at your neck, work my tongue all over those beautiful breasts, and bite a nipple on my way down. I love the sounds you make when I do that. Then I'd climb between your legs and fuck you with my tongue until your thighs shook against my face. After you came in my mouth, I'd slide inside you and ride my way to heaven."

Her eyes fluttered as she moaned, but I spied a little sadness mixed with the lust in her gaze.

"Jake, I want to touch you in front of people and not hide it. I want people to know you're mine. I hate telling people about you but not being able to tell them you're you. Makes me feel like a dirty secret. And not the good dirty. I like our good dirty."

"I like our good dirty too, baby. And you're *not* my dirty secret. If you only knew how much you mean to me."

"How much?" A smile tugged at the side of her mouth.

"Everything. Sweetheart, I have never felt like this about anyone before you or wanted anyone like this. Being apart from you kills me, not only tomorrow but all the times I can't be with you. Not being able to tell everyone you're mine drives me up the goddamn wall."

I was about to say *soon* again, but she'd argue the point even in her blitzed state. We needed to get over to Keith's right after the weekend and tell him. I hated missing her and really hated how she'd reached for a glass of wine every time she wanted to tell people about us, but couldn't. I needed her too much to be able to hide it, so why keep playing this exhausting game? I was done.

I'd spent what seemed like forever trying to drudge up some kind of love in my marriage, going through the motions just to feel something, until I walked away, unable to pretend anymore. I thought I was broken until I stumbled upon a beautiful woman who lit me up from the inside. I'd meant it when I told her she was made for me.

The best thing that ever happened to me aside from my son should never have been a secret. We were a truth, a bigger truth than I'd realized. If I couldn't touch her right now, I'd have to take the next best thing.

"Lie back and slip your hand inside your panties. But before you do, move the phone to the edge of the bed so I can see all of you."

The screen shook again as she adjusted the angle, and instead of ducking her hand inside, she dragged her panties down her legs and tossed them to the side of the bed.

"That's my girl," I growled. "Nice and bare for me."

"You too," she whispered. "Let me see it. Only fair."

I pulled my pants down until my cock sprang free. I was already hard as a rock, a drop pooling at the tip as my dick angled toward the screen. My pull to this woman was visceral and involuntary.

"Slide your fingers up and down, just like I would. You wet for me, sweetheart?"

She shut her eyes and nodded, bucking her hips off the bed as she rode her hand.

I glanced down, wishing I'd pulled on black sweatpants instead of gray to hide the evidence of the glorious mess we were about to make.

"God, I wish I could taste you. Slide a finger inside and inch it out just like I do."

I squeezed my cock at her drawn-out moan.

"You love that, I know. Now, faster. Swirl your thumb around your clit and go faster. Pretend you're fucking me when you come. That it's me moving inside you." I slid my hand up and down in long strokes as her legs spread wider on the screen. "That's right, sweetheart. I see you. Come all over me and make me yours."

She slid her hand up her shirt, pinching one nipple between her fingers before her head fell back with a silent scream. After she mewled my name a few times, I followed, my release coming in long spurts across my stomach and soaking my T-shirt.

I dropped my head back, sinking into the cheap mattress as I chased my breath. I couldn't even control myself on a video call with Peyton, much less in person.

"Does this mean you're mine?" she asked with a yawn. Her chest rose and fell as she sighed against the pillow.

"Yes, but I already was." I laughed as I tried to dab at the large spot on my pants with a paper towel. I'd need a change of clothes after we hung up. "I've been yours a lot longer than you know."

"Good. I love you, babe. Good night." She blew a kiss at the phone before she drifted off to sleep.

I sat up, watching her for a few long minutes before I ended the call.

Would she remember what she'd said? What was worse, if she did or didn't?

I peeled off my clothes and found another pair of sweats and a T-shirt, uneasy and jumpy but not freaked out.

At all.

Shouldn't I have been?

Keeping women at a distance was always easy—until her. With Peyton, I couldn't get close enough. I'd sworn never to cause another woman any more pain when I found out that my heart wasn't in it again.

But it was this time.

Because I loved her too.

But how?

It had only been a few weeks, after months of skating around the intense feelings we had for each other, but it was too soon for any declarations or feelings of love.

Yet, here I was. Here *we* were.

I trudged up the stairs, ignoring the walk of shame feeling on the way to my mother's kitchen.

Mom and Kristina were at the kitchen table, eyeing me with a suspicion I couldn't pinpoint.

"Who is she?" my mother asked as Kristina cringed.

"My sister hasn't spilled to you yet?" I fell into a seat at the table across from them.

"When Mom asked who you were calling, I told her I had a good idea, but didn't say who she was. *That* you can tell her."

"Not that you're forcing my hand or anything."

Kristina rolled her eyes. "Aren't you tired of keeping this in-plain-sight secret?"

"Could the two of you stop being so cryptic? I just wanted to know who my son is seeing. Why is who she is such a big deal?"

I rubbed my temples and groaned. After the post-phone-sex epiphany I'd had, I hated that I couldn't just tell my mother I'd fallen in love with someone. It had to start with who she was connected to, not how we felt about each other. I didn't blame Peyton for getting drunk tonight because this was ridiculous and taxing as fuck.

"Jake Thomas, I'll ask you again. Who is she?"

Kristina and I flinched at the same time.

"Her name is Peyton. She's a lot younger than me, but she's beautiful and amazing—and I think I'm in love with her."

Mom's gaze softened as a slow smile crept across her lips.

Kristina's brows shot up. "Wow, Jake. You think, or you know?"

"I know." I gave her a slow nod. Kristina's smile was

tempered with sympathy, reflecting my big realization on the way up the stairs.

This all was now even more complicated.

"Ever since the divorce, I've been so worried about you. I was afraid you'd never get close to anyone because you blamed yourself. This is wonderful." Mom clapped her hands together, beaming at me. "So, she's younger than you. What's the big deal?"

Mom caught Kristina cutting me a look.

"Okay, what else aren't you telling me?"

"She works at the high school as a guidance counselor."

"With Mikey?" she asked, her brow furrowed. "Okay, that's a little messy, but manageable, right? And Mikey likes her?"

"Yes, she's actually been great with him—"

"Okay, so fine. Not ideal, but not such a terrible thing, right?"

"Hit her with part three," Kristina whispered.

"What did you just whisper?" Mom asked, glaring at us with an impatient huff.

"She's . . . Keith's niece."

"Wait a minute," Mom said, her eyes losing their shine. "Your best friend Keith's niece? Donna's daughter? The last time I saw her, she was Emma's age. Keith's mother, rest her soul, would always tell me how Keith was more like a father than an uncle to her and Donna got jealous of how close they were. Has that changed?"

"No," I said, cringing when I met her widened eyes. "It hasn't."

She fell back in the chair, exhaling a long breath.

"Well, shit."

I couldn't help the laugh that slipped out of me.

"Pretty much, Mom."

"All right," Mom started, holding up her hands as she

stood and made her way to my end of the table. "I'm guessing because of who she is, you didn't come into this lightly, am I right?"

"No, I tried like hell to stay away from her, but I just . . ."

"Just couldn't." She laughed and took the seat next to me. "Sometimes that happens. If you're lucky. Love can be very inconvenient at times." She draped her hand over mine. "I'm happy for you, honey. I don't envy you, but I'm happy for you."

We laughed when I lifted my head.

"I'm assuming Keith doesn't know yet. I can . . . speculate on what his reaction will be, but don't make it worse by lying. That's a nice long friendship you kids have. Don't ruin it. If you love Peyton, go all in and be out with it."

She pushed off the table, groaning as she straightened.

"Bring her up here. I want to get to know her." She kissed the top of my head. "All I want is to see my children happy."

Kristina nodded with a sad smile.

"Working on it."

Mom tipped her chin at her before she shifted toward the hallway, shooting me a quick glance before she left.

"Can I give you a word of friendly advice?" my sister asked.

"Like what? Wear a bulletproof vest when we tell Keith?" I raised a brow.

"Well, *that*. I have spent years, what seems like forever, fighting to stay together because that's what we're supposed to do. But you've spent the past few months fighting to stay apart because you thought that was what *you* were supposed to do. We've been on opposite ends of miserable, but I'd much rather be where you are."

The big brother in me wanted to fix the sad gloss in her eyes, to fix it all for her just like when we were kids. If anyone deserved a distracting, undeniable love, it was my sister.

"I'm sorry, Kris."

She sighed, lifting her shoulder in a defeated shrug.

"I'll deal with it. But Mom is right. Love is very inconvenient, but if that's how you feel, be out in the open with it. Whoever has an issue with the two of you together—including Keith—isn't your concern."

"That simple, huh?" I scrubbed a hand down my face.

"Yeah," she said as she pushed off the chair and swatted my arm. "It kind of is."

TWENTY-SEVEN
PEYTON

"This is a nice condo," my mother said, falling into a chair at my dining room table as if she were admitting some kind of defeat.

"You sound surprised," I quipped as I set the table. "It has a lot more space than my apartment in Brooklyn, and I have access to the yard."

"I didn't know what to expect when you told me it was flooded. Why I never liked ground floor apartments." She shifted in her seat, finally having backed off from taking over and setting up everything herself.

I shut my eyes and took in a deep, slow breath. She meant well when she nitpicked and I tried to remember that, but sometimes she'd get under my skin.

Today, I wasn't bothered at all. I'd woken up a little lighter, on top of my covers after my housewarming party. It wasn't until I kicked the phone off my bed that I remembered my tipsy phone call with Jake before I drifted off. I vaguely recalled his gorgeous face on the screen and coming to the sound of his voice, but not much else. Whatever we'd said, it seemed to alleviate some of the tension that had been weighing on me for the past few days, and while I still wished Jake were here today, most of what I felt was genuine excitement.

"You have to be nice to me, it's my birthday."

"I know." The smile playing on her lips matched my own.

We didn't have the same features, but we had the same expressions. When I was a kid, I'd raid her jewelry box and make faces in the mirror, pretending I was on my way to work like her.

"The day you were born fell on Thanksgiving too. Your grandmother put everything in containers, and we had dinner the next day in my hospital room."

"I don't think I knew that." A pang squeezed my heart at the memory of my grandparents. They'd died within a year of each other, my grandfather clueless as to how to go on without his wife. It was devastating for all of us, but that was the epic kind of love I'd always wanted for myself.

"And now you're making dinner, finally paying us back." She stood, cradling my cheek for a moment. "At least you let me bring your birthday cake."

"I'm back," Uncle Keith sang from my doorway. "Donna, you didn't rearrange everything yet? Don't tell me age has slowed you down already."

"No, baby brother, I haven't." She huffed, scowling back at him. "I think everything is great where Peyton already has it."

He stilled before stepping into the kitchen. "You feeling okay, D?"

She smacked his hand away when he cupped her forehead. "Move and let me see my nephews."

"Hi, Donna." Aunt Maya came up to Mom and pulled her into a hug. "It's good to see you."

"You too," she said, shaking her head when she pulled away. "It's annoying how you never age. Especially considering you're married to him." She jerked her chin at Uncle Keith.

"He's not so bad." She craned her neck to her husband, standing behind her with an arm around her waist.

"I'm great. My sister could never appreciate it."

"Aunt Donna!" Aiden ran up to Mom with Brian behind him. "Can we take the train home with you?"

"My God, you both got so big!" I caught her steady herself when they almost knocked her over. Brian gave her a shy smile as she cupped his chin. "So handsome. And yes, you can come and stay with me whenever you want. I'm lonely back in Brooklyn."

I took another deep breath, cutting Aunt Maya a look. I missed my mother, but she didn't understand why I had to move—and I didn't have the heart or the guts to tell her. To her, even though I turned thirty-three today, I'd run away from home *and* her.

"Everything looks great, honey. And happy birthday!" Aunt Maya wrapped an arm around me and kissed my cheek.

"Happy birthday, Peyton!" Aiden yelled as I was attacked with my own clobbering hug from both boys.

My head shot up at a knock at the door.

"Surprise guest?" my uncle asked, eyeing my front window.

For a minute, I panicked. Was Jake coming here, after all? Was that what he'd said? Any conversation beyond him ordering me to finger myself wouldn't crystallize in my brain.

"Peyton Miller?" A man peeked at me over the top of the large box in his hands when I opened my door.

"Yes?"

"This is for you."

The box wasn't heavy but was difficult to grip. I thanked him and kicked the door shut behind me.

"What is that?" Aiden asked as I set the box on one of my dining room chairs.

"I'm not sure. I didn't order anything." I grabbed a pair of scissors and cut through the tape on the top, finding a layer of dry ice. "I think someone sent me food."

"That's a big box of food," Aunt Maya noted from behind me as she helped me dig through the box.

I felt around the sides and found a folded card and more ice. Once I peeled the last layer away, I found five pints of chocolate ice cream and a box of cones.

Jake wasn't at the door, but this was still all him.

"Wow, who sent all that ice cream?" Brian asked as he tried to push past his brother to see.

"I don't know," I lied as I eyed the card in my hand.

"Well, aren't you going to open that and see?" my mother asked, narrowing her eyes at me.

I glanced at Aunt Maya, a tiny but knowing smile twitching at her lips.

"It's probably Claudia. She ate all my ice cream when she came up here to help me move and told me she'd replace it."

Mom's eyes thinned to slits, my nervous laugh most likely not helping my case.

Her eyes burned into my back as I unpacked the box and headed over to my freezer, shoving the pints in one by one.

"There's a ton of snacks on the table. Let me go call her to thank her."

I shifted toward the hallway when Mom caught my arm.

"Don't forget this." Mom held the card out to me, her thumb in the middle of the now-open piece of paper. My hope that she hadn't peeked died when I spied her lifted eyebrow.

Great.

"Thanks," I managed to croak out on the way to my bedroom.

After I shut it behind me, I leaned against the door and opened the card.

Happy birthday, sweetheart.

I hate that I'm not with you today, but I thought this could make you feel like I was, and maybe you'd finally forgive me for cheating you out of chocolate ice cream that day. We'll put it to good use when I'm there.

Love, J

I laughed, despite the nerves churning in my stomach.

Did he purposely leave off his name or run out of letters on the card? Mom might not have equated Uncle Keith's Jake to my Jake if he'd written his whole name.

Only the people who were paying attention while they were in the same room with us would do that.

So much for a nice family dinner without a million questions. And now Uncle Keith was tipped off that I was seeing someone. When would I learn that lies never lasted and sneaking around never worked?

Apparently, when I turned thirty-three.

I grabbed my phone and dialed Jake. The anticipation of seeing his face once again trumped my dread over the repercussions that would meet me in my kitchen.

"Happy birthday!"

A wide grin split my mouth at Jake's crooked smile.

"I'm sorry I didn't call you earlier. Wrangling these kids all morning was a two-person job."

"No need for apologies. Thank you so much for my present, *J.* It just came a few minutes ago."

His smile faded as his eyes grew wide.

"That was supposed to come early this morning so no one would be around when you opened it."

"Oh, they were *all* around. My cousins and aunt helped me open it while my mother glared at me. She also saw the card, so I'm sure she's going to ask me who J is a few hundred times."

"Unca Jake, who are you talking to?"

Jake disappeared, a ceiling fan in his place as he whispered to someone off-screen.

"Sorry about that." He returned with a beautiful little girl on his lap. She stared back at me with the same blue eyes as Jake while twirling the ends of her long brown hair.

"Peyton, this is my youngest niece, Emma. Emma, this is Peyton."

"Hi, Peyton!" she yelled into the phone.

"Hi, Emma. Nice to meet you."

I'd watched Jake be a great father for months, and it was one of the things I loved the most about him. An unexpected but overpowering yearning washed over me at the sight of him holding a small child. I loved kids and always planned for them in the far-off future, but the picture on my phone was too wonderful not to want in the present.

But first, I had to come clean about being with Jake to family and friends before I dreamed of having his babies.

"Who is Peyton, Unca Jake?" She scrunched her nose as she craned her neck toward Jake.

"She's someone I like. A lot." He grinned, holding my eyes. "And I think she likes me too," he told her in a loud whisper.

"Can she come to play with me? She's pretty."

Jake laughed, his deep chuckle squeezing what was left of my heart.

"She is *very* pretty. I told Grandma all about her, and she wants to meet her too."

"You did?" I asked, gulping down the surge of emotion that had grown over the last twenty minutes.

"Well, she's met you. But you were only this size." Emma

giggled as Jake tickled under her arm. "She wants to get to know you, if that's okay."

"It's very okay." My voice cracked as my chest flooded with both love and frustration. I took a few long inhales through my nostrils as I finally arrived at my breaking point.

"Jake, enough. I'm getting this over with and telling my uncle now."

"No. Together, and I don't want you to ruin today with any fights when I'm not there. I want this out as much as you do. One more day won't make a difference."

One more day maybe wouldn't do any more harm, but when one more day became a week and then a month until it became a lie of omission too big to run from—then it made a big difference.

I jumped at a knock behind my head.

"Peyton." Aiden's voice drifted through the door. "Aunt Donna said we need to put all the food on the table, and you're taking too long."

I groaned, my head falling back against the door with a thud.

"I better go. Call me tonight."

"Of course. I forgot to ask how you're feeling today."

"Okay, better than I should. Sorry I was a sloppy drunk last night."

"You were an adorable drunk. Happy birthday, sweetheart."

He pressed two fingers to his mouth and blew me a kiss. My ovaries exploded when Emma did the same.

"Happy Thanksgiving, babe."

I ended the call and took one more glimpse at the note inside my present.

Love, J

Love . . . I'd told him I loved him last night. My blood iced over in my veins as my foggy brain finally cleared. Did he say it back? He seemed fine on the phone, unbothered and even mentioning how he wanted me to get to know his mother, but what had he said after I'd blurted out I love you? As if I didn't have anything else to worry about today.

I let my head drop between my knees, taking a few deep breaths before I had to pretend this was a normal Thanksgiving and birthday.

I did love Jake. Deeply and completely. Maybe that was why I woke up lighter and not as mopey as I'd been after everyone left last night. It was fast and would look odd to some, but it didn't have to make sense to anyone else but us. Telling Jake I loved him, even if it took me a bit to remember that I had, gave me amazing and innate relief.

Now, I just needed to tell everyone else.

TWENTY-EIGHT

PEYTON

"I guess we'll just come here for Thanksgiving from now on," Uncle Keith quipped after I'd set out all the desserts. I'd made an apple crumb pie and brownies, and Mom brought cookies along with my birthday cake from our favorite bakery back in Brooklyn.

"No, you can have it back next year," I said, laughing as I fell into a seat at my table. "This was mostly to thank you both for letting me stay with you, and I wanted to host a holiday since this is the first place I've actually owned and not rented, but I'm perfectly fine bringing a pie and being a guest."

"How many times do I have to tell you," Uncle Keith said, "we loved having you stay with us. There is no need to thank us at all."

"I remember when you used to beg to live with Uncle Keith when you were little," Mom said, her eyes narrowed but stifling a smile.

"Because I'm awesome. Peyton was just the first one of you to realize it."

Mom rolled her eyes at her brother.

"Once, you even packed a bag and told me to call Uncle

Keith to pick you up so you could live with him, remember? You put on a jacket and waited by the door until I got him on the phone."

"I remember that," Uncle Keith mused. "You were five, I think. I was still living in a dorm at Binghamton, and your mother"—he nodded to Mom next to me—"called me and said I had to be the one to tell you no since you wouldn't believe her."

"You told her you'd see her when you came home each month. And every weekend, all she would do was ask, 'Is it Uncle Keith's weekend yet?' and 'How about now?'"

She laughed, but I spied a little hurt in her eyes. What I did remember from when I was that age was trying to get my father's attention during the day while my mother was at work. He'd go through long periods between jobs and would be home with me most of the time, but he hardly interacted with me. Whenever I saw my uncle, he'd scoop me up and I'd be attached to his side. We'd laugh and talk for hours, playing games at the table until my grandmother would shoo us away so we could eat. He'd leave and I'd cry, already waiting for the next time I'd see him.

Even if I didn't remember trying to go live with him that day, I did recall it being exactly what I wanted.

"Can we have ice cream, Peyton?"

After the reminder of how much Uncle Keith always meant to me, Brian's innocent question triggered a new pang in my gut over what I was doing with my uncle's best friend behind his back.

"Yes. Why didn't you put that out? You have five containers," Mom said before pushing off the table and heading toward the freezer.

"Claudia ate that much ice cream when she was here?" Uncle Keith's rumble of laughter only made me feel worse.

I noted a "Hmm" from my mother as she ran a scoop over the top of one of the containers and packed the ice cream into a cone.

I shrugged at Uncle Keith, praying we'd all just eat and drop it.

"Unless Claudia changed her name to *J*, the box was from someone else. I guess there are things your favorite niece doesn't even share with you, Chief."

Mom gave Brian a cone and set the open container down on the table, her handful of spoons falling next to it with a clatter.

"I guess you read the note in the box that was supposed to be just for her. I can't imagine why she wanted to come live with me when she was a kid, can you?" He turned to Aunt Maya and arched a brow.

"It was open, and I happened to look. I figured she'd explain eventually."

"She shouldn't have to," Uncle Keith said, his gaze on me. "She'll tell who she wants when she's ready."

I sucked in a long breath through my nostrils, sneaking a glance at Aunt Maya before escaping to the kitchen to grab the coffee. I never participated in my mother and uncle's squabbles, especially when they squabbled about me.

I reached into my cabinet, stacking mugs into the crook of my arm, when I heard footsteps behind me.

"Need any help, kiddo?"

"No, Uncle Keith. I'm good, thank you."

His warm smile added to my growing remorse.

"You don't have to say anything to anyone until you want to, even me." He took the mugs from my hands. "But whoever he is, it looks like he's making you happy, and that's all I care about. And all your mother cares about, even if she keeps it hidden under all that ball-busting."

Here was my chance. Jake wanted to tell him together, but maybe it wouldn't be so bad if I just came clean now. After a lifetime of telling my uncle everything, why was I holding back something and someone this important to me? The words were lodged in my throat, fear holding them hostage.

After thirty-three years of having my uncle on my side no matter what, thinking of the alternative was too paralyzing to find it in me to do the right thing.

"He is" was all I was able to croak out.

"I'm glad, and I'm ready to meet him when you'll let me."

No, he wasn't.

When I finally did muster the courage to tell him the truth, it would change everything. And I would never be ready for that.

Mom and I didn't say much after everyone left. We cleaned up my kitchen in silence, not making eye contact until I spotted two cups of tea on my dining room table.

I didn't hear any apologies from my mother growing up, but when she was sorry, she showed it with a gesture instead of words. My favorite lip gloss that she happened to find in the drugstore on her way home or a cookie from the bakery was how she extended an olive branch after a disagreement.

"Is this my 'I'm sorry' tea?" I asked as I sat down and wrapped my hands around the mug.

A tiny smile pulled across her mouth as she picked up the other mug.

"I shouldn't have looked." She held up a hand. "But I guess that's what I get for being nosy. I hate not knowing anything about you anymore."

"And I could be a little more open about what's going on besides work."

"And why you're here in the first place." She leaned in,

arching a brow. "I know about the principal at your old school, Peyton."

My heart plummeted into my stomach. I studied her, searching for what I'd thought I'd see if she ever found out. I couldn't spot anger or disappointment, only the same hurt I'd noticed when she told the story of me wanting to move in with Uncle Keith.

"What . . . How . . ."

"Doesn't matter how I know. What matters is why you didn't tell me."

"How was I supposed to tell you? Hey Mom, I had an affair with my married boss and didn't lose my job but couldn't do it anymore because I'd lost everyone's respect."

"If it's the truth, yes. Instead, you ran up here to your uncle instead of coming to me. Just like you always did. Did you think I'd judge you or not stick by you?"

"No, but . . ." I pinched the end of my tea bag between my fingers. "It's less likely I'll disappoint Uncle Keith than you."

Until now. My present relationship would tilt those scales significantly when it finally came to light.

When she didn't reply, I took a deep breath before continuing.

"I believed a lie that deep down I knew wasn't true, and I paid for it. You raised me better than how I acted. Uncle Keith doesn't know either, and yes, I ended up here, but I was just looking for a place far enough away to feel like an escape. I never meant to hurt you. Then or now."

I turned to stand when she caught my arm.

"I'm hurt that you were hurt, although your uncle not knowing either does give me a little satisfaction."

She smirked, and I let out a long exhale as I draped my hand over hers.

"I'm sorry for underestimating you, Mom. I should have let

you come to school and attack like you used to when I had problems."

"I would have if I'd known." My nose burned when I met her watery gaze. "I was thinking about moving back up here. It's not like I'm working anymore, and all my family is in this sleepy little town now. I may as well." She shrugged, an audible sigh leaving her lips before she peered up at me. "But you're happy? Work? The ice cream man? You're sure?"

"I'm sure, and if you moved up here, I'd love it. Sleepy can be nice."

She trudged over to the kitchen and dumped the rest of her tea into the sink.

"This town isn't sleepy, just fools you into thinking it is. Remember that."

My mother's words rolled around in my head all night, making it hard to relax enough to sleep. I was able to start to let go of one secret but still had to hold on to the other. It was mentally exhausting enough to keep me awake.

I'd started to drift off, just as the black sky outside my window turned gray, when my phone buzzed on the nightstand. I read 6 a.m. across the top when I squinted at the screen.

Jake: *Sorry, it's early, but are you up?*

Me: *More up than I would like to be. Is everything okay?*

Jake: *It will be. Come to the door.*

Did he send something else? It was a relief that my mother knew I was seeing someone if I snuck off for a phone call while she was here, but more gifts were going to lead to more conversations, and yesterday's revelations and fresh guilt had tired me out.

I tiptoed through my living room, and my heart leaped at the sight of Jake's truck in my driveway. I clicked the locks slowly, trying to make as little noise as possible before I found Jake on the other side.

"What are you doing—"

He crashed his lips down on mine as he pushed me inside and closed the door behind himself. We kissed as if it had been years, not days, since we'd last seen each other, a mess of lips and tongues as we tried to get as close as possible, all while I kept one eye open and on the living room behind me.

"The job started early. I left Mike with my mother and sister to come down today," Jake said, his words stuttering through his short breaths. "But I had to see you." My eyes fluttered as he sifted his hands into my hair. "You're so beautiful."

"Hardly," I whispered, running my hands up and down the front of his jacket. "I just rolled out of bed."

"I dreamed of you looking just like this in the morning when I wake up next to you." His lips came back to mine, and he glided his hands down my back, cupping my ass. "I hate that I missed your birthday."

"You didn't. I have a freezer full of you for my birthday."

"I wish you were full of me right now." Heat ricocheted through me and pooled between my legs at the wicked gleam in his eyes. "I missed you so much."

I slumped against him at the next kiss, Jake licking into my mouth with long, slow strokes and soaking my panties under my nightshirt. My mind was on keeping the needy whimpers to myself and whether the route to my bedroom or my driveway was shorter.

At the flick of the kitchen light behind us, we froze mid-kiss.

"I guess this is the ice cream man. Hello, Jake."

"Hello, Donna." Jake nodded at my mother.

"Um, Jake came to check the floor by the hallway since it's new . . ." The dumb lie died on my lips the second it came out.

"Checking your floor? That's one I haven't heard yet. You kids with your expressions." She waved a hand. "Now that I know no one is breaking in, I'll pour us some coffee if your surprise guest has the time."

Jake's lips twitched as he nodded.

"Sure."

"Have a seat while Peyton gets a robe on."

Mom's lips pursed before she shifted back toward the kitchen.

"I guess I'll be right back." I stole a quick kiss before I jetted into my bedroom to grab my robe from the back of the door.

Mom's reaction was calm enough to be unnerving. She almost seemed to get a kick out of it, probably happy to know another secret about me that my uncle didn't, but I knew her well enough to know that she wouldn't be this okay about it.

"I set up the pot last night so I could have coffee early, which I'm happy I did so as not to waste time." Mom handed Jake a cup as I sat next to him. "I'm assuming no one else in the family knows about this."

Aunt Maya knew, but I'd let my mother have this small win if she stayed amicable.

She set down a quart of milk and the sugar bowl, eyeing Jake as she sat across from us.

"No, not yet. Jake and I want to tell Uncle Keith together."

Or I just wanted to tell Uncle Keith period, and Jake's way kept increasing the inevitability of being caught.

"I see," Mom said, still looking between us. "So what are you doing with my daughter? Trying to feel young with a woman a decade and a half younger than you? My brother has said more than once that you'd probably never commit to anyone else after such a terrible divorce, so I think you understand my concern."

So much for amicable.

"Mom, I get this is a little bit of a shock, but that's uncalled for."

"I'm just warming him up for when your uncle gets a hold of him. Keith is easygoing, but when you both decide to tell him, he's going to flip out. So, what is it?"

Jake turned toward me, his eyes boring into mine as a smile drifted across his mouth.

"I love your daughter, Donna. I tried to stay away for Keith's sake, but I couldn't. And yes, I had a rough divorce and didn't plan on falling in love with anyone, but she's the best thing that's happened to me since my son."

I tried to speak over the lump growing in the back of my throat, but when I opened my mouth, no words came out. I grabbed the back of his head, pulling him to me with a shaking hand.

"I love you too."

When a wide grin broke out on his face, anything else in this room and in this world that wasn't Jake faded away.

"Not that I didn't believe you the first time," he said, cradling my cheek. "But it's nice to hear it without you slurring the words."

I laughed, leaning in to kiss him until my mother cleared her throat.

Her expression softened, the small smile curving her lips surprising me.

"I've never known you to be a bad guy, but if you hurt Peyton, my brother will be the least of your problems."

"Noted," he said with a slow nod. "But I would never and could never hurt her."

"So why the secret, J?" Her easy gaze narrowed to a glare.

"I want to tell him together. It's me he'll be furious with, and I'm ready to deal with it, but I don't want Peyton going through it alone."

"Well, the longer you wait, the worse it will be. If you're really in love, don't cheapen it by sneaking around behind Keith's back." She drained her mug and rose from the table. "Whether you believe me or not, I am happy for you, even if I wouldn't want to be either of you right now."

"I've heard that before," Jake said with a sad laugh.

"I'll let you . . . get back to it." Mom raised a brow before heading back to my spare bedroom.

"I better get going. I didn't even know I was stopping here until my car turned onto your exit almost on its own." He framed my face. "I guess I missed you that much."

"So, you love me?" I gave him a watery smile, tears still scratching at my throat.

"I do. So fucking much. I told you, sweetheart. As soon as this is out, it's all going to be fine." He inched toward me, grazing his bottom lip over mine as he closed the distance between us. "Nothing else matters but this."

My mouth melded to his as I took in the sweet lie.

TWENTY-NINE

JAKE

"Why did we have to come here? We could've just ordered takeout like we always do."

I smothered a laugh at my son's audible exhale.

"Because neither of us had plans for the night, and I felt like getting out of the house, maybe even attempting a conversation with you without your headset. I'll keep the torture brief, I promise."

I shoved his shoulder, spying the twitch of a smile at the corner of his mouth.

We followed the hostess to a table when she called us over. We ordered burgers from Salma's at least once every weekend, but I thought it was a good place for what I had in mind for tonight. A slight step up from the diner, but not too formal. The research and preparation for attempting casual exhausted me more than they should have.

"It's not torture. I guess it's okay to get out."

"I'm glad to hear it," I said honestly. That was the closest I'd gotten to a compliment from my son in a while, so I'd gladly take it—especially tonight.

"Can I ask you a question?" Mike asked with a deep furrow on his brow.

"You can ask me anything. You know that."

"Where do you go on the weekends? Do you hang out with Keith?"

"Sometimes," I lied, as I hadn't been at Keith's house in a long time. I wanted nothing more than to come clean to him about Peyton and me, but each time I'd try, the universe didn't want to cooperate. Whenever I'd suggested dropping by, either Keith had a late shift thanks to the new surge in carjacking up and down the thruway, or someone in the house was sick and Keith couldn't leave or have visitors. The frustration was wearing on both Peyton and me, and these covert meetings and missions were ridiculous but, unfortunately, necessary at the moment.

"Sometimes I meet up with a couple of friends of mine for a drink, nothing too exciting. Why?"

"No reason. You just always seem to be in a rush to get to wherever you're going." His eyes stayed on mine as he sipped his water.

Fuck. I didn't want to lie to my son, and now that he was picking up on something, I couldn't keep doing it for much longer.

"Hey, I guess you guys wanted a burger too."

Peyton grinned as she approached our table, sliding her gaze to me for a moment before facing Mike. Her dark hair was down, falling in chestnut waves over her shoulders, and she wore a snug hoodie over leggings. I had to fight to keep my eyes on hers and not sweep up and down the mouthwatering curves I'd memorized with my hands and mouth.

"Oh hey, Ms. Miller." Mike shifted in his seat.

"I was shopping in town and felt like getting a burger to go. I haven't been to Salma's yet but hear they're the best."

"They are. I always get the one with fried mushrooms," Mike told her without any prompting. "We usually order take-out, but Dad wanted to eat here instead."

"More of my bad parenting. I tried to have a meal and conversation with my kid." I tapped his foot with mine under the table.

Peyton's smile widened, and I hated not being able to pull her in for a hello kiss. Tonight was about baby steps, not rushing in.

"You could join us if you want," I said, attempting to sound casual while studying my son.

"I wouldn't want to intrude or anything. Is that okay with you, Mike?"

"No, it's fine," he said, scooting his chair over so Peyton could take the seat next to him. "I need to use the bathroom. Can you order for me if the waitress gets here?"

"No problem," I said as he pushed off the chair.

Peyton shook her head as she picked up a menu.

"What?"

She peered at me over the top of the menu.

"I'm thrilled to have dinner with you and Mike tonight, but as my freshman students say, this is a little cringey. And forced. Granted, this town doesn't have many amenities, but how many times can I bump into both of you accidentally on purpose?"

"This is the last time I'll try to make it look unintentional, I promise. Mike is already suspicious, so I don't think we can hide out in plain sight when it comes to him for much longer anyway."

"Did he say something?" Peyton whispered, darting her eyes back and forth from Mike's path to the bathroom to me.

"He asked me where I go on weekends and why I always seem to be in such a rush to get there. I hate lying to my son, but with all the change he's had this year, I wanted to ease him in, even if he's probably about to figure it all out anyway."

"You guys ready?" The waitress approached our table just as Peyton's brow furrowed. I knew most of the staff since I'd done some work here a few months ago, but this waitress was young and new enough not to try to poke for any details about the woman sitting across from me.

"We are," I said. "Two deluxe burgers with fried mushrooms, medium."

"Make that three, please." Peyton smiled as she handed back the menu.

"Where does he think you're going?" Peyton asked when the waitress was out of earshot.

"I said out with friends or Keith. He didn't press, but I get the feeling he may put the pieces together tonight. Mike is quiet, but he takes in a lot."

"You mean I wasn't convincing?" Peyton pressed her hand to her chest with an exaggerated gasp. "Do you know how long it took to pick an outfit that looks like I intended to go home but was presentable enough to stay out? I'm sorry I let you down, Mr. Russo."

I laughed and reached under the table to squeeze her legging-covered knee.

"You're beautiful, as usual. Although I prefer you in one of my shirts. Nothing underneath, all that easy access." My brows jumped when she met my gaze.

"Don't do that." She glared at me, a blush filling her cheeks and spreading down her neck as she reached under the table to push my hand off her leg. "I'm trying to stay in character. Stop distracting me."

"Did you order yet?"

We both jerked back at my son's voice. He sat down next to

Peyton and reached for his water glass, not seeming as if he'd caught us getting closer than he would have expected.

"Yes. I got your fried mushrooms, no worries."

"Good. I'm starving."

Peyton and I snuck a glance at each other as he drained the rest of his water.

"Me too. I've spent my afternoon working on the holiday festival, and I could use a burger and a mountain of fries myself."

"Holiday festival?" I asked, cutting a look at my son.

"It used to be a dance, but the school thinks calling it a festival will get more students to go," Peyton answered instead. "The gym will be all decked out like a winter wonderland, and there'll be music and games. It sounds fun, I've just been in the weeds of the food budget all day."

"Mrs. Lopez wants us to build something for it. Like a holiday train or something."

"Does she? That would be so cool. I know other clubs are donating stuff. So, this means you'll go, right?" She nudged his side. "All my research on finger foods won't go to waste if students come to eat it."

A shy smile pulled at his mouth. "My friends and I were thinking about it. It sounds a little cringey."

Peyton bit back a smile.

"It may be a little, but you could still have fun if you keep an open mind. It's on the last day before the break if you're staying in town for the holidays."

"I am. My mom wants me to visit her, and I said no."

"You can if you want," I said when I spied Mike's vacant stare. "It's been a while since you've seen her."

He shrugged. "It's not that I don't want to see her. I don't belong with her and my stepdad. I'm in the way. And all she does is complain about you, even though she dumped me here. I just don't feel like dealing with it."

"I absolutely can understand that. Have you tried telling her how you feel?" Peyton asked, her brows knit in concern as she turned toward Mike.

He nodded. "She always says that it's not true, that her husband is just set in his ways because he never had kids around, then says Dad puts things in my head. She keeps texting me to think about it. If I don't go, she'll be mad. I guess I have no choice . . ."

He fell back in the seat after he trailed off.

"You do," Peyton said, inching her chair closer. "Your dad isn't going anywhere, and yes, she's your mother, but you have every right to keep yourself out of a situation that makes you uncomfortable. It's hard, but you should never feel bad about that."

"I know you have to say things like that because you're a guidance counselor." Mike sighed and pulled apart the napkin in his hand, his frustration evident in each tiny piece.

"No, I don't." She tilted her head and leaned in. "I'm saying this as a friend who believes that you shouldn't ruin your holiday because you think you have no choice. You're old enough to know and do what you think is right, and for the adults in your life to respect that a no is a no and doesn't need further explanation."

"It's just . . . I don't want to hurt her."

My guilt over leaving Eileen prevented me from firing back at her like I should have so many times. I couldn't go back in time, but I could sure as hell protect my son now.

"I'll deal with your mother. You don't have to worry about hurting her or being caught in the middle anymore."

"I just want to stay with you. I've always wanted to stay

with you. I never said anything because I knew it would upset Mom."

I'd forgotten our dinner experiment as my eyes clouded. I rubbed at the emotion flooding my chest.

"So then, you'll stay with me, and you won't worry about anything else." I reached across the table and squeezed his shoulder. "Okay?"

Silence fell over the table as the waitress placed the plates in front of us and left.

"I guess I could go to the festival if I'm here. It's not a dance, right? It's this winter carnival thing instead?"

A slow smile stretched across Peyton's mouth.

"We may pipe in holiday music, but it will *not* be a dance." She held up her hand. "I swear."

"Aaron said he saw a student volunteer flyer somewhere," Mike said around a mouthful of fries. I took it as a good sign that his usual bottomless appetite was back.

"Yep. We have only a handful so far, but enough to help with setup."

"If I wanted to volunteer, do I need to sign up?"

Peyton's eyes lit up, flicking her gaze to mine for a second before she set her burger back on the plate.

"Nope. All you'd have to do is tell me."

"Okay. Let me know what I need to do."

She leaned back, squinting at him.

"What size do you think you'd be in a Santa suit?"

When he whipped his head toward hers, his eyes wide, both of us burst out laughing.

"Relax. All we need is some decorating and setup, nothing more." She squeezed his arm and popped a fry into her mouth.

I didn't come out and tell my son that Peyton and I were a couple, but we felt like a team—more than I'd ever felt sitting across the table from his mother. My sister had said when I found the one, she'd be good for both of us.

I was never so happy to tell Kristina that she was absolutely right.

"You get those burgers every week?" Peyton mused as she rubbed her stomach. "I think they're a once-a-month burger for me."

"My son has tried to order a second one a few times." I chuckled as we headed into the parking lot. "Where are you parked?"

"Way in the back. I didn't anticipate the lot being so full."

"Let me walk you to your car. Mike, you can sit in the truck."

"Okay. Good night, Ms. Miller." He stuffed his hands into his pockets. "Thanks, I guess. Again."

Her full lips curved up. "Thanks aren't needed among friends. Thank *you* for letting me eat with you."

He shrugged and slipped into the passenger seat.

I opened Peyton's car door when she clicked the key fob and pulled her into a quick kiss.

"Thank you," I whispered. "For running into us." I kissed the corner of her mouth when she smirked. "And being what he needed tonight. You have that way with both of us."

"*You're* what he needed, Jake." She skimmed her hand down my cheek. "I had a great time tonight. I look forward to our next accidental dinner." She pecked my lips and climbed inside, rolling down the window after she started the engine.

"Have I told you that I love you lately?" I asked as I leaned in the open window.

"Yes, but repeating it is fine." She grabbed the back of my head and pressed her lips to mine. "I love you too."

"Text me when you get home."

I shoved my hands into my pockets and watched as she

drove off. When I shifted back toward my truck, Mike was facing forward, but that didn't mean he hadn't turned his head and seen me kissing his guidance counselor. But I felt no panic or dread if he did. I loved Peyton enough to tell him the truth about anything he may have noticed or seen tonight.

"You can always talk to me about your mom or anything else. Don't take that burden on when you don't have to."

He nodded, focusing on the whiz of cars outside his window.

"I know. And listen, it's okay that Ms. Miller is your girl-friend. I like her. I think she makes you happy. It's really not a big deal."

It was time for me to whip my head around and my mouth to gape in shock.

"You figured that out tonight?"

He rolled his eyes in my periphery. "No, but I heard you the other night speaking to someone named Peyton and saying I love you. Plus, you guys always look like you're afraid to look at each other for some reason. I thought that was weird until I heard you on the phone." He shrugged when we pulled into the driveway. "I just hope she was kidding about that Santa suit."

My eyes followed Mike into the house as I gaped at him, in awe of my son and the wisdom beyond his fourteen years.

I pulled out my phone when he ran upstairs.

Me: *Mike told me it's fine that you're my girlfriend. Turns out he heard me say I love you to a Peyton over the phone and connected the dots.*

Peyton: *I rehearsed running into you all afternoon for nothing? What a waste.*

Peyton: *He's okay with it?*

Me: *He is. He said he's happy I'm happy.*

Peyton: *I'm happy you're happy too.*

Me: *You have no idea how happy I am right now, sweetheart.*

Me: *Next time, you have dinner here. Maybe even stay for the night.*

Peyton: *That's a big leap. Are you sure?*

Me: *More like it's about time.*

It had taken too long for me to find the guts to be happy. I wasn't wasting a second.

THIRTY
PEYTON

"Hey, beautiful," Jake murmured against my lips. His mouth had been on mine the second he'd stepped through my door.

"Hey yourself," I chuckled against his mouth. "Did you miss me that much?"

"Always." He framed my face, his blue eyes twinkling. "But I have a surprise for you."

"It's not Christmas for another couple of weeks, but okay," I said, trying to hold on to my wide smile.

The thought of spending the entire Christmas holiday keeping the man I loved a secret made me want to scream and cry at the same time. Neither of us had been able to get a hold of my uncle for weeks, and when I did see him for a few minutes, Jake wasn't able to be there. I was so close to breaking the promise I'd made to Jake and just telling Uncle Keith the truth. I'd gladly bear the brunt of his anger if we could finally be out in the open.

"How would you like to spend the entire weekend with me?"

"I'd love it, but where?"

He cocked his head from side to side.

"How about my house? Mike is going away with Aaron's family until Sunday, so for the first time in months, I have the entire place to myself." His hands coasted down my back and cupped my ass. "We could have tonight, all day tomorrow, and half of Sunday. Every room, every surface."

I laughed, catching some of his excitement despite my trepidation.

"What time is Mike coming back on Sunday?"

He shrugged. "Afternoon, I think, but it doesn't matter. He knows and he's good with it, so you don't have to run out so he doesn't catch you. It's a small step, but an important one." He pressed his lips to my forehead. "I can *finally* wake up next to you."

"That sounds like heaven," I said, drifting my hands down the front of his jacket. It really did sound like the best kind of dream, so why wasn't I running toward the door? I didn't know Jake's neighbors or how well they knew my family, although all of Kelly Lakes knew *of* my family. Two days where I didn't have to walk Jake to my door and wonder which night the following weekend I'd get to spend with him sounded amazing, but too brazen for my comfort.

"What's wrong?" Jake asked, his smile fading. "I thought you'd be happy to spend the weekend with me."

"I am, believe me. It's just . . . I hate that it feels like you're sneaking me into your house."

"Well, I'm not." He squared his shoulders. "My son will know you're there. You're walking in the front door, no one is going to recognize you as Keith's niece, and if they do . . ." He lifted a shoulder. "It's not their business. We're almost there. We just need to get Keith alone and get it over with. In all the years I've known him, it's never been this difficult to see him, but we'll tell him the first chance we get." His mouth curved in a crooked smile as he dragged his calloused thumb over my bottom lip. "So, please, come home with me."

"Okay," I whispered, and kissed his jaw. "Let me pack a bag, and we'll go."

"It shouldn't take that long. You don't need any clothes. You can have your pick of any shirt of mine that you want."

"I may steal some." I crinkled my nose and buried my head into his chest.

"All I have is yours, baby." He swatted my ass and nodded toward the hallway. "Let's go."

I knew where Jake lived, but this was the first time I'd ever been to his house. Taking what we had out in the open, or at least outside my condo, seemed like a significant step. I wanted to believe Jake that we were close to the end, but the more time we weren't honest with everyone—everyone being my uncle—the more we risked being caught.

"I didn't know your house was this big." I took in the simple gray house with the wide bay windows as Jake pulled into the driveway. "You never wanted to get something smaller?"

"We bought this house when Mike was born," Jake told me as he unlocked the front door. "When I divorced his mother, I considered getting a smaller place, but I like where I live and wanted Mike to keep his room. I tried to keep the constants in his life where I could."

"You've done more than try. I think you're the biggest constant in his life, period."

A blush ran up his cheeks as a shy smile stretched his mouth. "I tried. It's nice to have a little confirmation lately that I did my job, even if I couldn't fix everything for him."

"I'm surprised you didn't make it a full man cave like my uncle," I said, scanning the living room.

"I have my share of sports stuff." He pointed to the framed

hockey jersey on the wall. The gray leather couches and simple black furniture seemed lived-in and cozy, not what I'd expected from a man who'd lived mostly alone until a few months ago.

"I always hoped he'd come to live with me full time some-day, and even though it didn't happen until he was older, I kept the home he was used to."

Whenever he talked about Mike, I fell in love with Jake all over again. He never saw anything he did as a big deal, but he'd revolved his entire life around his son, even when he had limited custody. Jake had a huge heart full of love, and as much as he tried to fix everything for everyone, no one took care of him.

I wanted nothing more than to spend the next lifetime changing that.

"Mike left right after school. He came home to get his bag and texted me when they were on the road." His lips quirked into a smile. "I love having you here," he rasped, grabbing my hand and pulling me flush to his body.

I chewed on my bottom lip when I met his gaze.

"So, you're saying we're alone," I whispered, hooking my thumb into the belt loop of his jeans. "For two whole days." I drifted my fingers back and forth along the inside of his waist-band until I unbuckled his pants.

"We are." He groaned when I wrapped my hand around his cock, already hard and straining against my palm.

"I can do anything I want to you?"

"Fuck, yes. Please."

I sank to my knees, pulling down his jeans and boxers until his cock bounced against his stomach.

I kept my eyes locked with his as I took him in my mouth, loving how his eyes fluttered as I inched away and then brought him to the back of my throat. He was smooth and hard, velvet steel against my lips as he grew harder in my mouth.

"No, not yet. Get up here," he husked out, a growl rising from his throat as he grabbed a fistful of my hair and pulled me back before lifting me by my underarms up to stand.

"I thought you said I could do whatever I wanted," I said, jutting out my bottom lip in a pout.

"Oh, you can, sweetheart. We have all weekend. But first, I want you to ride my face before I fuck you on my couch."

I gasped into his mouth when he kissed me, hard and deep enough for my hands to quiver against his chest in anticipation. He unbuckled my jeans and dragged them down my legs, tapping my knee for me to step out when they pooled at my feet.

"Say goodbye to those until Sunday," he rasped, his mouth twisting into a smirk as he threw my jeans behind him.

"You're an animal, Mr. Russo." I yelped when he lifted me by the waist and carried me to the couch.

"Off," he said, his voice dipping low and husky when he sat on the edge of the couch and pushed my panties down my legs, dropping kisses along my thighs and down to my ankles until he peeled them off. His blue eyes bored into mine as he lay back on the couch and crooked a finger at me.

"Climb on, sweetheart."

I pulled my shirt over my head and let it fall to the carpet before I climbed onto the couch and straddled his chest. Before I could settle myself, Jake grabbed my hips and dragged me toward his face.

"So goddamn perfect," he hissed, his breath hot against my core as he positioned me over him. "Fuck my mouth, baby."

Jake lifted his head and dragged his tongue up and down my wet skin before taking my clit between his teeth and sucking hard enough for stars to burst behind my eyelids. I grabbed the arm of the couch for purchase, rocking back and forth as his lips and tongue worked me over. I folded when he snaked his tongue inside, darting in and out as his thumb stayed on my clit, tracing circles around and over it as his mouth destroyed me.

I blinked away a drop of sweat as I bucked my hips against him. Jake moaned as I moved, the vibration ricocheting down my legs and rolling through my entire body. My arms shook as I held on, the lower half of my body on fire as I chased the friction and the high I could only get from the man underneath me.

"Jake, I can't, it's too—" I screeched his name as I went over the edge, more sounds of sweet torture dropping from my lips as my head fell against the back of the couch.

I was a limp noodle as Jake set me back on the other side of the couch, his eyes hazy as he swiped his tongue along his bottom lip, still glistening from me.

"So good, baby. You have no idea how good you are."

He hooked my leg over his hip and entered me with one thrust. I sucked in a gasp, still sensitive from the waist down as he picked up the pace.

"I'll make love to you later," he grunted out. "But I can't be gentle now." He slid an arm under me and brought me closer. "I need you so much. Inside you is the only fucking place I ever want to be."

I grabbed the back of his shirt as he went deeper, pressure swelling between my legs and up my spine. We'd stopped using condoms when my birth control pills kicked in, and nothing was better than Jake bare inside me.

"This pussy was made for me. So. Fucking. Perfect."

His words were stunted as I clenched around him, Jake filling me with a growl right after, plowing me into his couch cushions until we both collapsed, his mouth finding mine in a sloppy and slow kiss, calming and soothing each other as we both came back to earth.

"Wow." I wiped the sweat off my forehead with the back of my hand. "That was some welcome."

Jake chuckled, pushing his hands into the couch on either side of me.

"Sorry if I was rough, but something about you in my house . . ." He traced the curve of my jaw. "We've waited for the simple stuff longer than we should have."

My heart fluttered when his smile faded.

"You were amazing." I ran my fingers through his damp hair. "Maybe the waiting makes it better." I roped my arms around his neck. "I love you."

"I love you too." His lips came back to mine with soft kisses, both of us still catching our breath.

"You're really keeping my jeans until Sunday?"

He nodded as he climbed off the couch.

"You can keep these." He plucked my panties off the floor, dangling the black lace from his finger. "Sometimes."

I laughed, stretching my arms over my head.

I already didn't want to leave on Sunday. It would be wonderful to have this all the time—granted, sex in the living room with our clothes littered all over the floor would be a novelty with a teenager living in his house.

He said we were close and I agreed, but to what outcome? I couldn't relax and enjoy what we had because I was too busy preparing myself for whatever "after" we'd get.

THIRTY-ONE
PEYTON

I couldn't remember the last time I'd slept with someone else. I'd had sex, sure, but actually sleeping next to someone and staying the night? It was so long ago that I couldn't even remember when or who it was.

Travis's promises of lavish weekends away were the same bullshit as all the other lies he'd told me. I was into him enough at the time to hold on to the hypothetical strings he'd dangled in front of me. When we were together—if you could even call it that—I'd wake up very much alone with only my broken spirit to keep me company under my sheets.

Sharing someone's bed and waking up in their arms was intimate in a way sex wasn't. I'd woken up feeling relaxed and safe, my soul as satisfied as my body. Yes, we had to keep the secret going until we were able to tell my uncle about us, but Jake never made me feel like he put me in a box or was ashamed of what we had. He was just as stuck as I was.

I propped my elbow on the pillow and rested my chin on my hand, oddly entertained and soothed by watching Jake sleep. An extra layer of stubble dusted his cheeks, the dotting of gray now more noticeable with the longer bristles. He stirred for a moment, tucking his hands under the pillow as his long lashes fluttered. My gaze drifted to the muscular cut of his arms and down to where the V of his hips disappeared under the sheets.

He was so damn beautiful, it hurt to look at him. Unable to help myself, I feathered the back of my hand down his cheek and over his scruffy jaw. I skidded my fingertips down his neck and over his chest.

His head jerked up as he caught my wrist before I could go lower.

"Taking advantage of me in my sleep? That's a little unfair. At least wake me so I can enjoy it."

He pulled my arm until I was splayed on top of him.

"I was ogling you in your sleep. Can you blame me?" I tilted my head, straddling his hips and grinding against him.

"Do what you want with me, sweetheart. I'm all yours." He drifted his hand up and down my naked back.

"Yeah?" I whispered, hovering over him as he peered up at me with hooded eyes.

"Yeah," he said, lifting his hips and grazing his hard length against my already needy core. "Did I mention that I'm glad you're here?" I moaned as he grabbed my ass and brought me closer, doubling the glorious friction between us.

"You did," I whispered, rocking back and forth. "On the couch, against the kitchen counter, the bed."

"We're a couple of animals, aren't we?"

His low chuckle settled deep in my chest. This was so much better than the random nights and afternoons we'd had at my condo for the past couple of months. What would it be like to have this all the time? Wake up in his bed and be with him officially all the time, not only in stolen moments.

The thought was as wonderful as it was distant. I wanted to ride on euphoria before I dwelled on the struggle. He grabbed my backside and yanked me closer, sliding into me with one slick thrust. I rolled my hips as I pressed my hands into his chest, fixated on the heat in Jake's eyes as they bored into mine.

"I will never get enough of you," Jake groaned, his fingers digging into my thighs as he sat up, cupping my neck to bring me in for a kiss. This wasn't the marathon we'd had last night. It was slow and sensual as we drifted together like two puzzle pieces. It was supposed to feel wrong between us, but it never had. Maybe this was why.

He bucked his hips off the bed, hitting a new angle as his thumb danced across my clit. My legs went rigid, my body already pulsing around him as I came. Jake sifted his fingers into my hair, taking a fistful as he plunged faster and deeper, groaning into my neck as he rode out his release. I looped my arms around his neck, holding on tight so I wouldn't fall. I'd never be able to let this man go, no matter what happened after people found out about us.

He was too perfect to give up—for anyone.

"You are better than coffee," he said, smoothing the damp hair off my forehead. "The best way to wake up." His smile faded for a second when he brought his lips back to mine.

"I love waking up with you too."

A grin split his mouth. "Good." He lifted me off him and slid out of bed, treating me to a glimpse of his backside.

"I'm guessing we're staying inside since I can't put pants on until tomorrow," I said, feeling around for the T-shirt Jake had ripped off me before we climbed into bed.

He shrugged. "I have nowhere to go. We have a kitchen full of groceries, and it's supposed to snow today. In fact, I may not let you leave tomorrow. Keep you in my basement for my own wicked intentions."

I laughed at his wry grin.

"I wouldn't fight you." I stood and wrapped my arms around his waist.

He cupped my cheek, shaking his head.

"You should have been here sooner."

We'd only been together a couple of months, despite the instant attraction from that first day. But it seemed long enough to resent the simple things we hadn't enjoyed yet.

"I'm here now, so I'm willing to make it count if you are."

Jake and I might have been secret, but we were permanent. The certainty thrilled me as much as it frightened me.

He insisted on making breakfast, shooing me out of the kitchen until he was done. After we ate, I ambled around the living room, scanning the pictures along the wall. I recognized his sister, Kristina, as she beamed at the camera with a baby girl in her arms and an older child at her side. Mike's school pictures lined half of the living room, his blue eyes almost translucent in each shot. I stilled when I recognized my uncle, standing next to Jake in a tuxedo.

"Mike hates that I still have his baby pictures up," he noted behind me. He handed me a cup of coffee when I turned around.

"Where was this from?" I asked, pointing to Uncle Keith.

"Prom. My mother found it a long time ago. My father took it before we got into the limo, and he called us gangsters."

"I don't see any friends from high school, other than when they pop up on Facebook and wish me a happy birthday. I met Claudia in college, so I guess she'd be my oldest friend."

"I met Keith when I was Mike's age." He folded his arms, still staring at the picture. "My mother and your grandmother used to joke that they shared custody of us since I was always at his house or he was at mine. I've basically known him my entire life," he mused before letting out a long sigh.

Bringing up the familiar undercurrent of guilt between us

was pointless. It was always right there, a given just as much as the combustible chemistry. We pushed past it, but we didn't ignore it. We couldn't. Uncle Keith was important to both of us.

Even if my greatest fear was realized and nothing was the same between me and the only father figure I'd ever known, we would still be family. He'd always be in my life, even if he decided to distance himself from me.

If Uncle Keith cut Jake off, even if Jake swore he would still choose me, regardless, it would break his heart. The closer we got to coming clean, the more I prayed it wouldn't come to that.

I nodded and headed for the couch, snatching the blanket from where it was spread over the back and pulling it over my bare legs as I held my coffee mug.

"If I can't put pants on, can I at least crawl under a blanket if I'm cold?" I scoffed.

"You can, if you let me crawl under with you," Jake teased, grabbing my ankles and draping my legs over his lap as he settled next to me.

"I hate this for you. For both of you." I rested my elbow along the back of the couch.

"I told you, I love your uncle like a brother, but I won't give you up for anyone. I tried and I almost lost my mind."

"I remember." I nudged his thigh with my heel and set the mug on the side table. A moan rolled through me when he pressed his thumb into the ball of my foot. "Stop distracting me."

"Like you haven't been a huge distraction since the day we met. Well, since the day we met again." He grabbed my other foot and held them both in his lap. "I believe that it may be bad at first, but he'll come around. Can we not think about that this weekend? Be us? The world is out there in the snow. All that matters until Sunday night is this."

I yelped when he grabbed my thighs and planted me on his lap.

"Okay, I can do that. Try to, anyway." I cupped his chin, scratching my nails along his extra day of stubble. "I can get into this, the rugged mountain man keeping me captive and pantsless."

"Same here," he whispered, brushing my lips before bringing me to his chest.

"I didn't go to my prom. A bunch of us were single and didn't want to feel pressured to get a date, so we took a limo into the city instead. I always wondered what I missed out on."

"Not much."

I rolled my eyes.

"You're a guy, of course you think not much. We had fun, I guess, came home drunk as hell thanks to our friend's twenty-one-year-old sister who was supposed to 'watch us.'" I held my fingers up in air quotes. "I think the dress and monkey suit are rites of passage. But I get to go to the Kelly Lakes prom."

"See? Never too late to make a dream come true."

"Some dream." I shoved his arm when he laughed. "I'm faculty. A chaperone." I shook my shoulders in a mock shiver. "Depressing."

"I could take you." He tightened his hold around me.

"Really?" I crinkled my nose. "You'd want to? Don't get me wrong, the idea of you in a suit is too sinful to contemplate, but you'd really want to waste a night in the high school gym?"

"No night with you is a wasted night. You could live the dream, I'll get you a corsage and even put out at the end of the night. You'll get the whole experience."

The idea of walking anywhere on Jake's arm, even to a high school prom, sent a thrill through me.

"We'll see," I said, my gaze drifting to another picture of Mike on the end table behind Jake. A grin split his chubby baby cheeks while he sat on Jake's lap.

"That's a great one."

Jake craned his neck around, laughing to himself as he lifted the photo off the table.

"He was my baby. Why I drive him a little crazy. He's my only one. Who else can I hover over?"

"You didn't want more kids?" I panicked when he squinted back at me. "I mean, it's none of my business, of course, but you're so good with Mike. I'm surprised he's an only child."

"I always wanted him to have a brother or sister, but . . ." He shrugged. "Timing was never right. We wanted to wait until he was two for another one, but by then, we were fighting all the damn time, so bringing a baby into all of that wasn't a good idea. I wish things were different, but he has his cousins and has made a nice group of friends up here. Certain things can't be planned for."

"You're probably done, right? You wouldn't want more kids at this point?"

Where the hell did that come from? Sure, we'd moved at warp speed since the end of October, but even the idea of this conversation was too soon.

"Why? Because I'm old?" He pinched my side. "How old have I seemed to you since I brought you here?" He traced his finger along the collar of my shirt—his shirt—before pressing a kiss to my throat.

"I didn't ask because I thought you were old." I squirmed away. "Trust me, I can barely keep up with you there. I just thought that with a fourteen-year-old, starting over from the beginning wouldn't be something you'd be interested in doing."

His brow furrowed, as if he were mulling it over. His hesitation triggered an ominous pang in my gut.

"My nieces are almost a decade apart. Emma, the one who's dying to meet you, surprised the shit out of my sister. But we love that she's a baby we can all enjoy without the first-time kid fears and mistakes." His lips curved as he drifted his hand up and down my thigh. "If I'm lucky enough to have forever with someone and a baby came along, I'd love it."

My heart fluttered in excitement and relief. Hearing Jake say he'd love it if it happened filled me with a pure if confusing joy.

Maybe Jake hadn't called me his forever, but I already knew he was mine.

THIRTY-TWO

JAKE

Even before Mike moved back in with me, I was an early riser. I'd work out for a while in the basement and ease into the rest of my day, even on the weekends.

But since I'd brought Peyton home with me, I had trouble getting out of bed. I had no clue when I'd fallen asleep or what time it was now, my eyes still adjusting to the light and unable to make out the numbers on my alarm clock.

Peyton mumbled in her sleep, grabbing the sheet and pulling it over her shoulder without opening her eyes. I smiled when she buried her head into the pillow and groaned.

"You're grumpy when you get up in the morning," I teased, running my lips over the exposed inch of her shoulder. "I wouldn't have guessed." I smoothed her hair off her nape and dragged openmouthed kisses down her back. I'd feasted on her all night and still woke up hungry.

She leaned into me, rubbing her sweet, naked ass against my cock.

I still couldn't believe she was here. It felt like the craziest dream yet so damn natural at the same time. I'd thought spending the weekend with her would make it easier when we had to part ways, but I already didn't want to let her out of this bed, my house, or my sight.

She belonged here. With me.

I'd said we'd tell Keith together, but it was taking too long. I planned to stop there alone this week, let him say or do whatever he needed to so we could move on. I didn't want to ruin a friendship I'd had for most of my life, but aside from my son, Peyton was before anything. Who she was related to didn't matter more than who she was.

Mine.

"Could we do it this way?" She mumbled into the mattress as I cupped her breast, her nipples already rigid against my thumbs. Peyton seemed tiny, but once I got her clothes off, she was all soft, mouthwatering curves. Her breasts spilled out of my hands as she writhed against me.

"Do what, sweetheart?" I kicked the sheet off both of us and drew her closer.

"Make love like that," she said, her throaty voice still groggy from sleep. "You behind me, touching me. I need it, Jake."

"Well then, I need to take care of my girl. You ready for me?" I slid my hand between her legs. "Fuck, sweetheart," I hissed. "You're drenched. Did I give you good dreams?"

"So good, so—yes, please, Jake."

I slid inside from behind, trying to go slow and fight my urge to pound into her as I had on my couch. She reached back, hooking her elbow around my neck, and kissed me, sloppy and desperate, as I inched in and out.

I'd never been so hooked on anyone. I wanted to keep her here, blow off my job and anything else that would take her out of this bed and away from me. This craving for Peyton wasn't new. She'd done this to me from day one. The only difference now was that I embraced it instead of fighting it.

I held off until her body shook against me, clenching around me until she took all I had. I dropped my head to the crook of her neck as we rode out the aftershocks.

"I almost wish I'd packed my work clothes." She turned and buried her face into my neck, painting kisses along my throat and sifting her fingers through the dark trail of hair on my stomach.

"You can go get them if you want. I'll drive you back to pick up whatever you need for tomorrow. We'd get one more night."

She pushed off my chest and sat up on her elbows.

"If I stay one more night, I won't be able to leave."

"What's wrong with that?" I chuckled, not really kidding at all.

"A conversation needs to happen with someone before we start talking about extended stays."

She swung her legs over the side of the bed and grabbed my T-shirt off the floor. I'd had my mouth and hands all over her from the time she'd walked in, but my gaze still tracked her body, following the hem of the shirt as it fell halfway over her thighs.

"Sweetheart, soo—"

"Soon, yes, I know." She cut me off, breathing out a heavy sigh, weeding through the clothes on my carpet until she plucked her panties from the corner and pulled them up her legs. "And we aren't supposed to talk about it until tonight."

I pulled on my boxers and followed her, pulling her back before she made it to the staircase.

"I'm as frustrated as you are. But I promise this is almost over."

She turned, meeting my gaze with a sad smile.

"I'm not frustrated with you. With the holidays looming . . . either we're keeping a secret or dealing with the fallout. Not exactly what I was hoping for."

"I know," I said, grabbing the back of her head and leaning my forehead against hers. "Either way, I want you to come with me on Christmas Day. Be with me and my family. This is it, this is us." I cupped her cheek. "I'm not begrudging us one single thing, not anymore. Hell, I'll put a sign in my office window saying that I'm in love with you, so there's no question from anyone anywhere."

Her face crumpled before she dropped her head against my chest.

"You're always so damn impossible to resist."

I laughed and pulled her tighter.

"Right back at you."

I was tempted to bring her back to bed, but followed her downstairs into the kitchen. We'd fallen in love, and it was no one's business but ours, yet all we'd done about it up until this point was tiptoe around how others would react.

I hoped Keith would understand eventually, but if he didn't, I'd still choose Peyton without a second of hesitation.

"Can I put pants on after breakfast?" Peyton asked when I handed her a cup of coffee. "Mike knows about us, but walking in and seeing me half naked with you may be pushing it just a bit."

"He texted this morning and said they wouldn't be back until tonight, but I guess I can't stop you," I grumbled as I mixed pancake batter on the counter.

"Wow, Sunday pancakes and everything. Do you treat all your guests this well?" She raised an eyebrow over the rim of the mug.

"My son has had Sunday pancakes from me ever since he

grew out of baby food. Besides him, I don't see many guests other than my nieces."

"Many?" She slid onto one of the stools next to the counter, the sides of her mouth quirking up.

"I don't make pancakes for other women, if that's what you're hinting at," I said, setting the spoon next to the bowl. "In fact, I never have women here. Keeping it casual is easier when you get to leave whenever you want, and that's hard when you bring someone home. So, I didn't."

"Really? You never had anyone here?" Her brow knit as she studied me.

"I lived here when I was married, but after that, no." I leaned over the counter and kissed the tip of her nose. "Is that the answer you were looking for?"

A slow grin split her mouth.

"Yes," she whispered, cupping my chin and brushing her lips over mine. "That was a *great* answer."

A wide smile ripped across my mouth as I set a pan on the stove. Just as I was about to turn on the burner, my doorbell rang.

"Shit," Peyton sputtered her coffee and popped off the stool. "This is why you should've let me put pants on." She glared at me before racing up the stairs.

I peeked out the side window, my eyes wide as they landed on my ex-wife.

"Eileen? What's going on?"

She pushed past me without looking at me when I opened the door.

"Where's our son?" She scanned the living room before shifting toward the stairs.

"Not home," I told her when I caught her arm. "He's away with his friend and his family, and he won't be back until tonight. What are you doing here?"

She swiveled her head, her nostrils flaring.

Eileen hadn't been this angry when we'd first met. Her easygoing personality was what originally drew me to her. She'd have a tantrum here and there, nothing I found concerning, but maybe I'd misread some important signs early on. While I accepted her anger toward me, what she'd done to my son's head all these years was unacceptable and unforgivable. I was grateful Mike wasn't home and was at least spared from witnessing his mother's wrath this one time.

"Max had to come to Albany for a quick trip, and I planned to surprise Mike today. Is he really not home, or are you keeping him from me?"

"Mike is old enough to make his own decisions, and I'd never keep him from you. I know you hate me, and I'm sorry about that and can't change things, but do you know what you've done to his head by trying to poison him against me all this time? What happened between us should have stayed between us. Using him as a pawn to hurt me ended up hurting *him*."

"Telling him the truth about his father, the hero, was using him as a pawn?" She scoffed. "You left us."

"I left *you*, yes. You know staying together wasn't working, but I never left my son. I appeased you so that you'd let me see him, and I was wrong. I thought I was sparing my son by not putting him in the middle when *you* were doing it anyway. You forced him to make a new life, and he's happy here with me, but do you think you can just come here for a visit and he'll drop everything?"

She rolled her eyes and opened her mouth to say more before something caught her gaze over her shoulder. Her eyes thinned to slits when she turned back toward me.

"So that's why Mike isn't home. I see you had a friend to entertain for the night."

My head fell back as I scrubbed a hand down my face. I exhaled a frustrated gust of air and reached behind me toward where I figured Peyton was standing.

"Sorry," Peyton mouthed when she sidled up next to me.

I shook my head and took her hand.

"Peyton, this is my ex-wife and Mike's mother, Eileen. Eileen, this is my girlfriend, Peyton."

Fuck that. She wasn't going to make the woman I loved uncomfortable in my house.

I spied a flash of hurt in Eileen's eyes, but I had to ignore it. Atoning for so many years for something I'd had to do had made things worse for all of us.

"*Girl* is right," she said, her shoulders shaking with a humorless laugh. "Find a nice older man to buy you a drink, honey?"

"Stop," I told her through gritted teeth and pulled Peyton behind me. "Mike isn't home and won't be coming back until tonight, so you have no other reason to be here. I'll tell him he missed you. I'm sorry that you came here for nothing, but it's time for you to leave my house."

"I remember when it was my house too." She shook her head and approached Peyton, looking between us for a second. "Be careful. He builds you up so high that the fall is a real bitch."

She gave me one last scowl before stalking out the door and leaving it open behind her.

I pushed the door shut, rubbing my eyes as I tried to calm down. So much for a perfect weekend. If Peyton and I were in this for the long haul, she needed to know what baggage she was taking on. An ex-wife I'd never be on friendly terms with was more than half of it.

I sucked in a breath, not wanting to meet Peyton's gaze yet. After trying to prove to her how different she was from Eileen or anyone else I'd ever known, I was afraid Eileen's ugly words had planted a seed of doubt.

"I'm sorry about that. I had no idea she was coming here, and neither did Mike."

"Hey, stop it." She rubbed her hands up and down my arms. "I'm fine. She's not the first one to imply I'm a young whore."

"*What?* Who called you that?"

"Travis's wife, when it all came out. She showed up at my apartment and said a whole lot worse for much longer. But what could I say? He lied to her too. I felt sorry for her and ashamed of what I'd done. And while Eileen has no excuse for making her son suffer for her own anger, I honestly feel sorry for her too." She feathered her hand down my cheek. "I imagine you're difficult to come back from."

"I love you, more than I ever loved her, as terrible as it sounds. Please don't think that I'm—"

She pressed her finger to my lips. "I love you too. And I know what kind of man you are. The best one I've ever known. I think you've punished yourself enough where she's concerned, and now you take care of yourself and your son and hope that she finds a better way to deal with her unresolved feelings toward you. But that's her problem. As much as you'd like to think so, you can't fix everything."

"I'm so fucking lucky," I rasped, grabbing the back of her head and hauling her to me. I covered her mouth with mine, bringing her flush to my body, and that still wasn't close enough.

She laughed against my lips before she pressed her hands into my chest.

"So am I. Especially if I still get pancakes." She peered up at me, quirking an eyebrow.

"I'll give you whatever you want." I kissed her again before looping my arm around her shoulders and heading back to the kitchen.

I'd never come back from Peyton. She gave me a certainty and satisfaction I'd never known, and I was done keeping it to myself.

THIRTY-THREE

PEYTON

"That's a great tree," I told my aunt as I eyed what looked like a six-foot Christmas tree taking up almost the entire corner of their living room.

"It's a *big* tree. That's why it only has lights so far." Aunt Maya dragged her gaze up and down the tree, shaking her head as she pinched one of the branches between her fingers.

"It's fantastic." Uncle Keith wrapped an arm around her waist. "The boys expect a big tree."

"This boy expects a big tree." She pointed a thumb at my uncle over her shoulder. "The two upstairs just care what's under it on Christmas Day."

"Speaking of," Uncle Keith said, keeping his arm around his wife. "Are you bringing someone with you on Christmas? You know you can. I'll only show him my gun once." He laughed when Aunt Maya elbowed his side.

"Maybe," I said, pushing a smile across my lips.

While my frustration grew, I was relieved at every reprieve. I paid closer attention to all the laughs we'd have when I'd see my uncle, compared to how I imagined things would be when he found out. Everything was about to shift, and I wanted to hold on to the simpler times before they all got too compli-cated to remember.

But it had gone on too long, and Jake and I had come too far to take anything back. My uncle deserved the truth from us, and we'd carried the lie on for too long. Jake would be mad at me, but he'd get over it. I'd had a small break between dismissal and when I had to head back to school tonight, and all I could think of was coming here and getting it over with.

"Actually, can I talk to you about that, Uncle Keith?"

"I am going to the garage to see if we have that other set of lights," Aunt Maya said as she stepped to the side. "I think this is the fourth set." She chuckled, her brows lifting when she glanced in my direction. "I'll be back."

Part of me wanted to go with her, delay this conversation once again, but I'd explode if I waited another minute.

Lying to my uncle cheapened what should have been the happiest time of my life, and I was sick of doing it.

"You can always talk to me, you should know that. I told you, the ice cream guy is welcome here if you want to bring him."

I stifled a laugh. He had been, but I doubted he would be for a long time after what I was about to say.

"I never meant to keep this from you," I began, my stomach coiling tight as his smile faded. "But for the past few months, I've been—"

He looked away when his cell phone went off in his pocket.

"Shit, it's the station. One second, P." He lifted the phone to his ear, his mouth flattening into a line as he nodded at whatever was said on the other end. "Okay, I'll be right there."

He shook his head as he stuffed his phone into his pocket.

"I'm sorry, I have to run in."

"Everything okay?" I asked, relief and rage flooding

through me. Just when I found the guts to come clean, my uncle had to leave.

"This small town is seeing more activity than I would like lately. Since we go away for the weekend tomorrow morning, I need to take care of this before I go. Is everything okay? You looked like you had a bomb to drop just now." He snickered and squeezed my shoulder.

"No, it can wait. Go be chief."

He grinned as he pulled on his jacket.

"I'd tell you to hang around, but I don't know how long I'll be."

"I have that parent workshop tonight anyway. I wanted to stop by to see you while I had the chance."

He kissed my temple. "I'm glad you did. We miss having you here. Let me go tell your aunt I was called in, so she can yell and get it over with. You're sure you're okay, though? You have me a little worried."

"I'm fine. It can wait."

Like it had been for months.

When he left, I fell back on their couch, propping my elbows on my knees as I dropped my head into my hands. I was already keyed up from preparing for the workshop tonight and anticipating how to be professional with Jake in the same space. The rise and fall of adrenaline all day had me breathless.

What would it be like not to have a perpetual knot in my stomach about what people were saying or what they knew? The memory was too distant to recall.

"Peyton, are you okay?"

I lifted my head to Aunt Maya's voice.

"I'm fine. A little stressed, but nothing I can't manage." I smiled and attempted a cheerful shrug.

"You shouldn't be stressed. Being in love is supposed to be a happy time, right?"

My eyes bugged out for a moment. I'd known she had a feeling, not that she was sure.

"We'll be home on Sunday evening. You'll both come here, we'll get it out, and move on." She cupped my cheek.

"It's a shame you don't have daughters. You're spot-on with advice on men." I leaned into her palm for a minute.

"I have one, or she always felt like one to me." She smiled and came closer. "Which is why I want you to revel in the joy instead of making yourself suffer over it."

"Revel in joy, what's that like?" I chuckled, giving my aunt a watery smile.

"I think you know." She gave me a slow nod.

It was Friday night to Sunday morning and every stolen hour and moment before. It was pancakes and ice cream and pure love that would confuse everyone else but made perfect sense to us.

"Tell Jason I said hi," I said before I stood.

"Oh, my brother and your uncle will be too busy picking up the bromance for the weekend to hear me, but I will." She kissed my cheek. "Go do what you have to do."

I nodded, even if I wasn't sure what that was.

The guidance department made the event open to all parents, but as we suspected, only a handful from each grade showed up. Deirdre and I did presentations on depression and anxiety, how we'd step in, and when we'd contact the parents if their child had an issue. A few were interested enough to ask questions, but most sat back and listened. It was a decent turnout overall, but my mind was on the one parent I couldn't acknowledge. My neck heated each time I felt his eyes on me, but I managed to stay cool until it was all over.

"I'm surprised some of the senior parents showed up,"

Lena, the senior counselor, scoffed. All the parents were separated into clusters, some sipping their free coffee from the paper cups.

Jake spoke with another father in the corner, my peripheral vision focused on him even though I couldn't look directly at him. As anxious as I was throughout the day, I took a little comfort in knowing that I had at least started the ball rolling. My uncle knew something was going on, and I'd have to explain on Sunday night. For the first time, I felt the beginnings of a resolution.

Even if it was the disaster I feared, that was still a resolution. I'd deal with whatever came to be, as long as it was over.

"The ones who care show up, especially if their kids have had a history of issues. I try not to be jaded," Deirdre said, turning to me with a quick eye roll.

Lena shrugged. She was nice enough at the department meetings we had each week, but had little interest in doing anything other than what was required in a school day. She was older than us, I'd guessed in her late forties, with striking green eyes and long auburn hair that fell almost to her waist. The leather skirts she liked to wear to school turned more than a few heads, but she was all business with her students.

"You see Jake Russo's son, right? He's a freshman, so I assumed."

I tensed up at Lena's question.

"I do. He's a good kid. You know him?"

Something about how her mouth curled into a smile made my skin crawl.

"I know his father," she whispered, her grin still wide.

Deirdre snuck me a glance, her brows raised. Lena never made small talk with us, so for her to get this personal was strange—and who she was getting personal about unnerved me even more.

"Speaking of . . . Hey, Jake," Lena said as Jake approached our table to throw his coffee cup into the trash can on the side.

"Hi, Lena. This was a lot of good information. Scary, but good." He smiled at us but avoided direct eye contact with me. It was the game we'd played since the beginning—and I was over it.

"Good, I'm glad. It is scary, but we like to remind parents that we can help but we need them to pay—"

"I meant to call you," Lena began, turning toward Jake and cutting Deirdre off. "My deck needs a little refresh. Maybe we can get coffee at the diner after this is over and discuss it. Or now. We're pretty much done, right?"

"We are," I said, the rage searing through my veins taking away most of my voice.

"Good, the diner is all that's open now, so I'll meet you there. Nice job, ladies," she told us as she motioned for Jake to follow her, my heart free-falling into my stomach when he did.

I gathered up the rest of the pamphlets and stuffed them into an envelope, missing the opening to slide them in, my vision clouded by white-hot anger.

"I can clean this up if you want to go kick her ass," Deirdre whispered with a sad smile.

I stilled, letting out a slow breath before turning my head, too focused on Jake's exit with Lena to think up a pointless denial.

"Thanks, but it's fine."

Lena didn't know anything about Jake and me. She was a single woman, and to her knowledge, Jake was a single man. I couldn't begrudge her for simply going for what she wanted. I almost laughed at my panic over the possible stigma of dating a parent when Lena had basically picked one up at a school event. I would have if I weren't fighting with the bile in the back of my throat to stay down.

I raced to my car after we were done, forcing myself not to check if his truck was still in the parking lot, and headed home.

Jake had seen women before me. He'd never hid it or apologized for it. Maybe he followed Lena to keep up the ruse that he was still single and not spoken for, that he wasn't seeing *me* in whatever spare moments we could get.

I piled into bed when I got home, trying to get lost in my Kindle, but the romance heroes who always soothed me couldn't help as I didn't register a word on any page. Every moment that I didn't hear from Jake, I pictured him still at the diner with Lena, and it made my stomach turn over each time.

I hated being this jealous shell of a woman. After eleven, I'd given up and thrown the Kindle on my nightstand. I shut my eyes, hoping but doubting that maybe sleep would somehow come, when the buzz of my phone made them pop open.

"Hello," I said, devoid of my usual happy greeting when I spotted Jake's name on the screen.

"Hey, sweetheart. I'm sorry about tonight."

"Sorry for what? Leaving with a woman you used to hook up with?" I hated the words and how they came out of my mouth. I knew Jake would never do anything with Lena, but the sting of watching him walk away with her triggered something in me that I couldn't control.

"Peyton, you know damn well I'd never look at or touch anyone else. How could you even think that?"

I didn't answer as I sat up in bed, the silence doubling the tension piercing my chest.

"Why didn't you just say no? Say 'Meet me at the office,' say 'I'm seeing someone'?"

"I know Lena enough that she wouldn't let it go, and I

wouldn't have been able to get her out of the office if she came. I made it very clear that I wasn't interested beyond business."

It was the right answer, but my focus was on "I know Lena enough."

"Sweetheart, come on. After all this time, you don't trust me?"

"It's not that." I groaned as I sorted out the sour concoction of feelings hitting me from every direction to pinpoint which one was irritating me the most. "If we were together out in the open, I could have told her to back off, or she wouldn't have approached you in the first place. Maybe. Paralyzed is the best way that I can describe the shitty way I felt tonight."

"You shouldn't have felt like that."

"So you wouldn't feel like that every time Ron comes to school and asks me out on a date?"

"What do you mean, comes to school? Is this hypothetical or actually fucking happening?"

"Uncle Keith has someone come to school once or twice a week on their lunch hour as a favor to him. He thinks the kids who want to pick fights may think twice if they know a uniform could stop by at any time. They just stop by and leave, but when it's Ron's turn, he lingers until I make something up and shut my office door."

"The fuck he is," he growled, drawing a surprised chuckle out of me.

"And what are you going to do? Tell him to back off because we're together? That he has no right? I know you wouldn't have done anything with Lena the same as you should know I blow off Ron every single time, but it's the same thing."

"No, it's not. I don't want him coming near you."

I could almost hear his teeth grinding and picture the tic in his jaw.

"I come from Brooklyn and worked at schools all over the city during my master's. Do you think I can't handle a guy who hasn't even grown into his gun belt?"

Another long silence.

"I was disappointed and hurt tonight. It wasn't your intention, it's something we have to expect if no one is supposed to know about us. It's hard to get used to, even though it's all we've ever done. And after tonight, I'm very much over it. Good night, Jake."

I hated cutting him off and ending the call, but I was too exhausted to have the same conversation for what seemed like the millionth time, and I feared I'd say something I couldn't take back.

As much as Jake and what we had meant to me, either we were out in the open or nothing at all.

THIRTY-FOUR
PEYTON

I was on my second cup of coffee and still struggling to make it through the morning. I'd drifted off to sleep somewhere around 3 a.m., two hours before my alarm went off. A slew of texts from Jake littered my screen, but I still hadn't looked at any.

I told my friends that I had work to catch up on in my office during lunchtime and couldn't join them. Sitting at my desk and stewing over the new tension between Jake and me seemed like a more tolerable option than answering questions about how off I probably looked. Deirdre would want a full explanation sooner or later about what she'd noticed last night, but I didn't have it in me today.

I raked a hand through my hair before finally picking up my phone and facing whatever Jake had said between last night and this morning.

Jake: *I love you. I love you more than I ever thought I could love anyone.*

Jake: *That's what I would have said had you not hung up on me.*

Jake: *It was wrong to leave with Lena. I should have just dealt* *with her at the office. If I had to watch you go anywhere with Ron, I would have lost my goddamn mind.*

Jake: *Or lost it again like I did at your uncle's house.*

A smile tugged at my lips. I guessed there were two possessive fools in this relationship.

Everything would be over Sunday night—or at least, the secret would be. Jake was wrong, but so was I. The constant pressure of the past months had finally come to a breaking point. I knew Jake would never lay a finger on Lena, but jealousy and frustration had gotten the best of me. We'd come too far for silly insecurities to derail us. We were in love, and that was a certainty no matter who did or didn't know. After all this time being angry about keeping what we had to ourselves, in the end, we were the only ones who mattered.

I'd never loved anyone else like I loved Jake, and it was time to take my aunt's advice and revel in the joy rather than fear the reaction or judgment of others—including Uncle Keith.

I left my office for a quick walk outside, hoping it would clear my head enough before I called Jake back. As I pushed the back door open to head out, I stilled at loud shouting behind me. Sure enough, I spotted three students at the end of the hallway, two boys getting louder as they got in each other's faces.

"What's going on?" I asked as I jogged over. I found Selena, her face crumpled as if she were about to sob, standing next to an open locker as the boys continued to argue.

"Nothing," the boy facing me sneered. I recognized him from the sophomore class but didn't know his name. "If Aaron wants to talk to this weirdo, it's his own business."

My heart sank when I met Aaron's gaze, his face red as if he were ready to kill.

This would be his second fight this semester, and the principal wouldn't go as easy on him this time. Even if it appeared to be provoked, nothing I could do would lessen his punishment if it came to blows.

"Guys, stop it," I said, getting between them and holding out my arms to keep them separated. I took a quick glance around us, wondering where the hell security or the cafeteria monitors were, and huffing out a frustrated breath when I found no one. "Go back inside the cafeteria and cool off."

I gave them both what I hoped was a glare of warning before I turned to walk away.

"What is he going to do? Tell his mommy the teacher on me?" The boy's voice dropped to a baby's whine. "I guess trash stays with trash."

Aaron lost it and dove for him before I could jump in and pull them apart again. I was so concerned with holding Aaron back from throwing a punch that I didn't notice the one heading for him. The boy's fist missed Aaron's face as it slammed across my cheek. I jerked back from the blow, and in what seemed like slow motion, my head hit the open locker door before I tumbled over.

I registered a whispered "Shit" behind me and Selena yelling for help. I lay there for a few long moments, the wind knocked out of me as I landed on my other cheek. I pushed off the floor, relieved when my arms and legs were able to move, but as I began to roll up to stand, blood dripped off the tip of my nose and onto the floor. Sudden and searing pain across my forehead made me stumble back as the side of my head that took the punch started to throb.

"Peyton, are you all right?" Deirdre crouched on the floor next to me, her voice shrill with panic as she gently took my face in her hands and lifted it up. I winced at the movement, the rest of my head pounding along with my cheek.

"Can you stand?"

"I could, but my head is killing me, and the room is spinning a little."

"Why were you the only one in the middle?"

"I was the only one around." I touched my dripping forehead, jerking back from the sting when my fingertip grazed against the cut. I felt around for my phone to check the damage in the camera lens. I was sure I looked as beaten up as I felt.

She met my eyes, studying my face as I squinted at Erin and Cam behind her. "One of the students burst into the faculty room to get us, saying you were hurt. I think someone may have called 9-1-1 for you already because I hear sirens."

"What? No, I don't need an ambulance." I went to sit up and fell right back down. A hand behind me lifted me up by my biceps as a towel was pressed to my forehead.

"You can't drive, and this will get you there faster. Plus, you'll need this documented for the fuck-ton of incident paperwork later," she whispered and squeezed my shoulder, her sad smile almost making me laugh.

"Peyton! Are you all right?"

I held in a groan when I recognized Ron's voice.

"Good thing this is my day. I'll meet you at the hospital."

I hissed at the agony from just trying to shake my head. The paramedics swarmed around me, asking my name and the date and anything else I guessed they used to gauge a head injury. Even in miserable discomfort, I sensed Ron as underfoot as usual, but had no energy to swat him away. I wanted to tell Deirdre to call Jake, but I was strapped onto a stretcher and taken out of the school before I could say anything.

I was worried about Aaron and Selena and that I wouldn't be here when they handed out punishments, but my head spun too much to focus on anything except keeping the dripping blood out of my eyes.

"Don't you worry, Peyton. I will personally stay with you the whole time once I get there," Ron said as he headed for his cruiser.

"Ms. Miller, we're going to lift you in," one of the paramedics said. "How's the headache?"

A sad laugh fell from my lips.

"About to get worse."

THIRTY-FIVE
JAKE

I sat at my desk, grumbling through paperwork for the day in between checking my phone every five minutes for a reply from Peyton. The second Lena suggested coffee, I should have said no. Yes, she wouldn't have let it go and I would have had to make an appointment with her eventually, but it should have been on professional terms in the office, just like Peyton said.

I'd thought getting it over with and not causing a scene at the high school was easier, but I should've known better. If it were reversed, I would have lost it seeing Peyton walk off with another man. Lena must've made a comment about our fling that lasted just short of a month. She'd sworn she was on the same casual page as I was, but whenever I ran into her, she always tried to make me stay.

The only woman I wanted to stay for was Peyton, and my split-second bonehead decision may have caused a rift between us that we didn't need right now.

I almost left Keith a message saying that I needed to speak to him as soon as he got back, but he would have called me right away, and I wanted to tell him in person that I'd fallen in love with his niece. I owed him that much respect and would accept whatever happened with us later, as long as I still had Peyton.

That, not Keith's reaction, was what kept me up most of the night.

I leaned back, scrubbing a hand down my face before I jumped at the buzz of my phone. My hope turned to dread when I read my son's name on the screen.

"Mike, what's wrong? Are you okay?"

"I'm okay, but Ms. Miller got hurt. Aaron got into a fight at lunch, and she got hurt trying to break it up. I didn't see what happened, but there was blood on the floor after the ambulance came."

"She left in an ambulance?" I yelled, leaping out of my chair and grabbing my jacket and keys. "How long ago was this?"

"I don't know, right before lunch ended. I called you as soon as I heard."

How bad was it that my son saw a pool of blood where it happened and she left in an ambulance? My own blood ran cold thinking of her hurt and alone.

This was one way of letting the town know about us if they didn't already, because there would be no doubt left in anyone's mind once I got there who Peyton was to me.

She was everything—and until I knew she was okay, nothing else mattered.

"Thank you." I locked the door behind me since I was the only one due in the office for the afternoon. "Please do me a favor. Call Aunt Kris and ask her to pick you up at home after she gets the girls. I need you to stay with her tonight."

I jogged to my truck, jumping in as soon as I clicked the key fob and started the engine.

"Okay. Can you text me to let me know if she's okay?"

I smiled, taking in a deep breath to calm down enough to drive.

"I can do that. I'll text you as soon as I know how she is."

I hung up and battled the urge to do ninety for the twenty-minute drive to the hospital.

"Peyton Miller," I yelled at the poor girl at the intake desk of the ER, breathing heavily from running from the far end of the hospital parking lot. "She came in by ambulance."

She scanned a clipboard and nodded before lifting her head. "She's in triage. I can have someone update you when I know more."

"She's my girlfriend. Can you just let me back there so I could stay with her?"

My stomach sank when she pursed her lips.

"No one is allowed back there unless you're immediate family."

"Jake? Hey, man. What are you doing here?" Buck, an old friend of my sister's, slapped my back. "Is Mikey okay?"

Buck was an ER nurse, and I thanked God for this fucking small town and its endless connections that made it seem even smaller.

"My girlfriend was brought in by ambulance. She got hurt at the high school. Peyton Miller."

"Head injury, yes." He glanced over my shoulder before jerking his chin to the ER doors. I kept pace behind him but didn't run to avoid calling attention to myself.

"Curtain two," he mouthed before heading to the nurse's desk.

I sprinted over when I spotted the number on the top of one of the curtains and ripped it open.

"Shit, sweetheart." I cringed when I spotted the bloody rag draped over Peyton's forehead. Her eyes widened when she noticed me.

"Jake," she squawked out in barely a whisper, reaching out to me and dropping the bag of ice she was holding.

"Hey, shh. It's okay," I crooned, kissing the top of her head as I scooped up the bag and brought it to her bruised cheek. It was red and raw, but not swollen. I was more concerned about what was behind all the blood on her forehead. "So what does the other guy look like?"

She laughed, squinting as she reached for me again. I caught her hand and kissed the back of her wrist.

"I'm sorry, sweetheart."

"Me too," she said. "And I'm glad you're here. How did you know?"

"Mike called me. He's worried about you."

She smiled and shut her eyes. "I'm worried about Aaron. I tried to hold him back from throwing a punch, and I got punched instead. My reflexes didn't use to be such shit."

I chuckled and rubbed her arm.

"You're a guidance counselor, not an MMA referee."

"You'd think." She smiled, lacing her fingers with mine.

"Okay. I think while we wait for the doctor, we can start the incident report. Oh, hi. Jake, right?"

My jaw clenched so hard, pain shot down my neck at Ron's clueless smile.

"She has a head injury. Can't this wait?"

"Procedure. Emergency services were called, and I have to get her statement."

"Her uncle is the chief. I'm sure you can make an exception," I said through gritted teeth.

"Excuse me, only one person at a time." A nurse peeked in, leveling her gaze at both of us.

"We'll only be a minute," Ron said, settling into a chair next to her bed.

"No, you won't." He jerked his head up as I stepped closer.

"Feel free to blame it on me, and I'll speak to Keith or even the mayor if I have to, personally. I'll take care of my girlfriend from here. You can go."

His brow shot up before he stood. I wanted to make it crystal clear he was no longer needed and to stop bothering Peyton in general or I would shove him out of this corner of the ER if I had to, weapon or not.

"Well, all right, then. Feel better, Peyton. Expect a call in the next couple of days." He shot me a glance, his mouth turned down as he made his way out.

"Such a caveman," she said, her voice scratchy and her eyes closed.

"That's the third time I've said girlfriend since I walked in."

She opened one eye. "Really?"

I'd have to call Keith in the morning and tell him about us over the phone, which I hadn't wanted to do, but it was better than him hearing it from someone else. And since the entire town would know by the time he'd left his brother-in-law's house, I needed to get to him soon.

The woman I loved was okay and with me. This was all that mattered, and I'd make damn sure we'd never be sidetracked again.

"Yep, I told you soon. Looks like out in the open is right now." I skidded my thumb back and forth along her jaw. "You're pretty much stuck with me."

A tired smile stretched her lips. "Nowhere else I'd rather be."

THIRTY-SIX
PEYTON

"How's the head?" Jake asked me as we pulled up in front of my condo, studying me with caution.

"As good as it can be, I suppose." My cheeks protested when I tried to smile.

"That's why you're going to get inside and climb into bed." He shut off the engine, the slam of the driver's side door reverberating like a loud boom around my sensitive head.

"I'm fine. You should get home to Mike," I said, my voice weak as he opened the passenger door and held out his hand for me.

"Mike is staying with my sister tonight. I'm not going anywhere. Keys?"

"Sure," I said while fumbling in my bag, the simple act of tilting my head forward causing a wince of pain.

Jake took my purse out of my hands and rooted around until they jingled in his hand.

"Come on, sweetheart," he said, holding my door open. "Change and get in bed. I'll join you in a few."

"Demanding," I joked, my chuckle shooting pain across

my face. One punch had laid me out, and every part of my body protested. My arm and cheek were bruised from the fall, and my other cheek was sore from the blow.

"If only I'd moved out of the way that one second . . ." I shrugged out of my coat and set it on the coatrack.

"You expected students to hold their punches when faculty was between them. Aaron is a good kid, but once you got in the middle, he should have backed off."

"I will say this is a first. I've heard stories of teachers hurt in fights, but this is rare and extreme. Jesus," I hissed when I caught a glimpse of myself in my hallway mirror. "I can't go to work like this." The bandage on my forehead was the least of my injuries. My face was raw, with an angry bruise across one cheek and a scrape on the other.

"That's why you're not going if you aren't feeling better by Monday. And tomorrow, you're coming home with me. If you do have a minor concussion, I want to watch you for a couple of days."

"I can't do that," I protested as I trudged into my bedroom. "I don't want Mike to feel weird."

"Mike won't mind." Jake came up to where I sat on the edge of the bed. "He made me text him updates from the hospital. Both of us are happy to take care of you for a weekend. Now, strip and get under the covers."

"You say that a lot." I managed to smile without pain as I eased up to stand and lifted my dress over my head. I peeled off my tights and unhooked my bra, grabbing the T-shirt Jake handed me.

"So you know my hiding place for all your stolen shirts?"

"You can steal as many as you want this weekend." He grabbed the hem of the shirt when I struggled to get it over my bandaged head and eased it down my body.

"What a show, right? I'm a mess."

"You're beautiful, always." He pulled down the sheets and pointed to the mattress. "And even though I'm supposed to be taking care of you, I couldn't take my eyes off your naked body just now." He leaned over and pressed his lips to my forehead. "Nothing but dirty thoughts, baby. But tonight, we sleep. No stimulation like they told you."

"That's going to be hard to do if you're getting in bed with me." My weary head sank into the pillow. "Hopefully this is the worst of it and I feel like a person again over the weekend."

"You're not going to worry about that." He sat next to me and rubbed my back. "You'll rest as much as you need to for however long it takes." He dipped his head to kiss my shoulder.

"I guess this is one way to have you stay the night." I snickered, cupping my head at the sting from leaning on my stitches.

"Now we get a lot of nights. Finally." He drifted his thumb back and forth over my jaw, the one bruise-free spot on my face. "Then, when you're better, I can take you out and let everyone know you're mine."

"I think half of Kelly Lakes already knows that. You didn't have to yell at the doctor to come to take care of your girlfriend."

He narrowed his eyes at me. "The woman I love was bleeding and in pain. I did what I had to do. Plus, I've known Paul since high school. It's not as if I made a scene in front of strangers."

"Paul?"

"The doctor. He used to come to Keith's house for weekly poker games."

"Uncle Keith had poker games?" I squinted at Jake, my head already too heavy to lift off the pillow.

"Before the twins. Maya didn't want cigars in the house after that."

"Wow, is there anyone in this town the two of you don't know?" I had to laugh. "It feels good that it's out, though. Mostly." I shrugged. I wished my head felt clearer, but maybe the distraction was a good thing.

"We have to call Uncle Keith," I said, pushing into the mattress to sit up.

"I already left him a message." He climbed in next to me and drew me into his chest. "Let me take care of this, okay?"

My head hurt too much to fight him. My eyelids grew heavy as the all-day rush of adrenaline dissipated.

"I wish I could sleep with you every night. I miss you all the time." I yawned into the crook of his shoulder.

"I miss you too, sweetheart. I hate when I have to leave you. I should have kept you in my basement like I wanted to."

"Safer there anyway. Maybe one day, neither of us will have to go home. We can sleep in *our* bed, not mine or yours." My eyes bugged out at what I'd let slip. "And if that just freaked you out, I hit my head and probably can't think or speak clearly." I peered up at his crooked smile.

"I wish for all of that too. Maybe it hasn't been long for us, but I can't remember a time without us. We fit. My house feels empty without you, and that's with a teenager leaving his shit all over the place. I'd love it if you never left."

My smile grew wide despite the ache in my cheekbones.

"But if that scares you, you have a head injury and probably didn't hear me right." I laughed at his raised brow.

"God, I love you. So much." I pressed a kiss to his chest.

"You can't begin to know how much I love you." He kissed the top of my head. "That's why I want you to stay with us until you feel better and are cleared to drive. We'll do whatever you need for a few days."

"I'll never want to leave."

"That may or may not be my secret plan," he whispered into my hair.

Jake and I *did* fit. My unexpected turn had led me straight to him—where I was supposed to be.

THIRTY-SEVEN

JAKE

Despite a shitty night of sleep, I was up even earlier than usual. Every time I'd woken up, I'd nudged Peyton to make sure she was okay. The doctors said it wasn't completely necessary since they weren't certain it was a concussion. Considering how light-headed she said she was when they first brought her in, my anxiety had me up and checking her anyway. She'd look at me and whimper into my chest until she drifted back to sleep.

I kept one arm around her waist as I reached for my phone. Still no text from Keith, which was unlike him. My message had been simple but cryptic, and I was shocked he didn't call me back the second he'd seen it. The minute he got back into town someone would tip him off. Hell, all he'd have to do was call into the station, and Ron would be all too happy to fill him in.

Looking back at these past few months from where we were now, the secrecy seemed even more pointless. Instead of searching for the right time to tell Keith together, we should have just told him a long time ago. We still would have had to keep sort of quiet while Mike was her student, but there were ways around that. Keith was the biggest obstacle, and our blatant lies of omission would upset him more than anything else.

I was almost relieved our hands were forced, but we needed to get to him first. As the minutes ticked by, the more I feared we'd probably lost our chance.

I rolled out of bed at eight, making sure I was gentle enough not to jostle her too much. Even with the bandage across her forehead and bruises already fading to purple on her face, Peyton was the most beautiful woman I'd ever seen. I'd meant it when I told her I never wanted her to leave. Time was bullshit when you met the one, and I had zero doubt in my mind that was exactly who she was.

While the phone was still in my hand, I texted my son to let him know I wasn't coming home alone.

Me: *I hope you didn't stay up all night playing video games with Chloe. I wanted to let you know that I'm bringing Ms. Miller home with me and she's staying with us for a few days until she feels better.*

I was surprised to see the three dots pop up, as I was sure he'd still be asleep on a Saturday morning.

Mike: *Is she okay? Aunt Kris is taking us for donuts. Does she want any, or can she not eat?*

I smiled as pride swelled in my chest. Despite all we'd put him through, I had a damn good kid.

"What time is it?" Peyton croaked out, her voice still rough with sleep.

"Eight. When you get up, we'll pack and head to my house." I sat back on the bed, brushing the hair off her face to get a better look at the bandage. "How are you feeling?"

"The stitches are pulling. My cheeks are probably still ugly, but not as sore. I can smile, see?" She peered up at me with a sleepy grin.

"Nothing about you could ever be ugly." I took her hand and kissed the top of her wrist.

"You sound like you have it bad, Mr. Russo." Her hand drifted down my face.

"I do," I whispered, kissing her fingers when they grazed over my mouth. "It's incurable."

"Are you sure Mike is okay with me staying with you?"

I nodded. "I just let him know, and this is what he said." I turned my phone screen for her to read his text. "He's fine with it, and I'd like to point out that he didn't offer *me* any donuts."

She squinted at the screen, a slow smile spreading on her lips.

"Tell him anything chocolate, and when we're outside of school to please call me Peyton." She yawned, sinking her head back into the pillow. "Can I have a few more minutes?"

"Sure, sweetheart." I brushed a kiss to her lips and pushed off the bed.

I let out a yawn as I trudged into her kitchen and toward the coffee machine. I was used to functioning on little sleep, but I needed to wake up until I brought Peyton home with me. If her pain subsided and she wasn't dizzy, I was all for an hours-long nap when we arrived at my house.

When I turned on the faucet to fill up the pot, a loud knock behind me jolted me awake enough for tension to radiate across my shoulders. I wasn't surprised when I spotted Keith's SUV in Peyton's driveway as I peeked out the window.

"Hey" was all I said when I opened the door, steeling myself for whatever his reaction would be.

"Hey! Thanks, Russo," he said as he slapped my shoulder and pushed past me to go inside.

Thanks? I studied him as I shut the door behind me.

"What are you doing back?"

"I called the station to check in, and they told me about the fight at the high school and how my niece was a casualty." He snickered as he leaned against the counter. "Poor kid, I bet she didn't count on punks this brazen when she moved here from Brooklyn."

"I guess you heard everything."

"Mostly," he said with a shrug. "The officer I spoke to said that Ron didn't get her statement because you told him Peyton needed treatment and to rest. The guy can't take a hint, so I'm sure she was grateful. How did you know she was there?"

"Mike called me."

"Oh, right." He nodded. "One of the kids was his friend. I didn't know the other name they told me. Anyway, Maya and I took two cars in case I got called in, so I left her at Jason's with the boys. Donna is in Atlantic City, and honestly, my niece probably has enough of a headache already without her mother coming up, so I didn't even tell her. I came back to take care of her myself. If she's got a concussion, she shouldn't be alone."

"I agree." I folded my arms, surprised Ron didn't rat me out to everyone, but I guessed Keith only knew whatever was in the report I hadn't let Ron finish.

"Thanks for staying with her. It's good that the boys are gone so she can rest in the quiet."

"I told her to stay with me for the weekend."

"I appreciate it, but that's not necessary. Besides, isn't your spare room still used as an indoor toolshed?" He chuckled. "Where would she sleep?"

"In my bed."

His brow furrowed for a moment before he shook his head, still not absorbing what I meant.

"That's generous, but I'm back now to take care of my niece. You don't have to put yourself out—"

"Babe, I take it back," Peyton called out, trudging into the kitchen with her hands over her eyes. "I said my head didn't hurt, but that was before I sat up. I need to eat something before I take the pain pills they gave me."

Recognition drifted over Keith's features, his easy smile giving way to a tight jaw and narrowed eyes as he glared at me. Peyton leaned on me, still in nothing but my shirt as she groaned into my shoulder. My gaze stayed locked with Keith's as I rubbed her back, soothing her in advance for what she was about to see. The hour we'd been avoiding and dreading was upon us, and she still had no idea her uncle was two feet away.

"Ah, this wasn't just a 'you take care of my kid like I would take care of yours' gesture? You meant she'd stay in your bed ... with you ... like she was last night."

Peyton gasped as her head shot up, wincing when she noticed Keith.

He stepped closer, scanning her face as his jaw ticked.

"How many stitches?" he asked, his gaze cutting from her to me before she answered.

"Three. The bruises on my cheeks are from the punch and the fall. What I'm feeling now is the slice of the cut, but my cheeks aren't that sore anymore."

"Good," he said, his tone clipped, but I had the feeling that was more directed at me. "Give Jake and me a few minutes alone."

"No," Peyton said as she squinted at Keith. "Whatever you say to him, you can say in front of me."

"Peyton, please," I begged. "I told you, let me handle this."

"No. You're both not sending me out of the room like I'm a child. I'm an adult, fully aware of all the decisions I've made up until this point. I'm sorry we waited so long to tell you—"

"That was my fault," I interrupted. "I wanted us to tell you together, but we couldn't get a hold of you for a month."

"For a month." He leaned back with a slow nod. "Exactly how long has this been going on?"

"We've been together since the beginning of November," Peyton offered before I could answer. "But it was brewing long before that."

"Right." He clicked his tongue against his teeth, nodding again. After knowing him for most of my life, I couldn't get a read on him. This cool and eerily calm facade he'd stepped into unnerved me. "You want to stay since you're an adult, fine." His gaze slid to mine. "Let's put aside the fact that you've both been lying to me for months," he said, leveling his eyes at me. "What are you doing, Russo?"

"What's that supposed to mean?" I asked with a defensive edge to my voice that I couldn't help.

"It means that she is a hell of a lot younger than you and vulnerable. I'm not saying you took advantage—"

"You better not be," I said through gritted teeth. "I'm sorry we waited so long to tell you, but I'm not sorry we're together. If I weren't serious about her, I never would have come near her. I love Peyton. Maybe it doesn't make sense to you, but it doesn't have to."

"I love him too, Uncle Keith. He's your best friend. You've known him for most of your life, and you know what kind of man he is."

Keith coughed out a laugh. "I actually don't at the moment. I've known you since the day you were born, and I'm not sure who you are either."

Peyton straightened and ambled up to Keith.

"I'm sorry you feel that way, and again, I'm sorry we didn't tell you, but I don't regret one second with Jake. I know you're in shock, but can't you be happy for me? For us?"

Keith's eyes clenched shut for a moment. "I know what happened in Brooklyn. With the principal. I was waiting for you to tell me, but I guess you don't tell me much anymore."

"I couldn't tell you." She took in a deep breath after her voice cracked. "I didn't want to tell anyone, especially you. I was scared you'd be disappointed in me. Just like now. If you only knew how hard we fought against this—for you. But we couldn't. Loving each other doesn't mean we don't love you."

"You just don't respect me." He sucked in a long breath as he looked between us. "You're okay, and you're not alone. I'm going to head back up to Jason's." He glanced at me before turning toward the door. "I'm not needed here."

"That's not true. Uncle Keith," Peyton called out before he shut the door behind himself.

"Fuck," she groaned, pressing her palms against her forehead. "That was exactly how I didn't want it to go."

"He'll come around." I rubbed her shoulders. "If not for me, then definitely for you. Give him a minute."

I wished he would have just clocked me across the jaw and gotten it over with. This was not the way I wanted him to find out either, but I always feared he'd see my being with Peyton as the worst kind of betrayal. He'd come here thinking I was looking out for his kid as he'd always looked out for mine and now, most likely, believed the exact opposite. All the time that passed without telling him the truth made it that much worse. But no matter when we told him, the fallout between Keith and me would have been more or less the same.

Still, I loved Peyton too much to regret anything—even if it cost me my best friend.

THIRTY-EIGHT
PEYTON

"**I**s the festival canceled?" Mike asked me as he lounged on the floor. The three of us had a movie marathon from the time Jake had brought me back to his house yesterday. Mike was waiting for us with a box of donuts and an innocent smile, and I tried to stay upbeat for his sake, even if my mind was a million miles away.

"No. I'm not that important." I shifted on the couch and adjusted the blanket around me. The only lights in the room were the flickering bulbs on their Christmas tree. It took up the entire corner of their living room—exactly like the one Uncle Keith had picked out.

My eyes stung whenever I thought of my uncle, which was almost every minute since he'd left my condo. My uncle never raised his voice to me or made me feel like he was anything but one hundred percent on my side for my entire life. It was something I always took for granted because I was never without it, or him.

Now, everything was so uncertain and unsettled. I wished he would have yelled at both of us and stormed out. Instead, he'd just left. No fighting, no anger, just disappointment.

It was far worse.

"I'd say you're pretty damn important." Jake handed me a cup of tea and kissed my cheek before settling next to me on the couch. "How's the head?"

"Stitches are itching, but better. I can go to work tomorrow."

"But you're not driving," Jake said, lifting a brow. "Mike can sleep an extra half hour tomorrow, and I'll give you both a ride to school."

"Sweet," Mike said. "This week is BS anyway. Only two and a half days."

"Enough with the language."

"I abbreviated."

A chuckle slipped out of me when he shrugged.

"Sorry, Peyton."

"I'm off the clock and wouldn't write you up for letters, so don't worry."

If I weren't so distraught over my uncle, spending the weekend with Jake and Mike would have been wonderful. Transitioning from his guidance counselor to his father's girl-friend wasn't awkward or forced. Mike didn't seem to flinch when I cuddled next to his father on the couch or disappeared into Jake's room at night. Being this open with affection for each other was still a new thing for us, but with Mike around, it felt natural and comfortable. I could see myself here long term—with both of them.

"Aaron can't go back until January. Not that he cared about the festival anyway. Sorry." Mike flinched when he raised his head. "He feels really bad that you got hurt."

"Tell him he can make it up to me by not getting suspended again in the next three years."

I was tempted to take another day off, but I worried about Selena. She hadn't asked to have lunch with me in a few weeks, and that may have been thanks to Aaron, but I feared whatever reaction the students had to the fight would set her back.

My eyes drifted toward where my phone buzzed against the couch cushion, my stomach tightening when I noticed my uncle's number.

"Hello?" I said after I scooped it up and ran to Jake's kitchen. If this was an argument or another intense conversation, I didn't want Mike to overhear or get Jake upset any more than he already was, despite how he'd pretended to be fine since he'd brought me home with him.

"How are you, honey?"

I relaxed at the sound of my aunt's voice, despite my fallen hopes that it was Uncle Keith. Even if he'd call to argue, at least that would mean we were talking.

"Okay. Bruises are turning an odd shade of purplish-green," I joked. "Stitches are pulling, but I guess that means it's healing. I'm fine to go to work tomorrow."

"I wish you'd give yourself another day. Recover from it all."

I shut my eyes, not wanting to acknowledge what *it all* meant.

"I think, in my case, going back to work is the best thing. Jake won't let me drive, so I'll be fine."

"Good. He's coming with you on Christmas Eve, right?"

"Oh . . . I . . ." I stammered, caught off guard. "I'll ask him, but I wasn't sure if I was invited."

"You're serious? Of course you are. Your uncle just needs to marinate on this for a bit. He'd *never* not want to see you on Christmas."

"How is he?" I whispered.

"Quiet," she said after a long minute.

"Oh God," I groaned as my head fell back against Jake's

refrigerator. Uncle Keith was never quiet. To me, that meant I'd broken his heart, and that broke mine.

"He will come around. I'll set the table for two extra places, and we'll all get through this. I know it seems tough, but it won't last. You are too important to your uncle for him to cut you off for any reason, so stop thinking that's what he's doing. Let him be, and do all you need to do."

"Okay. I love you both."

"We know that, and we love you too. Rest and heal."

I ended the call. It was difficult to find any encouragement in what my aunt had said because who knew how long Uncle Keith needed to process all this. Would he ever truly be okay with it, or forgive me for what I'd done and how long I'd lied about it?

"That was Maya?" Jake asked as he wrapped his arms around me from behind.

I nodded without looking back at him. "She said she's setting two places at the table on Christmas Eve for you and Mike, if you want to come." I craned my neck toward him. "I'm still invited too."

"Why wouldn't you be? There isn't anything Mike could do to make me cut him off. Keith sees you as his own, so it's the same for him."

"What about you?" I asked when I turned around, playing with the loose string on the collar of his T-shirt. "What if he cuts you off?"

"In time, he'll see what we have is real and get used to it. Like I keep telling you," he began, taking my face in his hands. "I don't regret a thing. I'll deal with whatever I have to, as long as I still have you."

"You do," I whispered. "Always."

"Back at you," he rasped, a slow smile creeping across his lips. "It's nice to be public." He drew me closer.

"About that," I said, looping my arms around his neck. "I'm speaking to my boss tomorrow to see if they can assign Mike to another counselor after the new year. He can always talk to me, but if issues come up, I'd feel better if the school saw his advocate as impartial. I should have done this a while ago, but I guess I didn't want to be known for who I was dating again." I shrugged. "I could thank Lena for that. She didn't seem to have an issue with picking up a parent *at* school, so why not be honest."

"She didn't pick me up." I stifled a laugh when his mouth flattened to a hard line.

"Whatever. Let's go watch the rest of the movie."

He grabbed me when I tried to step away and tightened his hold.

"I love you. You are all I'll ever want."

"Am I allowed to go home tomorrow after work, or are you holding me hostage for a few more days?"

A smile tugged at his lips as he cupped the nape of my neck and brought me in for a soft, slow kiss.

"You're staying here until the doctor clears you to drive. After that . . ." He brushed my lips again. "I'm thinking about it."

THIRTY-NINE

JAKE

I went straight to Keith's house after I dropped Peyton and Mike off at school. I'd called the station to make sure Keith was off today, and I wasn't going anywhere until he agreed to talk.

I hated that Peyton was hurt, but I'd loved having an excuse to keep her with us for an entire weekend. She seemed as if she'd always been there with us and I hated the thought of her going back to her own condo, but things were different now. We'd get more than just the stolen moments and nights that we were used to. We belonged to each other—officially and publicly.

Nothing had ever felt so damn good.

Keith was free to hate me for as long as he wanted, as long as he made up with his niece. I knew the rift between her and her uncle was killing her, and Peyton had carried around enough guilt for too many things for far too long. It was finally our time, and she deserved to be happy. And I knew she was with me, but I hated watching her force smiles for the entire weekend because her mind was on her uncle.

I waited for a good five minutes after I rang the bell twice, a smile pulling at my lips at Keith's reluctant shuffle on the other side. Maybe he was being a little spiteful, but he wasn't ignoring me. I'd take whatever I could get.

"Something you want, Russo?" He lingered at the door, leaning his elbow against the frame.

"Just a few minutes of your time, Chief," I said, tipping my chin toward his hallway. "Am I allowed in, or would you want to talk in the cold? I'm honestly good either way."

He shrugged and headed back inside. I shut the door behind me and followed, still creeped out by a quiet and indifferent Keith, but he didn't need to speak, only listen.

He fell into his chair, picking at a piece of lint on his jeans and looking everywhere but in my direction.

"Look, I'm sorry we waited so long to tell you. That is totally on me. Peyton was ready to tell you on Thanksgiving, but I stopped her. I wouldn't let her do it until we could tell you together. Finding me at her condo like that I'm sure was a shock, and not at all how we wanted you to find out."

He kept his gaze forward and nodded.

"That's all you're sorry about?" He finally turned toward me, glaring as he leaned forward.

"Yes, it is. If you're expecting me to apologize for falling in love with your niece, I won't."

"You're in love with Peyton? After only a few months?"

"You bought a ring for Maya after knowing her for three weeks. Sometimes, you just know. With her, I know. More than Eileen, more than anyone. She's it."

He leaned back, squinting at me.

"After ten years of swearing you'd only date casually because you didn't want the hassle, Peyton made you do a complete one-eighty? She's been through a lot."

"I know she has. I know about the principal at her old school too. That was another reason why we kept it quiet at the beginning. After what happened, she was afraid of having a reputation here for dating a parent."

"Glad she told you." He huffed out a laugh. "I wish I knew when she'd stopped trusting me."

"She trusts you more than anyone. She didn't tell you because she was afraid you wouldn't see her the same, just like she's made herself sick over the past few months about how you'd react about us. So, I'm asking you"—I leaned forward, resting my elbows on my knees—"hate *me*. Be pissed at *me*. Let her off the hook. I don't want to see her like this anymore."

"Like what?" Keith jerked back, a deep furrow between his brows.

"Like she's afraid you're going to cut her off."

He shook his head and scrubbed a hand down his face.

"Is that what she thinks? She's like my daughter. I could never—"

"Then tell her. I don't have to come on Christmas Eve if it makes it easier."

"No," he sighed and fell back. "She wants you here, and I overheard Maya invite you and Mike last night."

"You could punch me now if that helps. I won't fight back."

"Right." The hint of a smile drifted over his lips for a quick second. "Because that wouldn't make things worse with my niece *and* my wife."

"Your wife?"

"Maya told me to grow up and snap out of it last night and hasn't said a word to me since. I am glad you were there at the hospital and that she wasn't alone. Despite my hesitation with all of this, I do know you wouldn't hurt her on purpose."

"I won't hurt her at all. I can't. I told you, she's it for me. Why nothing has worked out with anyone else until now. I was waiting for her."

"Wow." His eyes were wide for a moment. "I never thought I'd hear you say that."

"Because I've never been this sure. I promise I'll ask you before I marry her."

His brows popped up before his eyes narrowed. "Don't push it, Russo."

I held up my hands. "Just trying to be upfront and honest."

"Well, feel free to hold some things back." He stood. "If this is really it for the both of you, I'm happy. Or I will be when it stops freaking me out, which may or may not happen."

"I will gladly take that." I stood and held out my hand. "We're okay?"

"Not yet," he said, taking it anyway. "But as long as Peyton is happy, maybe we will be."

Things probably wouldn't be the same between us, but I was fine with that. I didn't mind earning Keith's trust when it came to Peyton, because there was no one else for me, and there never would be.

Everyone would see sooner or later, but all that mattered was us.

FORTY

PEYTON

"Is Keith going to cook outside again?" Mike asked as we headed down my uncle's walkway. The railings on the front steps were lined with lights, as was the tree next to their house. Everything was cozy and festive, except my turbulent stomach.

"He may smoke something, I'm not sure," I told Mike, the knot in my stomach coiling tighter as we approached.

I hadn't seen or spoken to Uncle Keith since he'd found me in nothing but his best friend's shirt and left my condo. Aunt Maya said he still wanted me here, and while I sort of believed that, it wouldn't be like the Christmases of old tonight. It would be uncomfortable and forced, which never described anything having to do with my uncle before.

"Merry Christmas!" Aunt Maya said before she brought me in for a hug. "Let me see." She pushed me away and studied my face. "Just a little bandage. Beautiful as ever."

"Right," I scoffed and stepped into the house.

"Let me look," my mother said as she rushed up to me. I'd almost forgotten she was staying with Uncle Keith until the new year. I called her about the accident at school but didn't mention my falling-out with her brother, but I was sure she knew all about it anyway. "What made you get in the middle of a fight?" She sighed, shaking her head.

"It's my job. This"—I pointed to my head—"is an anomaly."

A groan rose from her throat before her gaze drifted over my shoulder.

"Merry Christmas, Jake. You must be Mike." Mike's brows drew together when she cupped his cheek. "Aren't you a cutie? Wow, Jake, he looks exactly like you did when I first met you and you camped at my house all the time. I'm Donna, honey. Nice to meet you."

"My sister is a rite of passage, Mike." Uncle Keith came up to Mike and slapped his back. "She's harmless. Mostly." His warm smile surprised me in the best way when he turned to me. "Bruises are all gone, I see. Just the scrappy bandage is left." He grinned and tapped my chin. "Merry Christmas, P."

A sob rolled out of me as my head fell into his chest, soul-deep relief flooding through me.

"Hey," he laughed and rubbed my back. "It's okay. Don't cry. And listen, I would never *ever* cut you off. I'll love you until the day I die, so keep that in mind the next time you're afraid to tell me something," he whispered, grabbing my arms to push me back. "Okay?"

I nodded, wiping my cheeks with the back of my hand. "Okay. I'm sorry, Uncle Keith."

He shook his head and looped his arm around my shoulder.

"It's a holiday, no need to be weepy. Russo," he said, nodding at Jake. "Glad you guys could come."

"Wow," Mom said, chuckling at her brother. "You're really okay with your beloved niece with your best friend? I knew before you did, by the way."

"Because you never mind your business. But if you want to hold this one thing you found out about Peyton before I did over my head, happy holidays, D."

"You're really fine with this?" She peered at him, shaking her head. "No cleaning your gun for the hell of it tonight?"

"Honestly," he started, rolling his eyes. "You're probably going to be his mother-in-law. I would think a bullet would be less painful."

Mom glared, despite the twitching of her lips. When we sat at the table, it was so normal I almost cried again. Uncle Keith and Jake were talking, maybe not as relaxed as they used to be, but there wasn't a current of tension evident between them. Between the twins and my mother, poor Mike didn't have a moment to himself. Jake stretched his arm across the back of my chair, and the simple gesture was so surreal. We were here and together, and while my uncle didn't seem to be over the moon about it, he appeared to be rolling with it for our sakes.

This was the resolution I'd prayed so hard for, even when I'd thought it would be impossible.

"Oh, I have some news," Mom said, setting down her fork. "After the holidays, I'll be back in Kelly Lakes permanently. I found an apartment a few minutes from here. All I have to do is settle things back in Brooklyn, but it's not as if I'm working or anything. I can help out with the twins or any other kids that come along in the family." She lifted a brow at me and raised her wineglass. "So, Merry Christmas."

My gaze flicked to Uncle Keith, his brows shooting up to his hairline.

"We *should* all be here and together," he said, raising his beer bottle. "I'm happy to have you with us, sis. For the boys, for Peyton, and whoever else."

I shared a silent laugh with Jake. My poor uncle couldn't

wrap his head around kids from Jake and me yet. I couldn't blame him since I wasn't quite there myself.

"Just try to call first before you come by."

"Cute." My mother scowled as she speared her fork into a piece of chicken.

"To family!" Aunt Maya raised her glass. "Both blood and found, together and permanent."

I sipped from my glass, a stirring of excitement in my belly rather than the usual dread. Guilt over so many things had weighed me down for so long, the relief was palpable. Maybe true happiness didn't have to come with a caveat after all, and unconditional love accounted for the unexpected.

"This is . . . normal," I whispered to Jake. "I mean, it's wonderful, but I agree with Mom that it's odd he's this okay with it."

Jake shrugged. "I may have stopped by a couple of days ago and asked him to put all the blame on me, so he'd let you off the hook. I told you, you're too important to him." Jake glanced at the end of the table, my uncle more into his plate than our side conversation. "Is he thrilled? No, but he's getting used to it for both of us. All we can ask, right? Merry Christmas, sweetheart."

Jake reached across my plate to grab a roll and kissed my cheek. We all turned to my uncle's exaggerated cough. Jake shot me a crooked smile and shrugged. I fell in love all over again.

Maybe I'd come here to run away, but I'd ended up coming home.

EPILOGUE

PEYTON

Five Months Later

"I am impressed," Deirdre said as she scanned the gym. "This really looks amazing."

I nodded in agreement. The wooden floor was draped with a white tarp, they'd removed the basketball hoops for hanging lights, and the chairs were wrapped in silver bunting that gave the entire room extra shimmer.

I'd finally made it to prom. At thirty-three.

"You look hot," she said as we traipsed around the space, keeping an eye on the students without snooping.

"So do you. Not that anyone notices the chaperones."

She wore a simple black cocktail dress with her hair up in a twist. I'd chosen a snug green dress that fell just below my knees and styled my hair in loose waves. I fiddled with the corsage on my wrist Jake had insisted on giving me and headed back to the table.

Most of the faculty came alone except for the few who brought a spouse along. I didn't have to bring anyone, but he'd offered and Jake in a suit was a prospect I couldn't refuse. As

Claudia once said, the man was hot as sin. When he peeled off his jacket after we'd first arrived, popping open the buttons on his sleeves to roll them up past his corded forearms, I checked the corner of my mouth for drool.

"I picked up some punch for you," Jake said when we sat down. "You both need to stay hydrated enough to pick out the couples that you need to pull apart."

Deirdre's head fell back on a laugh as she sat down. "I'm not getting involved in that. Let the senior faculty take that on. We only breezed through to make sure everyone is having fun and not setting anything on fire."

"Exactly. We're just pretty decorations."

"I wouldn't say that," he rasped, stretching his arm across my shoulders. "You're a gorgeous decoration," he whispered, tucking a curl behind my ear. "When we get home, I can't wait for that beautiful body to decorate my cock."

I slapped his thigh, my cheeks flushing red-hot as I shot him a scowl.

"You cannot talk dirty to me in school."

A wicked grin stretched his mouth. "It's not school. It's prom. And I do remember promising you I'd put out. All part of the package, sweetheart."

I shoved his shoulder, my cheeks aching from my wide smile. I'd just put my condo on the market this week. I spent most nights at Jake's house anyway, and when he'd asked me to move in and stop wasting a monthly mortgage payment, I had zero hesitation before I agreed. Thanks to all the work Jake had to do when the condo flooded, the real estate agent said I might be able to get a better price for it than what I'd originally paid due to the new floors.

Moving in together should have been a scary prospect, but it wasn't. The few nights I did spend per week at my condo felt off, like an annoying in-between until I could get back to Jake.

I'd worried about Mike's reaction when we'd told him that I was moving in, but he didn't even flinch. He was a great kid, and I hoped he'd work things out with his mother someday for his own sake.

"Thank you for being here. I know it's a little silly." I rubbed the top of Jake's hand.

"It's not. We haven't danced yet." He stood and held out his hand. "I'll do my best to keep my hands above the waist."

"What fun is that?" I rose from my seat and took his hand. I didn't recognize too many of the seniors, and it was dark enough for them not to realize who I was. Jake didn't blend in too well, but he never did. His presence always filled a room, the understated swagger undeniable and intoxicating.

Or maybe that was just his effect on me.

"I like the heels." He brought our joined hands to his chest. "They're hot."

"They better be. They're painful as fuck."

He laughed, the crinkles around his eyes illuminated by the flicker of the DJ's strobe lights. I couldn't see his blue irises, but they were committed to memory, deep and bottomless.

"Your uncle and I were at prom, right here in this gym. Back in the nineteen hundreds, as my son likes to say."

"Ouch." I winced.

"Exactly. We came here right after we took that picture you found on my wall."

"Who did you take?"

I laughed when his brow furrowed. "Her name was Alissa . . . Elaina . . . No, Alissa, for sure."

"You . . . don't remember?" I crinkled my nose at him.

"We didn't take girlfriends. A date was the price of admission, so we took girls we sort of knew, and we hung out with our friends for the night. Prom wasn't a big deal for us, just another place to goof around for the night, except we had to get dressed up to do it. Getting drunk in a limo like you did was the far better option."

I smiled, picturing Uncle Keith and Jake as teenagers goofing around as I had seen them do at the dining room table so many times. It had taken a while, but most of the initial tension between them had worn off when my uncle realized this wasn't just a fling for either of us. I was with Jake for good, so confident in my feelings that moving in with him didn't frighten me in the least. I couldn't help wanting even more—everything—when it came to Jake.

All those months of soaking up the scraps of time we could steal had given us an appreciation for just being together. I still dreamed big when it came to us, but not having to hide that we belonged to each other would always be enough for me.

"Feel like getting some air, or do you have to stay inside?"

"We can head to the parking lot for a minute if you'd like. It's a little crowded and stuffy."

We snuck out the front entrance and into the lot, the cool night air a welcome reprieve.

"I think I saw you for the first time again right here." Jake ambled toward the empty front spaces in the lot.

"Was it?" I swiveled my head back and forth. "The lot looks so different at night . . ."

I trailed off when I found Jake on one knee in front of me.

"That was the moment that my life changed. I just didn't realize it until later. You're the love of my life, and I never want to be anywhere but next to you. Please marry me." He flicked open a velvet box, the outside lights shimmering off the stone, but I couldn't make out anything through my cloudy gaze.

"I changed your life in a parking lot?" I croaked out, tears scratching the back of my throat.

"Started to. Resisting you was the hardest thing I've ever had to do, why I didn't last very long. I want us to have everything. Please, sweetheart. Say you'll marry me."

I'd never witnessed anything in life—at least not in my life —truly come full circle. I'd walked Mike out of school and to his father, knowing I'd see the man I'd crushed on as a kid, but clueless as to how hard I'd end up falling for him as an adult.

And I would never have thought in a million years he would be mine to keep.

I nodded, forcing out a yes in a voiceless whisper.

Jake shot up and grabbed the back of my neck, hauling me to him and taking my mouth in a passionate kiss with too much tongue for outside of a high school, and for where I worked.

"Let's go," I murmured against his lips. "I'll tell Deirdre I'm sick. I've had enough prom, and I want to celebrate the rest of my life."

He laughed, his eyes twinkling.

"We can if you want. No rush. As I always told you, we have all the time in the world."

———

BONUS EPILOGUE

JAKE

"Dad, can you help me with this?"

I turned my head and held in a laugh at my son's obvious frustration. His necktie fell loose around his collar, wrinkled as if he'd been wrestling with it for hours.

"Sure," I said, slowing down my movements when I noticed him dip his gaze to watch me. "Guys your age don't wear ties much. They're a pain but necessary sometimes. You'll get used to it. Can you imagine having to do this every day before work?"

"Ugh, no." Mike scoffed. "That would be the worst."

"Then get good grades, find the job you want, and the only reason you'll ever have to wear a tie is if someone gets married or dies. There." I patted his chest. "You look good."

"Thanks. You too," he grumbled before he fixated back on his phone screen. That wasn't unusual, but he seemed more attuned to it today.

"Everything okay?"

"Yeah, working on my speech before the toast." He exhaled a frustrated breath, his brows pulling together as he scrutinized whatever he'd just typed.

"You don't have to give one if you don't want to." I squeezed his shoulder, the tension radiating from his neck and coiling his muscles obvious under my fingers.

"I'm your best man. Yes, I do."

"Listen to me." I grabbed his arms and turned him to face me. "You're standing next to me. That's all I care about, okay?"

He exhaled a long breath and nodded.

"I know, but I want to do it right. For both of you. I've only given one speech in history class, and when I forgot about whoever was staring at me, I was sort of fine." He shrugged before trudging to the couch and plopping down on the cushion with a dramatic sigh.

He was fifteen, but his voice had finally dropped that important octave to stop him from screeching. The peach fuzz on his lip had turned into the beginnings of actual facial hair, and I'd had to give him a quick shaving lesson this morning. He was in that awkward stage of not a kid anymore, but not a man yet either, and while the outside showed signs of growing up, the inside was still my Mikey. He was unsure and tentative, but his soft, good heart was something he could never hide.

"Maybe if I made the toast with actual champagne, it would, I don't know, relax me a little."

I leveled him with a glare when he lifted his head.

"You're underage at a wedding with the chief of police. So that's a no." A smile pulled across my mouth as I shook my head. "Nice try, though."

Mike and I had made sure to be out of the house early and had been hanging out in one of the bridal suites until everyone arrived. When we'd left, it was still dark, and Peyton was in a deep sleep. I didn't have the heart to wake her up, even though not seeing her awake yet had me a little antsy.

My sister told us at the rehearsal dinner last night that she'd never seen a groom so hopelessly gone for his bride. She was one hundred percent right, and I didn't see that changing in my lifetime. We'd been living together for almost a year, but claiming each other as husband and wife thrilled me in a way my first marriage never had.

Any jitters I had were from wanting to marry the love of my life as soon as possible.

"Good morning, babe!"

My body relaxed, a wide smile tearing across my mouth at Peyton's voice in my ear.

"You're in a good mood," I teased.

"Well, I get to be Peyton Russo in a little while. Why wouldn't I be? Aside from my fiancé not kissing me goodbye this morning."

"I did. You just don't remember it because you were sleeping."

"Why didn't you wake me up?"

"Because you need the rest."

"*Ugh,* are you going to baby me this whole time?"

I laughed when she groaned in my ear.

"Probably. But I promise when I kiss you today, you'll be awake and remember it all. I was less babying you this morning than saving your energy for tonight. You won't get much sleep—or any at all."

"Don't threaten me with a good time, Mr. Russo. How's Mike?"

"He's a big man today. Shaved this morning and is working on his toast. Are my nieces behaving?"

"Yes. Chloe has been a huge help, but Emma keeps making herself dizzy twirling in her dress." She laughed before the phone rustled in my ear. "She called me Aunt Peyton just now," she whispered.

"That didn't bother you, did it?"

"No, not at all. I loved it. Just, you know, shit is getting real."

"That it is. I love you. Hurry up and marry me, okay?"

"That's my plan. The car is here, so I guess I'll see you in a few. I love you too."

"How are we doing today?" Keith's voice drifted into the room after he knocked on the door. The twins barreled in, gravitating toward my son, who was still too into his phone to notice anyone or anything going on around him.

"We're good. Peyton said they're on their way so . . ." I shrugged and held up my phone before stuffing it back into my pocket. "Looks like it's all systems go, *Uncle Keith*."

He let out a groan as he scowled at me.

"Cut that out. You seem relaxed, at least a lot calmer since the last time you were getting ready to do this."

"I am." I nodded as my gaze drifted to Mike. I couldn't regret my first marriage since he was the result, but today felt like less of a logical next step and more like one of the greatest days of my life. "I told you, Peyton's it for me. I'm finally where I'm supposed to be."

"I'm glad, and I know." He slapped my arm. "Both of you were meant to be, even if it took me a bit to get on board. I know you love her, and I'm glad she ended up with someone this crazy about her. I'm happy for her, and I'm happy for you. You both deserve this."

"Wow." Keith and I hadn't really discussed Peyton and me since the day I'd gone to his house after he found out. He'd thawed out little by little since then, and we were mostly back to how we used to be. While he'd stopped scowling at me when I showed any type of affection toward Peyton in front of him, he'd never fully expressed his blessing before.

"Thanks. That means a lot," I said, my voice cracking a bit. I'd choose Peyton every time, no matter what the consequences were, but I was happy and relieved that I'd managed to get my best friend back.

"No need to get all sappy," he teased. "I'm happy you guys are together. Which is why you'll still be in one piece when I walk my *pregnant* niece down the aisle to you today."

My jaw dropped at his lifted eyebrow.

"She told you?"

He rolled his eyes, shaking his head.

"No, but when I dropped Maya off earlier and she suggested a champagne toast before I left, Peyton tensed up. She filled her glass with apple juice, claiming that she hadn't eaten very much and didn't want it to go to her head. Other than all that time she was sneaking around with you, I think I can read my niece pretty well."

I had to laugh. "I still don't know how you didn't pick up on it."

He shrugged, shooting me a scowl. "I didn't see it coming or expect it. Trust me, as an uncle and a cop, I couldn't be more disappointed in myself for being so fucking oblivious for so long." His brow furrowed as he scrutinized me. "You up for this again? I mean, with a teenager and all. The twins are only eleven, and I'm not even sure I'd want to go back to the baby days."

"With Peyton, I'm up for it all. Healthy before anything, but I've been thinking about a little girl." I smiled widely at the thought. I wasn't only up for this—I was fucking thrilled.

"A little girl for you would be karma, so I'm rooting for that too." He glowered at me before the corners of his lips lifted.

"I suppose it would," I said, chuckling as I adjusted my cuff links.

"So, double congratulations. I guess that makes me a great-uncle, grandparent level." He straightened, stuffing his hands into his pockets.

"And today makes me your nep—"

"I said stop it." He dug his buzzing phone out of his pocket. "Looks like everyone is here. Guys, let's go," he motioned to Aiden and Brian.

"Do we have to get married too?" Brian asked, his mouth pulling into a sour frown. "Mom said we had to walk down the aisle with a girl named Emma."

"You'll go home alone, I promise," Keith said, squeezing the back of Brian's neck before turning his head toward me.

"You ready, Russo?"

"I am," I told him with a slow nod. This day may have seemed to come quickly for some, but I felt as if I'd waited my whole life for this—for her.

"More than you know."

Peyton

"Okay, just hold still," Claudia whispered, worrying her bottom lip between her teeth as she untangled my curls from the edge of my veil as we headed inside the reception hall. "See, slow and steady, and no hair gets yanked out."

"Yes, thank you," I sighed. My hair was down in loose waves with a comb holding a short, but long enough to get tangled, veil. I didn't care about a big dress or a huge reception. We'd rented the only catering hall in Kelly Lakes, but tried our best to keep it simple and small. Rather than go to church, we were getting married in one room and the reception would be in the other. It was all details as far as I was concerned, as long as Jake had my ring on his finger and I had his last name by the end of today. He'd told me I didn't have to change my name if I didn't want to, but I had no allegiance to my father and wanted nothing more than to be a family with Jake and Mike.

"This is why your hair should be up." Mom *tsked* as she shook her head.

"I wanted my hair down," I explained, forcing a smile instead of arguing. "Today is supposed to be casual."

I sucked in a breath and exhaled slowly, my hand going to my still-flat stomach on reflex. I'd chosen a simple dress with an empire waist and spaghetti straps, a happy accident, as who knew I'd be walking down the aisle at six weeks pregnant? It wasn't apparent to anyone but me, but my jeans and skirts were growing tighter by the day.

We'd decided to keep it to ourselves until after the wedding, but I had an inkling my uncle either knew or was at least pretty suspicious after I'd so vehemently refused a glass of champagne this morning.

Secrets never stayed secret for long—at least in my family.

"Time to get paired up."

I turned to my uncle's voice, swallowing thickly when I spotted his proud smile. Pregnancy hormones mixed with wedding emotions were a dangerous combination. I had too many layers of makeup on my face to blubber my way down the aisle.

"Do I go now, Aunt Peyton?" Emma grabbed the basket of petals and jumped up and down.

"Yes, you get to walk with the boys," Aunt Maya said, pulling the boys over by the hands. "You'll all go down together, but don't run," she whispered before shooting me a grin.

Emma nodded, but I had no doubt she'd race down the aisle.

"See you there, Aunt Peyton," she said before barreling into my legs.

My chest flooded with warmth for my new niece, and I was fine with her jumping all the way down if it made her happy.

"See you there," I whispered, kissing the top of her head.

"You know, there's still time to make a break for it," Uncle Keith joked in my ear when I slipped my arm through the crook of his elbow as we lined up. "I'll radio for a police cruiser, and no one would find us."

I laughed at his cocked brow.

"Thanks for the offer, but no." My gaze drifted down the aisle, my little cousins moping as they flanked Emma, with poor Chloe in front of them, trying in vain to make them step in time together.

I locked eyes with Jake when we were halfway down the aisle, my heart climbing out of my chest when a slow smile drifted across his beautiful mouth.

"I'm right where I'm supposed to be."

"That's exactly what Jake told me this morning."

I turned to my uncle's glossy gaze and swallowed the sob wanting to break free.

"I love you, P. I'm happy for you. For both of you," he whispered before we made it to Jake, his own eyes wet as they locked with mine. Holding back the flood of emotions as I stood between them made my head ache. All the old fears of tearing them apart because of what I'd wanted so badly with Jake and didn't think I should have ran through my head, such a different picture from what was before me today. Jake was mine forever, and my uncle was happy for us.

All I'd wanted was his acceptance, but his blessing was the greatest gift I'd ever received, other than the man who was about to be my husband and the pea inside my stomach no one was supposed to know about.

"You're so beautiful," Jake rasped, stunning himself in a black tuxedo, as Mike looked on behind him. My uncle was signing our wedding license today, but Mike was the best man in all the ways that counted.

My hands shook around the stem of my bouquet as I handed it to Claudia. I slid my palms against Jake's and squeezed.

"I'm yours," I squeaked out, a tear streaming down my cheek as I lost the battle not to cry.

A grin split Jake's mouth as he took my face in his hands.

"Damn right, you are."

"You sure you're feeling okay?" Jake asked as he rubbed my thigh under our private table. The concern in my new husband's eyes was very sweet, but he needed to lay off before we sparked any more suspicion.

"I'm fine, babe. Stop looking at me like I'm sick or about to break." I kissed his cheek. "Before we tip anyone off."

"Your uncle already knows. Something about you saying no to champagne this morning."

I dropped my head into my hands. "Of course he figured it out. What did he say?"

"He told me double congratulations and hopes we have a girl because I need the payback."

"He's come a long way." I spotted Uncle Keith and Mom bickering over something, as usual, since she'd moved up here. Kristina twirled Emma around on the dance floor, her wide smile not making it up to her eyes. I couldn't help feeling guilty about inviting her to a wedding a month after her divorce was finalized.

"I'm only checking on you to make sure you're up for the wedding night," he whispered, draping his arm across the back of my chair and dropping kisses down my neck. "I'm peeling that dress off you and making you my wife *in every possible way*."

He pressed his lips to mine, light and soft but lingering longer with each kiss. The wicked gleam in his eyes was enough to make me forget where we were until the screech of the microphone ripped across the room.

"Hi, sorry," Mike stammered as he white-knuckled the microphone while keeping a death grip on his phone with the other hand. "This won't be long, I hate when speeches are long, especially when someone says they'll be short." He cleared his throat. "But the best man needs to make a toast. Don't worry, Dad." He put down his phone and picked up a tall glass. "It's ginger ale."

Quiet laughter drifted across the room. Jake shot me a glance and smiled.

"Peyton, I'm glad Dad picked you. You helped me more than you know when I first moved here. All the long talks at school and then later when you moved in with us—because of you, I felt less alone and less afraid. You helped me feel like I belonged here rather than was just dumped. And you always made Dad happy, even before he told me you were together. Or when I told him I knew already." More laughs fluttered across the room. "He deserves to be happy more than anyone."

His throat worked as his gaze landed on his father. I felt around for Jake's hand and squeezed.

"Dad, I'm sorry that no one ever put you first, and that I gave you such a hard time when I first moved in with you. You're the best father anyone could ask for. No one could ever make me doubt that or change my mind. I love you, and I just needed you to know that."

"Jesus," Jake whispered, swiping the back of his hand over his eyes. More tears threatened to spill down my own cheeks as I looked between them, Jake's gaze still locked on his son.

Jake had needed to hear all of that as much as Mike needed to say it.

How far they'd come.

"Anyway, I guess all that's left is congratulations." He raised his glass, a blush bleeding into his cheeks at the huge round of applause, before handing the microphone back to the DJ.

Jake stood when Mike made his way over to our private table.

"Was that okay? I didn't want to mess it up."

Jake shook his head and pulled his son in for a hug, too choked up to voice a reply. He whispered something in Mike's ear I couldn't decipher since his back was turned to me, but I spied Mike's smile as he nodded.

"That was the best toast I've ever heard." I wrapped my arms around Mike when Jake finally released him. Mike's cheeks were still red when I pushed him back. "I'm so proud to call you my stepson."

"Thanks," he said, a shy smile spreading on his lips when I cupped his cheek. "You too, I mean, that you're my stepmom. Not that anything has changed, right? We're all still just home."

Jake smiled when I craned my neck around to where he stood. He looped his arm around my waist and reached over to pinch the back of Mike's neck, flicking a quick glance to my stomach.

"That's right, we're all still home."

One Year Later
Peyton

"Jake, please . . . Oh God, right there," I moaned into my pillow, biting my lip to hold back a scream. He tightened his arm around my waist as he took me from behind, inching in and out as he drew wide circles around my swollen clit. Keeping an eye on the video monitor was next to impossible when both of them kept rolling into the back of my head.

"That's it, sweetheart," he grunted into my neck. "I love making you wet like this."

I turned my head, whimpering in protest when he took his fingers away and then again when he sucked them into his mouth.

"Best taste in the world," he rasped, his eyes fluttering as he continued to thrust inside me.

I grabbed his hand and brought it back to where I needed it as Keely's cooing over the speaker signaled we were running out of time.

"Hurry, please," I begged as he plowed into me, his thumb swiping faster over my clit until tremors rippled down my spine. Jake fisted the sheet as he filled me, growling into the pillow until we both collapsed against the mattress. Keely's gurgles were already morphing into whining.

Since I'd gotten my six-week clearance, Jake and I could only manage sex in spurts. Now that we'd moved our daughter out of her bassinet and into her crib, we'd progressed from five-minute quickies in the kitchen but still had to keep speed in mind.

"I'll get her," Jake panted against my neck, dropping a kiss to my nape after he swiped my sweaty hair away. "Give me a second."

"Take your time," I said when I noticed a dark figure blocking the screen. Her big brother had beat us to it, bouncing Keely in his arms as he whispered in her ear.

I lay back on the pillow, my cheeks aching from smiling so

widely. The beginnings of a wail had already eased into happy gurgles.

"I love watching them. He's so good with her."

"He's going to *hate* it when she starts dating."

I laughed and rolled toward my husband.

"Like you're not." I drifted my hand down his cheek.

"Of course I will. Thank God I have thirty years or so before either of us has to worry about that." He swung his legs over the side of the bed, plucking his boxers off the floor and pulling them on before he stood and shrugged into a T-shirt.

I had no doubt that *thirty years* wasn't meant as an exaggeration.

I slipped my nightshirt over my head and looked around for my panties. It felt as if it would be thirty years before I'd ever have a full night's sleep again, but my heart was too full of love for everyone in this house to care.

"Now that I've sent your brother to bed, maybe Daddy can get some attention," Jake crooned, and I melted, watching on the monitor as he kissed her baby feet while he lifted her legs for a diaper change.

Keely was the family princess and was already spoiled beyond repair at two months old. Everyone tripped over themselves for the chance to hold her, except for my mother, who never missed a chance to rub in how she'd have her all to herself when I went back to work.

She'd have her granddaughter all to herself until her brother stopped by between shifts, which I knew he would do as often as possible. They'd fight over her, and their tradition would continue.

"Everything okay?" I asked from the doorway. She was already asleep against Jake's shoulder, her heart-shaped mouth falling open as she drifted off.

"I think you like the attention," I whispered as I kissed her cheek. "You make a tiny little noise, and Daddy and Mike are right there." Her mouth curved up in a sly smile, as if she knew exactly how much they were both wrapped around her little finger.

"Mommy shouldn't be so jealous after *all* the attention Daddy just gave her." He kissed the top of her head, the wisps of dark hair sticking straight up no matter what we did. "I think she's just greedy," he said in a loud whisper.

"She's okay?" Mike asked from the hallway.

"I *have* done this before, you know," Jake teased. "She's fine, big brother. Go to sleep."

Mike shrugged, with Jake shaking his head at his departure.

"Soak it up, little girl," I said, rubbing her back. She was such a beauty, I couldn't blame them for being so in love with her because I was just as enamored.

"Your feet are never going to touch the ground."

Four Years Later
Peyton

"You're sure we can't drive you?" Jake asked as Mike loaded up his car.

"I'm fine," Mike said as he closed his trunk. "It's not like this is my first day of college. I have enough friends in the dorms that I know my way around, and I don't need much so I don't need help unpacking."

Mike had commuted back and forth his freshman year since the distance was less than an hour, but he'd asked to move in to the dorms since the back-and-forth was taxing and unnecessary if he could just stay there. He wasn't far away, but walking by his abnormally tidy room as he loaded his car sure made it feel that way.

"Tell your father to chill," Uncle Keith said after he'd pulled his cruiser in next to Mike. "We lived in the dorms in college, remember?"

Jake rolled his eyes before turning to my uncle. "I'd like to not remember that today if that's all right with you."

"So uptight in your old age." He shook his head and came up to Mike. "I just stopped by to see him off. He's a good kid, and your old man has nothing to worry about, right?"

Mike's lips quirked at the lift in Uncle Keith's brow. I'd seen his show of quiet yet firm authority with his officers and when he stopped by the high school a few times. He didn't have to raise his voice to prove he meant business. I still laughed when Uncle Keith became Chief McGrath.

"No, sir."

"Good," Uncle Keith said, patting his cheek.

"Stop looking so sad," Mike said. "There are a ton of holidays, and I'm close enough to come home for all of them." He shook his head and groaned. "You both look like I'm headed off to war."

"*Wait*," a little voice called behind us. Keely wore her rhinestone denim jacket, balancing two stuffed animals under her arm as she raced toward Mike. "I'm ready now," she panted out, dragging her Minnie Mouse suitcase behind her.

Mike's brows pulled together as she handed him one of the animals.

"Keely, what's this?"

She smoothed her hair away from her eyes as she peered up at him. "I'm coming to live with you."

Jake's shoulders shook as he stifled the same laugh as I was. Mike shot us a desperate glance while his sister tapped her foot. He eyed the stuffed bear in his hands and crouched down in front of her.

"Keely, you can't come with me. Where I'm going is only for college kids."

"I won't make any noise. I brought my headphones. You can leave me in your room when you go to college."

"I think Mom and Dad would miss you." He squinted at her. My heart went out to him as I spied the dread of breaking her heart in his gaze.

"You just said there are holly-days and we could come home." She shrugged. "Bye, Mommy. Bye, Daddy," she called behind her.

Mike clenched his eyes shut and grabbed her wrist.

"You can't come, K. I'm sorry. I'll miss you too, but I promise I'll be home as soon as I can."

Her suitcase fell back on the ground with a thud.

"But," she started, her chin quivering, "I want to stay with you." Her chin dipped to her chest as big tears cascaded down her cheeks.

"Don't cry," Mike pleaded, pulling her into his arms. "I promise I'll be back soon. And I think you'd miss Mom and Dad if you came with me anyway."

She shook her head, still crying into her brother's chest. "Not as much as I'll miss you."

Mike flinched as if he had been shot. I lifted my head toward my uncle, the only one of us laughing openly at this adorable yet sad scene in front of us.

"Come on, baby girl." Jake pulled her away from Mike, holding her around the waist as he peeled her hands off her brother's neck. "Mike needs to get going. I promise you'll see him soon."

She finally relented, leaning her head on Jake's shoulder as she hiccuped, the sobs muffled but still coming.

Mike scrubbed a hand down his face before leaning in to kiss her cheek. "I love you, and I'll be back soon."

"When?"

"This is a tragic retelling of history," Mom sighed as she came up behind me. "The only difference is the suitcase *you* packed to go live with your uncle was Strawberry Shortcake."

"Our first long weekend is October eighth. I'll be back then, and we can spend the whole Saturday together and do whatever you want, okay?"

Mike was his father's height, all broad shoulders with a jaw that had sharpened as he'd gotten older. He had no problems leaving when we'd asked him to stay, but disappointing his baby sister seemed to be killing him.

She nodded, heaving a dramatic sigh.

"Okay. I love you too."

"We all do," I said, kissing Mike's cheek. "Be safe, okay?"

"And call us when you get there," Jake added, pulling him in for a hug.

"I will." Mike sucked in a breath, exhaling a long gust of air before climbing into his car.

"Come on, kiddo. It's lunchtime." Mom tapped Keely's chin. She'd come by to see Mike off too, but I guess had stayed back to laugh at us before now.

"I'm too sad to eat." Keely dropped her head back on Jake's shoulder, her mouth pulling into a dramatic frown.

"Well, you need to eat something good before your daddy feeds you all that ice cream or whatever you ask him for so you can feel better." Mom pursed her lips and held out her arms. "Come with Grams."

Keely climbed from Jake's arms into my mother's. Mom patted her back, rolling her eyes at me before she went back inside.

"Are you okay?" I asked Jake as he collected Keely's stuffed animals from where they had scattered on the grass and picked up her suitcase.

"I wish I knew why both my kids want to move out so badly." He lifted his head with a sad smile, his eyes a little glassy when they met mine.

"Your daughter loves us, but I realized a long time ago that no one compares to Mike in her eyes."

I looped my arms around his waist and pressed my lips to his. "*I* don't want to move out. Does that make you feel better?"

He laughed, kissing my forehead.

"You're not going anywhere. Stuck with me."

"Same. It's okay if you need a minute."

He shrugged and turned toward the house.

"Don't you have to go back to work?" Jake asked Uncle Keith.

"I'm the chief." He shrugged. "All part of my jurisdiction." He smiled, crossing his arms.

Jake chuckled. "Of course. Thanks for being here." He waved and trudged toward the house.

I had two broken hearts to nurse tonight.

"Poor Mike is going to feel like shit for the entire drive." Uncle Keith's chest rumbled with a laugh. "At least I had the luxury of disappointing you over the phone. If I'd had to tell you face-to-face that you couldn't live with me, I probably would never have left."

"You never disappointed me. Ever." My gaze drifted down the street, Mike's car long gone. "I hope she doesn't get hurt if he doesn't come home on holidays."

"He will," Uncle Keith said, draping his arm across my shoulder. "The same as I always did."

"When he has a party to go to, or starts dating someone, he may not want to come home, or he'll forget."

"He won't." He pulled me closer and kissed my temple. "I'll

just have to warn Mike to keep Keely away from his friends when she turns thirty."

I laughed and wrapped my arms around his neck. Home always was and always would be Uncle Keith.

"I saw the look on his face just now."

My uncle's sad smile almost had me in the same sobs as my daughter. Memories of us flashed through my mind, and he was my hero in every single one.

"He wouldn't and couldn't forget. For her, he'll always remember."

ACKNOWLEDGMENTS

Thank you, James and John, my very patient and supportive husband and son. Thank you for loving me and believing in me, even when you mostly see my back as I'm pounding at the keys. I hit the jackpot for the two best men ever, and I love you both.

To my mother who still hasn't read a book of mine yet, but always tells everyone about her daughter the writer. Maybe you'll read this book since it's for Aunt Ro. Either way, you'll always be the woman I love and admire most.

To Najla Qamber Designs, who created this amazing cover and teasers. After seven years of covers, I never think you can top the last one, but you always prove me wrong. You are a super talented and professional genius and thank you for my new favorite.

To Lisa, thank you so much for the beautiful editing job you did, and for both teaching me new things and making me laugh in the editing comments.

Thank you to all my betas: Jodi, Lauren, Rachel, Lisa, Karen, Korrie, and Bianca. I was a bundle of nerves with this book, and your feedback and direction were exactly what I needed.

Jodi, my PA and basically my family at this point. Thank you for all you do for me, for always leading me in the right direction, and pushing me to be the best I could be. You do that every day and with every book, but I especially needed it with this one.

Rachel, your enthusiasm and love for this story pushed me through more than you know (you probably *do* know, but just in case.) Thank you for loving Jake and Peyton so much.

Karen, the wise one. I still don't know what I offer *you*, but your friendship, guidance, and the time you took to read through this story means the world to me.

Korrie, thank you as always for having my back as a sensitivity reader and as a friend.

Lauren, my Bronx sister, thank you for your awesome friendship and support and for always being within walking distance.

Lucy and Tim, you're both dream makers—or givers still not sure of the right term. Thank you for believing in me and for all you've made possible.

To Dan, Rick, and everyone at TWSS responsible for getting this book into readers' hands, your support is more appreciated than I could ever express.

To all the "awesome ass authors" I know, to LJ and Kathryn for being the best hype friends, to Melanie Moreland and Emma Scott for being wonderful friends and author idols, and all the author friends I've met on this journey. I'm honored and inspired to work alongside such amazing and talented humans.

For all those who gave me technical help, to my college bestie Candie for schooling me on what guidance counselors actually do and what fictional liberties would make sense, to Rhon for all her great help and information on small-town police departments, and to my brother-in-law Michael who very patiently answered question after contracting question to make the flood and repair in Peyton's apartment accurate.

To my beloved readers group, The Rose Garden, to Ari and my street team roses, and all the bloggers who took a chance on a girl from the Bronx who wanted to write, thank you so very much for all your support.

As I always said when I first published, if ten people not related to me bought a book, I'd consider it a success. To be here is a dream that was beyond my comprehension, even now. There will never be enough words of gratitude for how thankful I am.

AUTHOR'S NOTE

I can honestly say that writing a story to follow a top 100 book was not on my author life bingo card. While writing *Just One Favor* gave me the joy of writing back, the pressure I put on myself to make the next book just as good was crippling. Impostor syndrome times a million. Even though I'd been writing for seven years before that, I had never had a release like *Just One Favor*. Each time I sat at the computer in the morning I felt like the group who sang "Take On Me" in the '80s, a one-hit wonder. My poor friends and husband heard me lament daily over my constant inner turmoil and terror of disappointing everyone, and even with their daily reassurances, I was still a mess of self-doubt and whining.

My PA and one of my best friends, Jodi, suggested I write a scene far into the future of the story, knowing well how my pantser brain works since initial setup is always a challenge for me. I was this close to dumping the story until I wrote Jake and Peyton's first kiss and knew that I had to keep going. I made a slight tweak to Peyton's backstory, and it all—finally—began to click. Still, when I showed my first chunk to betas, I wanted to burrow myself in the cushions of my couch, fearing they'd say what I was most afraid of—that this book didn't measure up. It was the best surprise ever when I heard the exact opposite. They loved Tyler and Olivia in *Just One Favor*, but Jake and Peyton's forbidden and emotional romance nailed them right in the feels too.

While *Just One Favor* will always be special to me for so many reasons, *An Unexpected Turn* is the rich romance I always loved to both read and write. The close-knit found family rocked by a slow burn turned explosive attraction between two people who shouldn't be together but couldn't help themselves was a fun as hell story arc once I finally got going.

Then something else happened.

Peyton's Uncle Keith was modeled after my Aunt Rosalie in many ways. My mother was also a single parent who worked a lot of crazy hours and didn't have time to play or have fun because she was too busy making sure she had money for things like rent and tuition. My aunt was my mother's only sister and my godmother without children of her own. Growing up, especially when I was little, I became the child she didn't have. She loved to play and laugh and always took me on the best vacations. She also had a big thing for romance novels. My favorite thing to do was sneak read the paperbacks she'd bring whenever she'd visit.

Unfortunately, she was unhappy on and off over the years and went through months-long periods of not speaking to us. I'm thankful that we all made up last year and when she'd call from her house in Las Vegas, she was the aunt that I remembered. She loved the fact that I became a romance writer and was the only one in the family, other than my husband, who read my books. When *Just One Favor* hit #57 in the Kindle store, she was too sick for me to tell her and that will always break my heart.

She passed away just as I got halfway through my first

draft, and that's when I really noticed how much of my aunt was in Uncle Keith. It was almost sadly poignant how I'd given Peyton and Keith all the best parts of the relationship we had. Aunts and uncles are so important. That combination of parental unconditional love and friendship meant so much to me and has colored all my best childhood memories. Her passing is new enough that it still feels as if I owe her a phone call, and then when I remember she's not there, the grief resets.

My aunt was a social butterfly and excellent business-woman, so I can imagine her networking up in heaven and telling her new friends all about how her niece has a new book coming out. I'll smile at all the great moments a book launch always brings because I'll know she's helping me from the other side, because that's what she always did for her family while she was here.

Thank you for reading *An Unexpected Turn*. I hope you loved Jake and Peyton's journey, and I hope you had an Uncle Keith or Aunt Rosalie in your life who loved you enough to simply let you be a kid, leaving you with amazing memories that still make you smile when you're an adult.

And to my aunt: Rest easy, Godmother.

Much love,

Steph

ABOUT THE AUTHOR

Stephanie Rose is a badass New Yorker, a wife, a mother, a former blogger and lover of all things chocolate. Most days you'll find her trying to avoid standing on discarded LEGO or deciding which book to read next. Her debut novel, Always You, released in 2015 and since then she's written several more —some of which will never see completion—and has ideas for hundred to come.

Stay in touch!
Join Stephanie's Rose Garden on Facebook and sign up for Stephanie Rose's newsletter at www.authorstephanierose.com

Follow Me on Verve Romance @stephanierose

BOOKS BY STEPHANIE

The Second Chances Series
Always You
"Always You is the debut novel for Stephanie Rose and I have
to say she knocked it out of the park."- *Jennifer from Book
Bitches Blog*

Only You
"Paige and Evan's story was beautiful yet so very sad - stunning
in its romance, love and friendship. *-Jenny and Gitte,
TotallyBookedBlog*

Always Us, A Second Chances Novella
"Alpha daddy Lucas is a sight to behold...damn, I love that
man!" - *Shannon, Amazon reviewer*

After You
Some books make you wanna shout them from the rooftops.
After You is that book. - *Paige, A is for Alpha B is for Books*

Second Chances Standalone Spinoffs

Finding Me

"What a gorgeous book. Five whole-hearted stars." - *Emma Scott, author of Forever Right Now and A Five-Minute Life*

Think Twice

"Four people, two love stories, one amazing book." *Melanie Moreland, New York Times and USA Today Bestselling author*

The Ocean Cove Series

No Vacancy

No Vacancy is undoubtedly the feel-good romance of the year. Stephanie Rose has all your needs covered in this delectable love story - *Marley Valentine, USA Today Bestselling author*

No Reservations

"No Reservations is *"second chance" GOLD!* Tragic, heartfelt, sensuous, touching and romantic......This is your next 5 star summer read!" - Chelè, 4 the love of books

The Never Too Late Series

Rewrite

"Rewrite gripped me from the start and never let me go." - *Award-winning and Bestselling author, K.K. Allen*

Simmer

"A slow-burning romance about friendship, family, love and the true meaning of home. I absolutely adored this book." - *Kathryn Nolan, Bestselling author*

Pining

"One of my favorites! Comics, and steam, and redemption. It doesn't get better than that! Five stars!" - *Award-winning author, A.M. Johnson*

Standalones

Safeguard

Safeguard, a standalone novel in the Speakeasy series in Sarina Bowen's World of True North

Just One Favor

"Just One Favor by Stephanie Rose is heartwarming, panty-melting perfection." - Brayzen Bookwyrm

Made in United States
North Haven, CT
26 June 2023

38252604R00200